THE DEATHBED GAME

Secrets and Promises

Book 2

Anna Wilcoxson

FROM THE TINY ACORN...
GROWS THE MIGHTY OAK

The Deathbed Game
Copyright © 2022 Anna Wilcoxson. All rights reserved.

Printed in the United States of America.

For information, address Acorn Publishing, LLC, 3943 Irvine Blvd. Ste. 218, Irvine, CA 92602
www.acornpublishingllc.com

Cover design by Damonza.com

Interior design and digital formatting by Debra Cranfield Kennedy

ISBN—979-8-88528-002-0 (hardcover)
ISBN—979-8-88528-001-3 (paperback)
Library of Congress Control Number: 2021924266

Author's Note

The characters in this novel are fictitious. Historical references and depictions are strictly the author's interpretation of these events.

To Scheggino
and all the joy it brings me

Preface

I stumbled upon the apartment on the last day of my vacation. It was just a sliver of stone nestled between two larger apartments at the top of an old castle. It had a weather-beaten door with a *Per Vende* sign posted on it and a pot with a dead plant on the front step. If I hadn't guessed the view potential from its second story balcony or caught the sun glinting off the low iron gate of the villa next door, I might have passed it by.

As I stood on the doorstep looking out on the Umbrian valley of Scheggino, it felt like home.

Visiting Scheggino had been a last-minute idea, a chance to connect to my Italian ancestry and bring to life the stories my grandfather had told us about the little town where he was born. Little did I know that visit would uncover a part of Spirito Urbino's life that I knew nothing about: a vengeful murder, a secret love affair, and two sons from a woman who was not my grandmother. One son was dead, but the other, my Uncle SJ, was very much alive. I had brought my brother, Tino, to meet him.

Fate, and my impulsive nature, had tempted me back into the bosom of my family's checkered past.

Italy 2015

Chapter 1

Getting There

"SO, WHO'S driving?" Fabio, the Europcar rental agent, dangled a set of keys in front of us.

"I am," Tino and I answered at the same time.

We were at the rental car desk at the airport in Fiumicino, outside of Rome.

"*You* drive?" Tino snorted. "I don't think so. I can count on one hand how many women I'd let drive this car in a foreign country and have fingers left over. He held up three. "I don't see the name *Anna* on any of them."

"Even in Italy, that comment is sexist as hell," I replied.

"And your driving skills leave much to be desired. Weren't you the one who told me you learned how to drive a stick on the *autostrada*?"

My brother had raced cars in the days before he thought about what smashed up body parts looked like. Two years older than me, at sixty-one, he had become safer, if not wiser . . . even if there were a few male chauvinist issues he still needed to work out.

Fabio handed over the keys to Tino. "I would suggest letting the *signora* navigate," he said. "You may need her to read the signs. They come up fast."

"I have a better idea," I said. "You drive, I'll nap."

"Oh, no you don't," Tony fired back. "The last time I drove to Umbria was forty years ago. Someone has to stay awake . . . besides me, of course."

"It is comforting to know you intend to stay awake." I yawned.

We left the rental car desk and headed toward the parking lot to pick up our car. A shiny red Maserati GranCabrio convertible sat a safe distance away from the Fiats and Lancias like a diamond among zirconium.

"Nice," I said. "I'm glad I let you pick the car. I always rent Cinquecentos."

"Umbria's full of narrow cobblestone streets," Tino said. "The GranCabrio has a width four inches less than the Fiat Cinquecento."

"I'm *sure* that was the deciding factor," I said. "Chicks drive Cinquecentos; real men drive Maseratis. Isn't that a more accurate assessment?"

"Now that you mention it . . ."

We shot out of the airport car park and onto the ramp leading to the Autostrada A1. The sun was playing peek-a-boo between a bank of ominous clouds.

"Looks like it's going to rain," I said, reclining my seat to a flat position and getting comfortable. "Hey, you got this, right, bro? I feel an overwhelming need to rest my eyeballs."

"MapQuest. Piece of cake."

I looked at the complicated dashboard. "I hate to break this to you, but I'd be surprised if MapQuest has even heard of Umbria much less our ancestor's Podunk little town of Scheggino."

"Podunk little town. Hardly a ringing endorsement for someone who just bought a piece of property there . . . even if it is a run-down hovel that the rest of our family won't ever want to set foot in."

"I am not without hope that someday Terry and her family might come to visit."

Tino looked doubtful. "If you are talking about the only sibling who hasn't been to our ancestral village, don't hold your breath. She might actually request a working bathroom."

"Very funny. We'll see what you say when I fix it up. You'll be asking to bring your lady friends to visit. I charge a hundred dollars a day. Of course, I might consider offering a special discount to *certain* family members."

"Does that include me?"

"It depends on how I feel at the end of this trip," I said.

The soft patter of rain caressed the windshield as the sky darkened. Up ahead, near the long, flat stretch of Sette Bagni, a flash of thunder cut through the clouds. The weather in Italy in November could be dicey.

"Remember," I said pulling my jacket over me, "look for *Firenze*, then L'Aquila, and get off at Orte. Wake me when we get to the toll booth."

"Where the hell are we?"

I heard my brother's frantic voice and my eyes opened. We were on a dirt road, and a bunch of cows were staring at us in complacent astonishment. They were wondering what we were doing there too.

"Did you pass the toll booth?"

"An hour ago."

I stared at my brother. "You're lost."

Tino nodded. I knew the admission wasn't an easy one.

"Sheesh. I doze off for a few minutes and the world falls apart. Let's see . . ." I glanced at my map, "You just took a wrong turn. Get back on the autostrada going south."

"Easier said than done. On- and off-ramps are few in these parts." Toni's mouth was a thin line, and sweat was dripping off his brow.

"Patience, I said. "We'll get there."

Patience. I had learned that word early in my Italian adventures. Nothing happened fast in small Umbrian villages like the one where we were headed, except, of course, the spread of malicious gossip. That traveled faster than the winds that swept through the valley in winter. In the years I had been visiting my ancestral village, some of that gossip had even been about me. Who was this upstart American asking questions about her family and uncovering secrets comfortably buried in the cemetery on the hill?

Patience, I said to myself as I tried to befriend the old ladies dressed in black who walked the streets at sundown enjoying the age-old tradition called *la passeggiata*. They stared at me with suspicious eyes no matter how many times I smiled and said *buona sera*. From their perspective, anyone who hadn't lived in the village since the turn of the century was considered a newcomer and not to be trusted.

Tino had been to Scheggino once before with our parents, but I had never set eyes on the village until my mom and I visited nearly five years ago. Besides being captivated by the gorgeous scenery, good restaurants, and well-groomed hiking trails, I felt drawn to the lifestyle of this rural Umbrian town. I was impressed that despite the increasing intrusion of technology, the inhabitants clung fiercely to their traditions. The saints' days, the festivals, and the importance of family in everyday life were things they cherished and fought hard to maintain. Being here brought into focus that my grandfather's story was my story, and without the events that had shaped Spirito's life, I would not be here. The more I uncovered, the more I wanted to know, and that included his imperfections. Knowing the truth about his secret love affair and the act of vengeance that changed his life made him human . . . and real. Instead of being ashamed, it made me love him more.

The apartment I had discovered was on the third level of a medieval castle with a labyrinth of stairs leading up to it. Built in 1000 AD as a fortress against marauding Saracen invaders, the castle's massive stone structure dominated the town. In the sixteenth century, a cardinal had acquired it for his own personal use, the many individual rooms functioning as living quarters for his entourage. In the last two hundred years, the rooms had gradually been subdivided, reconfigured, and sold off as private residences. My apartment had been requisitioned and put on the market by the town government after the previous owners couldn't pay the mortgage. It was a fraction of what a two-bedroom condo would cost back in San Diego. How could I go wrong? I put down a deposit to hold it until the paperwork was completed and I could return to sign the necessary documents and secure ownership.

I stared out at the landscape as the Maserati cruised past the city of Terni. Scheggino was less than an hour away. The rain had tapered off, allowing the sun to push through the clouds and dazzle the dewy fields with its brilliance. High in the hills, the stone walls of ancient towns shone bright and clean against the sky like freshly laundered linen.

I heard a growl. I glanced at Tino, and he grinned. His stomach was letting us know it was well past noon.

"Lunch is *after* we meet the realtor at the apartment," I told him. "Hopefully I will still have an appetite after I take a look at the inside."

Chapter 2

Cold Feet

WE CAME out of the tunnel into a blast of sunlight.

"That tunnel wasn't there forty years ago," Tino said as we turned toward the off-ramp to Scheggino.

"It was built in 1998," I told him. "Four kilometers. Two and a half miles long. Italians don't mess around when it comes to boring through solid rock."

"I was here in 1995," Tino said, "*My* back-to-our-roots trip with Mom and Dad. We had to travel the long way, over the mountain passes of Piedi Paterno. Our cousin, Brunetta, raced me from Spoleto to Scheggino's cemetery." Tino paused for a moment, remembering. "She had the gift."

"What gift?"

"The gift of driving like you could never die," Tino answered. A half smile played on his lips, and his eyes grew soft. "How is Brunetta these days?"

"Married. Her husband is in high end construction. He hauls marble up to mansions owned by Hollywood actors in Lake Como. Don't get any ideas about rekindling your romance . . . you could wind up in the hospital."

"It was wishful thinking on her part," Tino assured me, "I was still busy sowing my oats."

"Or spreading your seed," I muttered under my breath. My brother's first and only marriage ended a few years ago, and he had recently signed up for Match.com. I wondered if they had an Italian contingent.

Up ahead, we passed a sprawling complex with a big iron gate and a sign spelling out *Urbino Truffle Foundation* in bold black letters.

"Is that where they process the truffles?" Tino asked.

I nodded. "The plain-looking building is the warehouse where the truffles are cleaned and processed. Then, they are exported all over Italy and the rest of the world." I pointed to another structure with glass walls that ran from floor to ceiling. "This is where the offices and kitchens are located."

"Kitchens?"

"They do cooking demonstrations for clients. You know, to get them hooked. Truffles are an acquired taste. The first time I tasted them, I thought I was tasting dirt. Now I can't get enough."

Tino stopped in front of the gates and cut the motor "Sleek and classy," he said.

"Just like Agatha Altarocca. I chuckled. "She helped Claudio Urbino design it in the late 1940s."

"Agatha Altarocca," Tino repeated. "Spirito's secret love . . ."

"His *first* love. Before he met our grandmother," I reminded him.

Tino glanced at me. "I want to hear more about her. She sounds like quite a woman."

"Our Uncle SJ will fill us in. We're having dinner with him tomorrow night. It should be quite a story."

Tino started up the motor and we edged out into the road. "There are skeletons in every family's closet. I'm guessing ours is no exception."

"You guessed right," I said.

A few minutes later, we could see the outline of Scheggino's castle rising up against the mountains. Impenetrable, imperious, and oblivious of time. A crumbling stone wall edged its way up the outer perimeter, ending in a watch tower overrun with vegetation. A single tree grew out of the top as a testament to nature's winning battle against the intrusion of man. Towering over the red clay tile roofs, a construction crane carried a gigantic piece of stone to its final destination.

"I hope that crane isn't hovering over your new apartment," Tino said as we got closer. "A sudden gust of wind or a well-placed lightning bolt . . ."

I looked up at my window on the third story. It was right underneath it.

"Keep your eyes on the road," I said through clenched teeth.

The Maserati eased into a spot in the parking lot off the highway. Two bars, two restaurants. and a bank clustered around the modern fountain built in Pietro Urbino's memory by the Urbino Truffle Foundation. Pietro had started the Mom and Pop operation in 1910, in a small stone building near the *piazza*. By the 1940s, Claudio, his son, had taken it to worldwide recognition as one of the top distributors of truffles in the world.

"This fountain wasn't here twenty years ago either," Tino observed as he surveyed its saucer-like formation. "I like it. A contrast from the ancient feel of the castle. Demonstrates style and big bucks."

"The Urbino clan have plenty of both," I assured him.

"Are you sure we aren't related to that gazillion-dollar family? We have the same last name."

"'Same last name, no relation.' That is what Gabriella, one of the matriarchs, said to Mom and me when we first came here."

"Too bad," Tino said. "Still, I'd like to hear some of that early history and decide for myself."

"We'll ask SJ tomorrow night."

I looked at my watch. It took me a minute before I realized I was still on San Diego time.

"You'd better change that thing," Tino reminded me as he whipped out his cellphone. "I don't wear a watch when I travel. It singles me out and invites theft. I use my phone, and the time changes automatically. It's 11:45."

"What happens when your phone goes dead?" I asked him.

"Not likely. I keep close track of it. I suggest you do the same."

Siblings love to tell you what to do, I thought. "We have fifteen minutes before we meet the realtor. Let's grab a bite at Avelino's. My treat."

Avelino's bar was located right off the SS395 highway that passed through town. From 6:00 to 9:00 a.m. it was packed with brick layers and businessmen downing espressos before heading off to work. At noon, the place was deserted.

"Avelino, *Ciao!*" I called out to the florid-faced man wiping the counter.

He looked up and smiled. "Anna! The rising star of Scheggino . . . and now a property owner, or so I have heard." Avelino gestured to Tino. "American boyfriend?"

"Brother," I said.

"*Benvenuto, fratello*," Avelino held out his hand.

"*Piacere*. Tino Wilson."

"Wilson," the bar man repeated. "Nice Italian name."

Tino smiled. "My mother chose outside her elite gene pool. She married an American from California."

"So, you are American." Avelino countered. "I get it. And yet your sister has bought property here and brought you to visit.. Italy is a long way from California."

Tino's features darkened, and I could tell he felt insulted. Maybe it was the smug look on Avelino's face, like he was suggesting our

Italian heritage was much more important than our American one.

The two men eyed each other, arms crossed in front of them. A testosterone standoff if I ever saw one. Time to intervene.

"I will admit," I began, "there are some things about the American lifestyle that I don't agree with. Too much emphasis on being better than everyone else. 'The one who has the most toys wins' mentality. At the end of the day, we know how to make a buck, but we don't know how to enjoy life."

"*Brava*," Avelino said. "Spoken like a true Italian."

"*Grazie*. I will take that as a compliment. Now, tell me why everyone knows I bought an apartment when I haven't even signed the papers yet?"

"In small towns, news travels as fast as those who make it. Take your car, for example." Avelino gestured to the parking lot where a group of men were gathered around the Maserati. "Half the town already knows who that car belongs to. Tino, you are famous!"

Tino started out of his chair. "If they put even a finger on it . . ."

"*Tranquillo*, relax." Avelino reached into the display case, pulled out two sandwiches, and placed them in front of us. "Your car, she is like a beautiful woman, no? And who knows how to appreciate *la donna* better than an Italian man?"

Clearly unconvinced, Tino wolfed down his *panini di porchetto* and strode outside. He needed to remind those village idiots that the beauty they were salivating over belonged to *him*.

With a nod to Avelino, I hurried out the door after him. "Time to head on up to the apartment. It's three tiers from the bottom and all of it straight up."

Tino wasn't listening. His eyes were glued to a woman striding across the piazza in a pair of four-inch stilettos with legs that seemed to sprout from just below two perfectly shaped mammary glands.

Tony gave a low whistle. "Who is *that?*"

I put my hand over his mouth. "Pamela Urbino, the Mayor, and I hope to God she didn't hear you."

"You never told me that the Mayor of Scheggino is a sex goddess."

"There you go again, objectifying every female in sight. I know you have joined Match.com . . . I just hope you are modifying your *very* outdated dating strategies. If I were you, I'd leave off the *sex* part and just refer to Pamela as a goddess.

"Okay," Tino said. He sounded disappointed. "I can remember twenty years ago when a woman in Italy was complimented when a man pinched her behind."

"Those days are long gone, my friend," I assured him. "The sooner you realize it, the better. Besides, Pamela belongs to Giovanni, the heir to the Urbino Truffle Foundation."

"Married?"

"Very."

"A man can look, can't he?" Tino noticed that the group of men ogling the car had switched objects. "Look at them. They don't seem to be following a new set of rules."

"They're Italian. They can't help themselves. I'm just warning you. Look at your own risk. I have heard jealousy comprises 90 percent of an Italian male's DNA, and Giovanni is 100 percent Italian."

Tino wasn't listening again. He was focused on the swaying hips of Scheggino's top elected official as she disappeared into the office of the *comune*.

* * *

As we climbed up the stairs from one of four entrances that cut into the castle's perimeter, blood-red begonias cascaded from balconies, and blue and white tiles announced the addresses of quaint, well-kept apartments. Two-story, multi-balconied residences sharing walls with the humblest of cottages demonstrated not only a pride of ownership but also a sense of a shared community.

Tino stopped to catch his breath. "Did you *have* to pick a place near the top?"

"Quit whining," I said, giving him a shove. "Only three more sets of stairs."

At the top of a stone ramp, we came to a massive wooden door with a set of ancient iron bars locking it together. An official-looking crest with a shield, two doves, and a cross was barely visible over the top.

"Cardinal Graziani's private quarters," I said proudly. "Circa 1560."

We lifted the latch and pushed. Inside, there was a partially enclosed foyer with two arched doors on either side. "My neighbors," I said. Walking farther into the enclosure, on the right, we came to a low iron gate and an exquisite garden, basking in the sun like a miniature forest. Above the garden, a two-story villa towered over the castle's outer walls, commanding an unobstructed view of the valley.

"Not mine," I said, seeing Tino's astonished face. I pointed to the tiny sliver of stone next to it. "*That* one's mine."

My partially open front door was a water-stained gray that had once been polished oak. Pieces of broken cement lay strewn around the steps that had fallen from the balcony parapet above.

"Funny, I could have sworn it looked a lot better when I was here last."

"You mean, before you put down the deposit? When the stars in your eyes blinded your perception of reality?"

"Yeah, something like that," I confessed. A cold hand seemed to touch my shoulder. *What have I gotten myself into?*

"Signora Corti?" I said, stepping through the doorway into a big open space on the apartment's ground floor.

"*Sono quassù,* I am up here," a voice called from the railing on the second level. *"Un momento."* I heard a clatter of heels, and a well-dressed figure emerged from under the arched entrance to the stairwell.

"Ciao, Anna!" Francesca kissed me on both cheeks, Italian-style, and turned to Tino. "You are Anna's brother?"

"Sì, sono Tino." My brother held out his hand, his gaze swiftly taking in the tailored pantsuit and patent leather ankle boots.

Francesca Corti, my realtor, was well past forty but carried herself with an air of professional confidence. Her hair, a brilliant shade of auburn, was cut at straight angles across her brow and jawline. Red lips framed a big smile, and thick lashes shaded eyes that didn't miss a trick. Francesca's smile stayed in place as she gestured around the room. "What do you think of your new place?"

The first thing that struck me was a peculiar odor emanating from the walls and wafting down from the second story. "What is that smell?"

Francesca colored. "Just a small plumbing problem . . . upstairs."

"Just a small plumbing problem." Tino repeated the words as if I hadn't heard them the first time. There was a wicked gleam in his eyes.

"The toilet was not used for a year, and when we turn on the water," Francesca turned her palms up in classic Italian style. "an accident happened."

Seeing the look of horror on my face, she gave me a confident smile. "You can fix, no problem."

Almost fearfully, I walked the ground level area. The flooring was clay tile set in a herringbone pattern, and except for the stains, it looked to be in pretty good condition. A fireplace straddled one corner, blackened and filthy but serviceable. On the east wall were a series of holes where nails used to be and electrical wires protruding from sockets like atrophied snakes. Something was missing.

"Where's the kitchen?"

"The former tenants took it with them," Francesca said, casually, like it was the most normal thing in the world.

"They did *what*?"

"It was prefabricated and very cheap. IKEA, I think."

I pictured people hauling cabinets down to waiting trucks and speeding out of town in the middle of the night. I turned to Francesca. "Is this common practice in Italy? Portable kitchens? I'm surprised I have a toilet. Did they take the bathroom sink too?"

"Too heavy," Francesca said.

We climbed the ten stairs to the second level. As we neared the top, each step became increasingly steeper. Finally, we came to a huge block of marble that served as the stepping-stone between the landing and the bedrooms. *Good thing I'm a hiker.* Just getting to my bed every night would keep me in shape.

The first bedroom was oddly shaped, long and narrow, with a window at the far end and a view of the town below. As we passed the bathroom, we instinctively averted our eyes and held our noses. I decided to inspect it later, after the clean-up crews had come. The master bedroom, the one with a balcony overlooking Cardinal Graziani's garden was the prettiest room in the house. It had sixteen-foot ceilings, original rough-hewn wooden beams, and a French door with shutters.

"Nice," Tino whispered to me. The growing sense that I had made a terrible mistake ratcheted down a notch. At least the place wasn't a total loss.

There was a strained silence as the three of us descended to the first floor and headed for the front door.

"I will see you tomorrow, at the *comune*, to sign papers, *sì?*" Francesca's eyes were anxious.

I wasn't just getting cold feet. They were positively *frostbitten.* Part of me wanted to thank Francesca for all her trouble, walk away, and never look back. Then, I thought about my dream of putting down roots in my grandfather's village. Owning property in Scheggino meant owning a piece of my family's past and staying connected to its future. If that was my true purpose, then making four walls livable was the easy part. Besides, what two-thousand-year-old condo is going to be perfect?

I took a deep breath and smiled at Francesca. "Yes, I will see you tomorrow."

When I saw the look of relief on her face, I knew what she was thinking: *Only an American would be stupid enough to buy a disaster like this.*

"I have just one question before you go," I said, hoping she couldn't hear the tremor in my voice. "Do you happen to know a good plumber?"

Chapter 3

Old Friends

"CAPPUCCINO?" Tino said gently as we wound our way down through the Castle into town. The sun was on its downward slide heading toward the western rim of Monteluco. In three hours, it would be dark.

"A *grappa* would be more like it," I said. I was still reeling from the shock of what I had committed myself to. The apartment was little more than a smelly hovel with plumbing problems and no kitchen. What had I been thinking three months ago when I put down the deposit? It was obvious I had leaped before seeing how far down the bottom was. It reminded me of a few impulsive relationships of the human variety I had suffered through.

We found a table at Il Ponte, the restaurant and bar that ran alongside the Nera River. The swiftly flowing stream that passed through town followed a circuitous route beginning at the top of Monti Sibillini and ending near the little town of Orte, one hundred sixteen kilometers away. For hundreds of years, the residents had fished from its waters, irrigated their crops of corn and farro, and grown vegetables in the fertile land that lined its banks. Not much had changed, including the ever-present ducks that glided back and forth, constantly on the lookout for handouts.

"You could always back out," Tino suggested as he brought two glasses of grappa from the bar.

"Believe me, the thought has crossed my mind . . . but I would lose my deposit. Of course, I made a generous one to demonstrate what a serious buyer I was."

"I guarantee when you build your first fire in the *camino* and cook your first meal in your new kitchen, you will laugh about this day. *Saluti!*" Tino raised his glass. "Here's to adventures! May we never stop having them!"

I downed the liquid in one gulp. "Easy for you to say. You get to come here and enjoy it after all the hard work is finished."

A petite figure with a mop of red hair walked into the bar. "Anna, is that you?'

"Leonia! We arrived a couple of hours ago. Come meet my brother." I took her hand and led her to the table.

"Grappa?" Tino gestured to the bar.

"Per carità, no! Too early . . . even for me." She smiled at the bartender. "*Caffè, solamente,* Emilio."

"Tino, this is the lady I told you about. The daughter of Enzo Verrocchio. Enzo was just a boy when our grandfather came back here in 1923, for the reading of his uncle's will. That's the inheritance that helped our grandparents open the restaurant in San Diego."

Tino's eyes lit up. "So, your father is the one who told us about Spirito's secret Italian family. I would like to meet him."

Leonia's voice dropped to a whisper. "My papa died last year." She looked at me. "The same as your Virginia."

I nodded, my eyes filling with tears. I remembered the day, four years ago, when we had all met at the piazza for the first time. Enzo and Virginia had hit it off instantly. They were both in academics, Enzo, a retired Professor of history at the University of Assisi, and Mom, a language teacher. Through him, we learned the story of why Spirito was forced to leave his homeland in 1906.

"Condolenze," Tino said. "I am sorry about your father. I am still getting up to snuff on my sister's Italian adventures."

"You remember the story Enzo told Mom and me," I said to Tino. "Something about a duel?"

"Not exactly," I said. "Our grandfather shot and killed a man in cold blood. The man who raped his lover."

"A tragedy." Leonia said, quickly. "But because of it, Spirito was free to marry your grandmother, and that is why you are here. Strange, how so many things can change in a person's life because of one decision."

"Like my decision to buy a hole in the wall in a foreign country," I muttered half to myself.

From the window of the bar, I could see the sun edging closer to the mountains. Reluctantly, I got to my feet. "We have not even been to Villa Urbino to check in. It will be dark in an hour."

"You are staying at Villa Urbino? Leonia's eyebrows shot up. "You are brave. That is where your grandfather's troubles started. *In bocca al lupo,* as we say in Italy."

"In bocca al lupo," Tino repeated, "What does that mean?"

"In the mouth of the wolf," I told him. "It means good luck, but Italians use it when one is faced with a great challenge. For you and me, it has a more literal meaning. A hundred years ago, our grandfather killed the great, great uncle of the current owner.

"Okay, maybe you'd better refresh my memory." Tino looked uneasy. "How does Villa Urbino figure into all this?"

"In the summer of 1906, when Spirito was twenty-three years old, he and Leonia's grandfather, Enzo, were working as field hands at Villa Urbino. It was there, at the villa, where Spirito fell in love with a young servant girl named Agatha Altarocca. The owner's son, Armando, had his eye on her too. When he found out about Spirito and Agatha's love affair, he became enraged with jealousy and raped her one night as she lay asleep in the servants' quarters. Spirito, obsessed with revenge, devised a scheme that ensured Armando would pass by Spirito's house at a certain time. With Enzo acting as the lookout, Spirito aimed his rifle through the hole in his parents' storage room and killed Agatha's assailant."

"Did Nonno Spirito leave Scheggino to escape prosecution?" Tino asked. "Or was he forced to leave?"

"Both. Not long after Armando's death, Agatha discovered she was pregnant. Not knowing if the child she was carrying was Spirito's or Armando's, she made a decision to stay with the wealthy Urbino family and have her child brought up by them. She forced the Urbinos to pay for Spirito's passage to America. With vengeance inevitable, she knew his banishment would save his life."

Tino shifted uncomfortably. "Why in hell did you book rooms at Villa Urbino? We could have stayed here, at Il Ponte. We would have been a lot safer."

"Adventures are rarely safe," I reminded him. "Besides, SJ lives next door."

"I thought we had other relatives here, from way back, Spirito's uncle's people," Tino said.

"We do. Giorgio and his daughter, Renata. They live in the original family compound."

Tino looked interested. "In the same compound where Spirito fired the fatal shot?"

"Yep, the same place."

"I want to see it! Let's go visit them."

"Can I come too?" Leonia asked. "After all, I have a vested interest in this story."

I looked up at the sky. "Okay, we've got an hour of daylight left. Ready to start climbing?"

Tino looked like he was having second thoughts. "All the way to the top . . . again?"

"Just halfway. Be thankful it's only two levels, not three."

Tino stood up and patted his stomach. "At this rate, I'm going to be able to eat all the pizza I want and not gain a pound."

Giorgio and Renata's property was a large piece of land protected by a front gate and a high wall that formed the western edge of the castle. It sported a two-story residence, three storage buildings, and a courtyard.

"This is where our family used to live?" Tino asked.

"Before 1902. Spirito's uncle bought it from us after Spirito's mother died. He took care of our family and left them a nice inheritance. The shot was fired in that building on the far right, the one that shares the same wall as the outside of the castle. Spirito fired the shot from one of the old medieval rifle holes."

I buzzed the intercom, and a few minutes later, a woman in her early forties walked toward us.

"Renata! Sono Anna!" I called out.

The auburn-haired beauty smiled and opened the gate. "You are back!" She kissed me on both cheeks and looked at Tino.

"*Fratello,*" I said.

Renata gave her cousin a closer look.

"He wants to see where the shot was fired." I pantomimed firing a gun.

"And to meet my relatives," Tino added quickly. "I must say, Anna's description of you did not prepare me."

"What do you mean?" I said defensively. "I said she looked like Mona Lisa's sister."

"Sophia Loren, circa 1960, would have been more accurate."

Renata smiled demurely. "Come in, I will call Papa. Can you stay for dinner?"

As she started to walk toward the house, I stopped her. "We only just arrived and have to check into our rooms. Another day, perhaps?"

"Of course. But you must let Giorgio show you the rifle hole. He *loves* to play tour guide."

"Papa! *Americani! Vendetta di* Spirito!" Renata called out in a voice that Georgio, along with half the population of Scheggino, was sure to hear.

I winced.

A minute or two later, Giorgio's head popped out.

"Anna! You bring your brother! He hear about 'Spirito's Revenge,' *sì*?"

Giorgio was about five foot two inches tall and almost bald. He had the striking blue eyes of my grandfather, and by the size of his belly, it looked like he didn't skip any meals.

"You want to see where your grandfather shoot his rival in cold blood?" He looked at Tino and grinned.

Tino looked as wary as I felt. I could only hope "Spirito's Revenge" was not destined to become a major Umbrian tourist attraction.

"I don't know how he knew Armando was passing by at that exact time," Giorgio said as we walked over to the storage room. "I think about this for a long time. He must have had help."

Leonia's eyes were anxious. We both knew her grandfather had played sentry that night.

"I never heard anything about that," I responded quickly. "And after so many years, I guess we will never know."

Leonia reached out and squeezed my hand.

<hr>

The grand tour was over in less than ten minutes. The place was a hole in the wall of an old dusty storage building reeking of damp stone and manure.

With the appropriate *oohs* and *ahhs* and promises of getting together in a few days, we left Giorgio and Renata and started the climb down to the parking lot.

"That Renata sure is a looker," Tino said. "Doesn't resemble Giorgio at all."

I gave him a stern look. "She is off limits. You are related, even if it is remotely."

"Yeah, I have to admit, the thought of it kind of dries up the old juices. Although, in a town this size, I bet there is a lot of inbreeding..."

"No doubt," I said. "Maybe it's because I'm American but the *ick factor* is still there."

We crossed the bridge toward the piazza. A new group had gathered around the Maserati, and a few children were racing around the car, peering into windows, and trying door handles.

"Non tocare!" Tino's voice rang out with the authority of ownership. The children shrank back and regarded him with respect. We nodded to the crowd and got in. As the motor started up, everyone backed off, and Tino shot out of the parking lot with a theatrical squeal of tires.

"Show off," I said.

"Are they watching?"

I looked behind me at the contingent of slack-jawed males staring at the receding vehicle.

"Oh yeah, they're watching."

Chapter 4

In Bocca al Lupo

WE REACHED the entrance to Villa Urbino as the sun slipped behind the mountains.

Tino stared at the massive gates. "Is anyone expecting us? You made the arrangements."

I got out and peered through the iron rungs. The villa's clay tile roof was barely visible at the end of the long dirt road. I saw a man who looked to be in his late forties sweeping the front of a caretaker's cottage just inside the gate.

"*Posso entrare*? Can we come in?" I called out.

"Who are you?" The man said in heavily accented English.

"*Sono Anna,* the American from California. I booked rooms here for a week."

The man came out of the shadows, smiling broadly, and began unlocking the gate. "*Scusa*, I expect you earlier. This is off-season so you are our only guests. I am Agostino, you remember?"

"Of course, I remember. Four years ago, my mother and I drove up here looking for our relatives. The beginning of everything."

"You have brought Virginia?"

I shook my head. "*Morta*. One year ago."

Agostino opened the gate and reached out, the hard muscles in his arms encircling me in a spontaneous gesture of compassion.

He held me at arm's length and looked into my face. "*Condolenze.* She was a fine woman. I feel honored to have met her."

"*Grazie.* I miss her every day. I have brought my brother. Come and meet him."

Agostino turned to look at the sleek machine and its driver. "Maserati GranCabrio. *Bellissima*! Five- or six-speed transmission?"

"Six speeds, automatic, unfortunately. The two hundred sixty-seven horsepower more than make up for it, though," Tino said proudly.

"*Stupende.* She accelerates fast, *si?*" Agostino pantomimed stomping on a gas pedal and shifting gears.

"Gut punching." Tino shoved his fist into his hand for emphasis.

It is mind boggling the male bonding that can take place between two complete strangers in the presence of a beautiful automobile. Within minutes, Tino and Agostino were walking around the car, slapping each other on the back, swapping automotive details.

Trying not to feel upstaged by a piece of metal, I turned my attention to the caretaker's cottage. It was a saltbox-shaped building with a set of double wooden doors opening right off the private road, leading to the villa. Perched on an embankment, the cottage slanted at an angle to a lower level. Down below, another set of doors opened onto a front yard, with a table and two benches overlooking the fields and the town below.

"Who lives here?"

Agostino turned his head. "Many years ago, it was for caretaker, and in my teenage years, I turn it into my get-away pad. Now we rent it to guests during the summer. Only one bedroom but *very* private."

I had already pushed my way through the double doors and was eyeing the interior. To my right, an old bicycle sat just off the entryway. It looked a little rusty but serviceable. I couldn't wait to try it out. Farther on was a tiny bath with a toilet, sink, and shower. On the same level, there was a bedroom with a double bed, an antique armoire, and a series of stairs leading down to a kitchen and dining area. "I love it! Can I stay here?"

"Tonight?" Agostino eyed me anxiously. "The furnace is tricky. It is November. Very cold."

"You have blankets, right? I'll be fine." Not waiting for an answer, I walked to the trunk of the car and removed my suitcase.

Agostino watched me with an amused expression. "Don't say I did not warn you."

I'll be staying at the villa, Tino said. "The heat is in good working order there, I assume?"

"Each room has its own heating system. Very modern." Agostino looked at both of us. "Will you be having dinner? Tonight, *colombacci allo spiedo con tartufo.*"

Jet lag and hunger had been fighting a battle in my body for the last hour, but when I heard the word "*tartufo,*" I knew which side would win out. *Truffles.* Bedtime could wait.

Agostino brought my things into the *villetto* and turned on the furnace. It sputtered and hissed like a cranky old lady but eventually subsided into a precarious hum. "*Non tocare,*" Agostino warned me. "Temperamental."

Agostino got in the car, apologizing for the dust on his clothes, and we drove down the dirt road toward the villa. "The pig enclosure is there, on our right. The Urbino family still hunts with them, like in the old days, but more and more we use dogs. The dogs can be trained to find the truffle but not eat them."

"I thought pigs were smart," I said.

"They are." Agostino chuckled. "Smart enough to eat the good stuff before we can get to it. Ahead is laundry house. In the old days, water is pumped from the river, and everything was washed by hand. Next to it were the servants' quarters. Now, we use buildings for offices where we handle bookings. We do many weddings here from May to October. Later, I show you the two salons we added beyond the pool."

We parked and walked through a path that led to the guest rooms. They all had patios and a view of the valley and the Nera River.

"All guest rooms in the villa are named after my ancestors," Agostino explained. "Except for my private quarters in original part of the house. The villa was built in 1885, by my great grandfather Angelo and his wife, Mariella. In this wing, I name the rooms after my immediate relatives." Agostino stopped and unlocked one of the doors. "Here is *La Camera Gabriella*. I name it after my grand-mother."

"I think I met her," I said. "She has a villa down the road, doesn't she? You took Mom and I to her home when we first arrived here."

"I did."

"As I recall, our visit was cut short." I gave Agostino a wry look. "Her hospitality ended when I mentioned Spirito Urbino's name."

Agostino laughed. "My apologies if she was rude."

I waved my hand dismissively. "I understand. Not wasting time with pleasantries is a privilege reserved for the very old . . . one of the few perks of making it that far. Mom and I had just gotten here, as I recall, before I heard the story of 'Spirito's Revenge.' Now that I know he knocked off her uncle, I can understand why she didn't welcome us with open arms."

Tino gave me a "what the hell are you bringing that up for" look.

Agostino eyed me critically. "You are not afraid to speak your mind, I see. Don't forget Spirito's victim happened to be my great, great uncle."

"And don't forget why Spirito wanted revenge in the first place." I shot back.

For a few tense moments it felt like a standoff in a spaghetti western with Ennio Morricone music playing in the background. Then, our host smiled and put a hand on my shoulder. "Of course, I consider all this before I accept your reservation to stay here. The bad feeling between our families has lasted long enough. It is time to . . . how you say . . . kiss and make up?"

Before I could object, Agostino held out his arms and kissed me on both cheeks.

"I can't argue with your logic or your method of reconciliation," I said, blushing. "If only every conflict could be resolved so easily. Does this mean 'Spirito's Revenge' is now history?"

"*Ancient* history," Agostino replied.

"Whew." Tino wiped his brow. "I'm glad we got that cleared up. Now, can I see the other rooms? Maybe one of your male ancestors'? This one has a few too many doilies for my taste."

Agostino took us to the last room of the new wing. "This room is named Agosto, after my father."

The room was very masculine: a dark wood Chippendale desk and chair, a king-size bed dressed in a tartan plaid, and an armoire. On the walls were etchings of all the great monuments of Rome.

Tino set down his backpack. "This is more like it. It appears your father and I have the same great taste."

"I thank you for the compliment. Now, you must follow me to the kitchen. While I dress the birds, you can sample a glass of our *Grappa del Re*. The King's grappa. I guarantee you will like it."

From the guest cottages, we walked up a flight of flagstone steps to a large outdoor space where the pool and cabana were located. A broad elevated patio in front of a series of French doors led to the main house.

"*Colombacci allo spiedo*," Tino said slowly, his eyes on Agostino. "What exactly *is* that?"

"Roasted pigeon. I caught them myself this morning in front yard of the *villetto. Fresca,* Fresh."

Tino paled. "Pigeon?"

I shot my brother a warning look. "Sounds delicious, Agostino, I'm starved. I knew you were a farmer, but I had no idea you were a chef."

The kitchen of Villa Urbino proved to be a purely functional space: shelves loaded with condiments, gigantic cans of pomodoro sauce, and tins of Urbino Olive Oil. There were knives the size of daggers lining the walls and a meat slicer that looked like it belonged in a butcher shop. There were no marble countertops and not a single built-in microwave in sight. I noticed that Tino had positioned himself as far away from the sink as possible as our host pulled feathers from dead birds.

As I watched Agostino work, I noticed the muscled arms, broad shoulders, and sun-weathered features of a man who had worked outdoors every day of his life. There were wrinkles in the corners of his eyes and mouth, and his hair stood out at odd angles like he had just gotten out of bed. It was a look I found not entirely disagreeable. His smile was quick and his gaze direct. He was a man who didn't know, or care, how to be anything but himself.

I leaned against the counter, sipping my grappa. "Tell me about the servant girl, Agatha Altarocca. The blonde beauty all the Urbino men were in love with."

Agostino shot me a quick look. "Always it is about the past with you. Why Agatha?"

"She fascinates me. My grandfather and your great uncle Armando lost their heads over her, she gets pregnant, and instead of getting thrown out on her ear, she becomes this indispensable business asset for the Truffle Empire. Quite a story, you have to admit."

Agostino had just sliced open a pigeon, the guts spilling out into his hands. He put down his knife and turned to face me. "Yes. I know the story. Tell me, why do you want to bring it all up now?"

"Agatha was an important part of my grandfather's life. The details may lead to a better understanding of my ancestors and, ultimately, who I am."

"Some history should stay buried, is my thinking," Agostino said, "But I live here. Not all families have a past they are proud of."

"I could say the same thing," I responded. "It doesn't stop me from wanting to know."

Agostino's brow furrowed. "Let me prepare the meal in peace. Too many chickens squawking," With his hands covered in blood and feathers, Agostino shooed us out of the kitchen like a henpecked rooster. "Go and light the candles. We will talk while we eat."

Colombacci allo spiedo might have had the humblest of origins— pigeon being the one bird the upper classes had no taste for—but in Agostino's capable hands, it was a gastronomic masterpiece. The meat was slightly roasted with garlic and rosemary, and the truffle infused dressing, made with farro, kept the flesh moist and succulent. My plate was empty in minutes, and even Tino, after taking a few tentative bites, polished off the first serving and asked for seconds.

"Empty plate means the food is good, *sì?* It is a great compliment for a chef."

"I will never look at a pigeon the same way again," Tino said with his mouth full.

I studied Agostino as he cleared the dishes and brought out a bottle of limoncello and three glasses.

"You cook like this for one?" I had noticed the absence of female paraphernalia in the rooms we had passed through.

"Sometimes for two." His eyes twinkled. "There is a small kitchen in my private quarters upstairs. Only those with a personal invitation are allowed to visit."

"I would love to see it sometime," I blurted out. I felt my face turn red.

Agostino looked pleased. "I am sure that can be arranged."

"You promised us a story," I said quickly.

"Ah." Agostino leaned back in his chair and regarded me thoughtfully. "The story of the beautiful and mysterious Agatha Altarocca. She die before I was born, of course, but the memory of her beauty and her accomplishments live on. She is said to have looked like one of Botticelli's Madonnas: fair, blue-eyed, and with skin so pale it was like milk. Back then, many in the village were curious, like you, about the child. Was the father Armando or the young field hand named Spirito who left for America soon after she become pregnant? Maybe that is why she went to live in Spello. Too many tongues talking."

"So, you think she left Villa Urbino to get away from gossip?" I asked.

"It is one reason. There was also talk in my family that Claudio, the heir to the truffle foundation, was in love with her. We expect he ask her to marry him, but then she left with Santo for Spello."

"Maybe she did not want to encourage him?" I suggested.

"Then why did she decide to stay in the fancy home that belong to Claudio? The villa in Spello was in his family's name."

"Sounds complicated." I offered Agostino another theory. "*I think she was still in love with Spirito but used whatever means she had, in this case, Claudio's feelings for her, to get what she wanted.*"

"And what did she want?" Agostino asked.

"A better life for her . . . and her son."

Agostino looked at me as if he had not considered that before. "You may be right."

"So, I take it Claudio did not pine away?"

"He married the daughter of wealthy merchants in Florence. Olivia's family would be good for the Truffle business—many important contacts. It worked out. They have two children right away, Lidia and Marco, twins, and later, more children."

"I'm glad their marriage was a good one," I said. "And Agatha's child, Santo, grew up close to that family, right? I understand Claudio and Olivia helped Santo learn the business and become an executive."

"Then you know Santo end up marrying Lidia, Claudio's daughter."

"Yes. SJ told me all this."

Agostino was suddenly alert. "You met SJ? How?"

"By coincidence, in the cemetery on my last visit three months ago. He invited me to his villa."

Agostino looked suspicious. "He invite you to his home? How did you manage that? He is a very private person."

I gave Agostino a big smile. "Let's just say we had a lot in common."

It was almost midnight when I finally left Villa Urbino and headed up the road to the *villetto*. The cold night air felt good against my flushed cheeks, and looking up, I saw the clouds had obscured the moon and spread a soft gray blanket over the countryside. I realized it had been hours since I thought about the status of my cellphone or how many messages I had missed on Facebook. Back home, my devices would have been clamoring for my attention every waking moment. As I gazed out at the fields, still and calm in the silence of the night, the tech wizards that demanded my allegiance seemed very far away.

Chapter 5

Survival Instincts

I TURNED the key in the lock and pushed open the wooden doors to the *villetto*. The lights had been left on and the room was toasty. I looked around my private little domain with satisfaction. *This is what it will be like when I get my place fixed up.* I imagined myself in Scheggino each season: gathering wild asparagus on mountain slopes in spring, drinking wine *al fresco* in the warm summer evenings, and cooking sumptuous meals in my brand-new kitchen. So far, Umbria's winter chill had not been unbearable and, if anything, it was a refreshing change. Back home in San Diego, no matter what time of year it was, the weather rarely dipped below sixty degrees.

I reached into my pocket for my cell and, just as I suspected, it was deader than the proverbial doornail. I thought back to the last time I had seen my charger, maybe at the airport when we landed? Digging into my carry-on, I felt the familiar cord and pulled it out. Now, to find my adapter, that annoying plastic thing with holes on one side and two prongs on the other—I needed it to make the European electrical socket recognize my America devices. I dove back into my bag and retrieved the precious item. The only outlet I could find was next to the furnace, and right after I plugged the adapter in, I heard a distinctive *pop*. A flash of light next to the outlet followed, and seconds later, all the lights in the house went out.

Shit. What do I do now? The pitch-black room offered only an uncomfortable silence. Figuring a fuse must have blown, I thought briefly of calling Tino or Agostino. I glanced at the useless phone lying next to me and sighed. I was on my own, with only my survival instincts to rescue me from a night without conveniences.

Then I remembered the flashlight I had brought for just such an occasion. I reached my hand back into the carry-on, trying to identify the objects by feel. Lipstick, mascara, deodorant . . . When my fingers felt a hard object with a rubber grid on one end, I breathed a sigh of relief. I unearthed it, flicked on the button, and groped my way to the bathroom, the pinprick of light illuminating an impressive three inches in front of me. I stopped when my shins hit the toilet rim.

The last thing I remember as I slid between the sheets was that I no longer heard the hum of the furnace.

Sometime later, I woke up. For a split second, I had no idea where I was, what time it was, or why I had all my clothes on. All I knew was that I was freezing my ass off. Then I remembered. I pulled the covers over my head and assumed the fetal position. I huddled, in denial, for a few minutes before I assessed the situation. The furnace had to be checked, I needed to get another blanket out of the armoire, and I needed to pee like a racehorse. All those things required me to leave the confines of my bed, the only place in the house where I wasn't likely to die of hypothermia.

I sighed. There was only one way to do it, like taking a dip in the Pacific Ocean in winter: I held my breath and counted to three. One . . . two . . . I popped my head out, swung my legs over the side, grabbed my flashlight, and headed for the toilet.

Shivering in the darkness, I was painfully aware of how quickly a cozy cottage can turn cold and miserable without heat or electricity. It dawned on me how naïve I was. I didn't know the first thing about how to live in a foreign country. Who would I call if my own furnace broke in the dead of winter?

What time is it? I felt my wrist and realized I had my watch on. I held it close to my eyeballs. Seven-oh-five. I looked up at the tiny window above the shower stall. It sure didn't *seem* like five after seven in the morning. I hit my head with the palm of my free hand. I never changed the time. Italy was nine hours ahead of San Diego. It was 4:00 a.m. in Italy.

I figured I had two choices. I could grab another blanket and crawl into bed, or I could find my tennis shoes and hit the trails. Running, even in thirty-degree weather, I would be warm in less than an hour. Then I remembered the bike. Maybe I could take it for a spin on the old Roman road. I walked over and shined my flashlight on it. The paint had probably been bright turquoise once but over the years it had faded it to a pale grey. The handle bars were rusty, the basket was frayed and all the tires were flat. I sighed and groped around for my tennis shoes. It looked like it was going to be a run after all.

It was 4:45 a.m. when I finally stepped out into the pre-dawn air. It was not as cold as I thought it would be, probably because I was already acclimated. The temperature inside the *villetto* was the same as the temp outside. I squeezed open the unlocked gates, turned my flashlight on, and headed uphill toward the cemetery. The tiny pinprick of light skittered across the old Roman road, barely illuminating the mix of stone and crushed rock under my feet. After thirty minutes, I began to thaw out, and by 5:30, I could see a light growing in the eastern sky. The canopy of darkness paled, slowly transforming itself into recognizable shapes. Farm buildings, fence posts, and dog kennels, all became comforting landmarks as I ran past them. The sounds of animals waking up carried across the fields, announcing that the day had begun, and it was time for breakfast.

I ran as far as St. Anatolia, the next village over, before turning back. As I reached the highest part of the road, I looked west, toward the river, and saw the rose-colored stone of SJ's villa catching the first rays of the morning sun. Its classic lines resembled a thirteenth century fortress from the days when kings and noblemen once ruled the land. *Agatha's Castle.* I thought about the story Agostino had told us last night, the story of a woman who had turned a horrific tragedy into an opportunity to save her lover and provide a better life for her family. In all that discussion, there was one issue we had not touched on. Agatha's life had been altered by Armando's brutal actions and drawn into the trauma of a family trying to survive a scandal. But what about Agatha the *victim*? What about the pain and suffering she must have experienced? I wondered how she coped with the emotional damage and if the success she enjoyed had ever made up for the loss of her innocence and the man she loved.

Looking down on the town of Scheggino, I suddenly felt an emotional connection with its people . . . their passion, their instinct for survival, and their willingness to make the best of life's difficulties. Agatha's story was a perfect example of that. Whatever hardships lay ahead or whatever changes I had to make to fit in, I knew that I possessed the qualities of my ancestors and that I belonged here.

It was nearly six when I reached Villa Urbino. I debated going into my little igloo and braving a shower, but my lack of confidence that *anything* worked in the *villetto*, including the plumbing, kicked in. I grabbed my phone and charger, adjusted my watch to the correct time, and headed down the dirt road to wake up Tino.

I knocked as loudly as I dared. After what seemed like an eternity, the door opened, and a disheveled version of my brother, complete with seriously rumpled pajamas, greeted me.

"You look like shit," he said.

"Thanks. I woke up at four and went for a run. You?"

"Three. But went back to bed. Nice and toasty in here."

"Soooo glad to hear it." I handed him my cellphone and charger. *"Postmortem rigor mortis."*

"Doesn't that bachelor pad have outlets?"

"I blew a fuse. Long story. Unless you want to stand here for thirty minutes, I'll tell you at breakfast. By the way, when is breakfast?"

"Eight o'clock."

Two hours from now. "I need coffee," I whimpered, looking inside Tino's room, hoping to see a pot.

"Go find Agostino. Farmers get up early."

The salon was warm, and the smell of roasted coffee beans filled the air as I walked in. Agostino sat with his legs propped on the dining room table, reading *Il Messaggero*, the Italian newspaper from Rome. He took a look at me and grinned. "Rough night?"

My eyes narrowed. This was the second comment about my appearance by a man before seven a.m. Since my need for caffeine far outweighed any outrage I was tempted to feel, I swallowed my pride . . . and my vanity. "Cappuccino, if you have it."

"Coming right up." Agostino swung his legs off the table and disappeared into the kitchen. A moment later, I heard the swooshing sound of steaming milk coursing through the espresso machine. I sat down, my sense of optimism restored. With a cappuccino in my hand, the world would be miraculously restored to order and last night's disaster destined to fade into memory like a bad dream.

Agostino placed the fragrant cup in front of me. "Do you want to talk about it?"

"Talk about what? Do I look that bad?"

"Let us just say, it is a good thing there are no mirrors in here."

Okay. That does it. My host is going to get the bad news without sugar. "Well, for starters, your furnace is out, an electrical outlet is burnt to a crisp, and the lights don't work."

"I'm fairly sure the problem is electrical, but I will defer to the experts. And by the way, the Italian name for plumber is *idraulico*. You had better memorize it, you may need to use it in the future.

"Thank you. Know any good ones?"

"I do. Now tell me, what happened in the *villetto*."

"I plugged my charger into the outlet next to the furnace." Even as I said it, I realized how idiotic it sounded.

"Do you remember when I told you furnace was temperamental?"

"I guess I picked the wrong outlet."

Agostino considered this. "I appreciate your honesty, and so I will be equally honest. This is not first time something like this happen."

"I feel marginally better. Don't get me wrong, the *villetto* is charming. And I love that adorable 1940s bicycle. If it weren't for the missing chain and flat tires, I would have ridden it this morning. Who did it belong to?"

Agostino's face changed. "It was Giulia's."

"Giulia." I repeated. "Who was that?"

Agostino took a while to answer. "Someone our family used to know."

The temperature in the room had grown chilly all of a sudden.

"Well," I said brightly "It is a very cool bike. I would love to ride it around the village while I'm here. Maybe you could fix it?"

Agostino's eyes met mine. "It is possible."

"Great." I said. "Now, If it's all the same to you, I'd like to stay in one of your ancestor's rooms tonight. I will be glad to pay for any damages."

"Oh, no. I'm sure you suffer enough." Agostino's grin was back. "I have two rooms available. Which one of my family members do you want to spend the night with?"

Chapter 6

Stilettos Rule

LATER THAT morning, Tino and I were standing in front of the non-descript entrance to the town's government headquarters. Totally at odds with its ancient surroundings, a neon sign with the word *Comune* hung over the top of the building and a modern sliding glass door that automatically opened and closed during business hours.

"Well, maybe they're already here. Shall we go in?" The doors slid open as Tino and I stepped into an unfurnished foyer with gunmetal-colored walls. "Hey," I said, touching his arm and giving it a squeeze, "I couldn't even imagine doing this alone. In case I forget to tell you . . . thanks for supporting me in all this. I feel better knowing you've got my back."

"Happy to be here."

I noticed Tino had dressed with special care this morning: khaki slacks and a button-down shirt under a smart leather jacket. The look went well with his strong jaw, blue eyes, and the gray but abundant head of hair.

"Do you think the mayor will attend the meeting?" Tino asked nonchalantly.

My brother's well-groomed appearance suddenly took on a whole new meaning. I smiled and wiped a few flakes from the shoulders of his leather jacket.

"You can bet on it," I said.

We walked up the narrow staircase to the first floor. The interior of the *comune* was drab and uninteresting; its bare walls and small cubicles reminded me of the 1950s' Bauhaus era. Either frills were not considered a government priority, or the *comune* had very little money to work with. I stuck my head into one of the open doors and inquired about our appointment. An overworked secretary pointed down the hall without looking up from her computer. A little farther down the corridor, a door opened to a large conference room. There was a long table with a podium at the far end and behind it, a framed picture of the current President of the Italian Republic. Two flags, one of Italy and the other a red shield with a castle, the symbol of Scheggino, flanked the podium.

"*Buongiorno*!" Francesca Corti waved and motioned for us to be seated. She was conferring with two men I did not recognize.

"Anna, this is Fabrizio di Lucca, the *notaio*. He has drawn up your title, the official document confirming your ownership of the apartment."

A gaunt man with impressive eyebrows nodded to me, looked suspiciously at Tino, and returned to his papers.

"And this is Maximillian Ladro, a real estate lawyer hired to represent the *comune*."

"Please, call me Max. I am honored to serve you." He put his hand to his chest and gave a slight bow.

Max had the look of a shyster and a manner more calculated than sincere, but maybe that was just my inherent distrust of anyone in the legal profession. I smiled and held out my hand, determined to give him the benefit of the doubt.

The sound of heels clicking down the hall put a halt to the pleasantries. A moment later, the mayor of Scheggino appeared in the doorway wearing a turquoise pant suit, a pink and white pin-striped shirt, and four-inch heels the color of cotton candy.

Tino was on his feet in seconds, pulling out the chair next to him and offering it to her. An uncomfortable silence followed, and everyone remained seated. It occurred to me that the chair Tony had offered was not the mayor's usual seat, and protocol had been disturbed. Like a parent with a well-intentioned child that had overstepped, Pamela smiled at him and sat down.

"*Nostra sindaco*," Max announced to the group, obviously for the benefit of the American contingent. Everyone else knew who she was.

"*Sindaco* means *mayor*," I whispered to Tino.

Max gathered his papers together and spoke. "As you know, the previous owners of the apartment had to default on their loan, and since the *comune* was the original owner, the property reverted back to them. Anna Wilson is here to sign the official documents as the new owner of Twenty-Seven Intero One, Via San Nicola. I have two money orders here from the bank, each for €40,000, totaling €80,000."

"Plus, the €20,000 already paid in the deposit," I reminded him.

Max looked at the papers and conferred with Francesca and the *Notaio*. "Yes, that is correct." He looked at me. "Italian Law states that, in order to purchase property, a foreigner must prove that he will actually live here, at least part time. One way to do that is to open a bank account. Which I see you have done. The government also requires an accounting of how the funds deposited were earned."

I groaned inwardly. I had gone through this three months ago when I opened the account where the money would be wired to the local bank. Endless questions about where the money had come from. I guessed it was a precaution against laundered funds from nefarious organizations.

"This is your brother, is it not?" Max indicated Tino. "The money, perhaps it comes from him?"

I felt my anger rising. Why did everyone naturally assume that it was the man that made the money? Before I could protest, Tino intervened. "The money is Anna's. Primarily inherited from our parents. None of it belongs to me."

Max turned to me. "Your parents? What line of work was your father in?"

I cleared my throat and addressed the group. "My mother was a schoolteacher, and my father a civil servant. They saved and sacrificed to provide a secure future for their children."

"Brava," the mayor said.

I looked into her baby blue eyes.

Then she turned her focus on the lawyer she had hired. "Enough with the questions. Signora Wilson is the kind of resident we want here in Scheggino. We must welcome her, not drive her out with silly discussion. Give la signora Wilson *i documenti* and have her sign."

Pamela's English may not have equaled her associate's, but the message was clear. The old ways had no place in the current administration.

My pen posed over the papers, I realized what a momentous moment this was. I was signing a legal document making me the sole owner of an apartment, and all the unknowns that went with it, in a foreign country. Earthquakes, natural disasters, and plumbing problems would all have to be dealt with by me. I took a deep breath and scribbled my name at the bottom where it said, *"firma."* Max looked over the signature and asked if I had any questions.

"Just one. As I understand it, the previous owners have no further claim on my property . . . Is that right?"

"That is correct."

"So, there is no chance I will come downstairs one morning and find my kitchen gone?"

Max stifled a grin. "No chance, but, just to be safe, I would lock my doors before I turn in for the night."

The mayor indicated the meeting was over. When Tino rose to

pull out her chair, she gave him a look that held more amusement than condescension. I even think I saw her eyelashes flutter once or twice. Maybe she was considering that, even in a nonsexist workplace, there might be a little room for chivalry.

Fabrizio gathered his papers, knitted his eyebrows more furiously than ever, and bid us a barely audible *buongiorno*. Francesca dropped a small white card into my purse. *"Idraulico,"* she said, and followed Fabrizio out the door.

"Would you be interested in a *caffè* at Il Ponte?" Max looked at Tino and me.

In Italy, an invitation to share a coffee after a business deal means one of two things: it can be a way of repaying a service without an exchange of money, or it can be an opportunity to conduct further business in a casual atmosphere away from curious eyes and ears. Max's invitation had all the earmarks of the latter.

The bartender at Il Ponte recognized our companion, but I noticed the welcome was not particularly warm. "Signore, e signora," Emilio said, his lips barely moving.

"Buongiorno," I said, returning the greeting. *"Due cappuccini."* I looked at Max.

"Campari, grazie."

It was barely 11:00 a.m., and our lawyer friend was already dipping into the sauce.

Max waited until the drinks were served before he spoke. "My wife . . . she has been diagnosed with a rare disease and an operation is needed. A very *expensive* operation." He paused. "It is a difficult time for our family . . . two children in university, many expenses. You do not have children, do you?"

I shook my head and glanced at Tino. Where was he headed with this?

"No, I thought not. You have an inheritance now, money enough to buy a second home in Italy. How fortunate for you."

I was too stunned to reply. Max rose. "If you will excuse me a moment. When I return we will talk."

I watched him walk down the hall to the bathroom. "What the hell?" I said to Tino. "Are you thinking what I'm thinking?"

"Looks like he's expecting a little "tip" for his "services.""

"Doesn't the *comune* pay him for doing this? Francesca said he had been hired."

Tino shrugged. "I noticed he's wearing a pretty snazzy pair of Manolos, so he can't be hurting that bad. He may have a little side business of extortion going on with poor little rich girls from the US. What are you going to do?"

"I cannot allow him to intimidate me. Who knows where this might end."

Max returned and signaled the bartender for another Campari. I had a good idea who would be expected to pay for it.

Max sat down and took a long pull of his drink. He had the confident expression of a man ready to close a deal. "Well, what have you decided?"

"I am sorry about your wife's illness. As far as any financial help, I will have to discuss it with my brother-in-law, Vito, and his *people* in Palermo." I raised my eyebrows a touch for effect. "I'm afraid they make all the decisions. If you will just leave your information with me, I am sure he will contact you directly."

There was a long silence. Max rose, finished his Campari, and gathered his things. "It was a pleasure." He nodded to both of us. "Wonderful to have met you." He turned abruptly and headed for the door.

"Give your wife my best," I called after him. "I will pray for her."

Chapter 7

Plumbers Are a Girl's Best Friend

I WALKED to the counter and paid for our coffees and Max's two Camparis. The bartender smiled sympathetically and only charged me for one. After leaving Il Ponte, Tino and I turned left and crossed the old stone bridge that spanned the river. Brightly colored rafts piled along the shoreline were waiting for the tourist season to begin. In June and July, with the humidity at its peak, the region would be teeming with families eager to ride the not-too-dangerous rapids. Now, it was deserted, the shack that housed oars and wetsuits buttoned up tight.

Tino leaned over the bridge, watching the play of sun on the water. "I hope our friend, the one with the fancy shoes, doesn't find out Terry's husband 'Vito' lives in San Diego and works for Sempra Energy."

I laughed. "I had to nip it in the bud. I don't want that weasel asking me to fund his new winery in Tuscany a couple of years from now. Seriously, I am surprised that a man with that kind of professional standing would resort to such methods. I confess, when I first met him I thought he was a little shady, but I hadn't pegged him as an extortionist."

"It could be he was testing your mettle, you being a foreigner and all." You've got to stand up for yourself or the villagers will cut you up into little pieces and feed you to the hogs. Speaking of prosciutto, when and where is lunch?"

I pulled out the little card Francesca had dropped into my purse and looked at it: *Luca Perdita. Idraulico per tutti i mestieri.* "I think that means plumber for all your needs. I need to check this guy out before the stink in my new apartment becomes permanent. I also remember Agostino saying he knew someone."

"I'd go with Agostino's man," Tino said.

"Why?"

"Let me put it this way. One plumber comes recommended by a realtor who just got her 3 percent commission and doesn't even live here, and the other, by a man who owns a working farm, five guest rooms, and a *villetto*. Who do you think has had more hands-on experience?"

I thought about last night's fiasco. "You're right. Let's go back to the villa. Who knows, maybe Agostino's cooking up something delicious for lunch."

As soon as we arrived, Tino and I followed our noses to the kitchen.

"*Zuppa de Lenticchie,*" Agostino announced, stirring a large pot of steaming liquid with a wooden spoon that looked like it had been in the family for generations. Nearby was a cutting board full of cooked pork ready to be added to the pot. The smell of spices and roasted meat made both of us realize how famished we were.

"Mom used to make lentil soup all the time when we were kids," I said, putting my face over the rim and letting the steam go up my nostrils. "But hers never smelled like this."

"The secret ingredient is the *lenticchie*. They come from Casteluccio, a town in the Apennine Mountains. The flowers the lentils make in *primavera* are famous. Someday, if you are lucky, I will take you there." Agostino winked at me.

I felt my face flush from the heat in the kitchen.

"So, how things go at the *comune*? Did you tip the lawyer?"

Tino chuckled. "How did you know?"

"Typical Italian business practice. Especially with Signore Ladro. What was it this time? His daughter's tuition to university?"

His wife's *very expensive* surgery," I answered. "Don't worry, I made up a story about my brother-in-law Vito from Palermo."

Agostino stopped stirring. "You have an uncle in the Mafia?"

I laughed. "No, but Max thinks I do."

Agostino resumed stirring. "You speak of your brother-in-law, but what about your sister? You have not mentioned her."

"Terry? There have been a few bumps in our relationship over the years."

"Ah." Agostino nodded his head. "No family path is ever smooth. I should know."

"Anna and Terry are close in age but have very different personalities," Tino explained.

"How so?" Agostino asked.

I thought for a minute. "I am the feather, and my sister is the rock. She never makes an impulsive decision while I . . . well . . . buy apartments in Italy sight unseen."

Agostino cut slices from a loaf of homemade bread and ladled the soup into large earthenware bowls. He pointed to an iron grater the size of a washboard and a triangle of cheese. "We will need some *Reggiano*. Meet me in the dining room."

Tino was making himself useful, having found a bottle of red wine and three glasses. "I could get used to this," he said as we all pulled up chairs and sat down.

Agostino gave him a pointed look. "As Anna can tell you . . . all this—" he gestured to the room, "comes with a price. Usually, a large bill from the *idraulico*."

I started to protest. "I told you I would pay . . ."

Agostino held up a hand. "No . . . no . . . What I mean is, tourists come here looking for a change, a life different than the one they have, but there is much that happens here to make that simple life possible. Harvesting the crop, cleaning the rooms, fixing furnaces . . ." He shot me a look. "Not to mention killing the calf for the *osso buco* that is served for dinner. Anna is going to find out soon what being a homeowner in our Italian village means."

"I'm beginning to see that. That reminds me, this morning you said you knew a plumber."

"*Sì*, the plumber. His name is GianPietro. He used to build villas up on Giro dei Condotti, the old road that crosses the mountains from Spoleto. He can fix anything, plumbing, electrical . . . but now he just works on small problems. Toilet, furnace . . ."

"Okay, okay, I get the drift. Where can I find him?"

"He's been working at the *villetto* all morning."

I walked up the dirt road after lunch, hoping to entice GianPietro to have a look at my apartment. The door was open, and I noticed that the bicycle was gone. There were tools spread out all over the bedroom floor and a figure, surrounded by a cloud of smoke, crouched over the furnace.

"*Buongiorno,*" I called out.

A head jerked up, and a pair of eyes regarded me suspiciously. A smoldering cigarette dangled between the man's lips.

"I am Anna."

GianPietro pointed to the burnt-out electrical socket. "You do this?"

I assessed my chances for escaping a serious dressing down from this character. He was male, about my age. *Maybe a little flirting might help the situation.* I batted my eyelashes. "I'm afraid so. Electrical things just baffle me."

GianPietro puffed on his cigarette and stared at me like I was an alien from another planet.

"When will you be finished?" I asked timidly.

"What, you need to shower?"

"No, I was wondering if you could look at a little problem I have at my apartment in town."

The plumber's jaw dropped. "You already make problem somewhere else?"

"Someone else made the problem. I just inherited it," I explained.

GianPietro wasn't buying it. I could tell. He took a last puff off his cigarette, flung it onto the floor, and ground it out. I winced. Good thing I was sleeping at the villa tonight. "I bought one of the apartments in the Castle, the one on San Nicola that's been vacant for a year. Do you know it?"

"But of course," GianPietro said. "I work on plumbing problem there."

Great. There's a plumbing history that precedes me. Nice to know.

"What problem you have?" GianPietro seemed interested.

" The toilet is stopped up."

"Stopped up?"

" You know. . ." I pantomimed flushing and then something that looked like confetti being thrown in the air.

"Ah, *sì. Un* backup."

Backup. Perfect description. I wonder where the Italians came up with *that* word.

GianPietro put down his tools. "You have *soldi*?" He rubbed two fingers of one hand together.

"You mean money?"

"*Sì*, moneee. You can pay *oggi*?"

"Yes, uh, *sì*, I can pay today."

GianPietro reached for his jacket. "*Andiamo*."

I didn't think I understood correctly. "You want to go now?"

"*Sì*, now," he repeated.

"*Un momento*. I've got to call, uh, *fratello*." I pantomimed using the phone. I dialed and waited. Three, four, five, six rings before a groggy voice answered.

"You asleep already?" I asked Tino.

"Just resting my eyeballs. What's up?"

"I'm with the plumber, he wants to go look at the apartment now. Want to come?"

I heard a snort. "What, and clean excrement? That job is reserved for homeowners."

"Okay . . . uh . . . can I borrow the Maserati?"

Long pause.

I sighed. "Didn't think so but I thought I'd ask. *Thanks*. I know, *I'm* the owner. Sweet dreams."

I hung up and looked at GianPietro. "Can we go in your car?"

GianPietro's car turned out to be a baby blue, three-wheeled 1990 Piaggio Ape van. In Rome, I had seen these toy trucks, loaded with bread and pizza, zipping through the tiny alleyways in the early morning hours. About half the length and width of a Ford-150 pickup, the Ape is Italy's answer to negotiating the ancient cobblestone streets built when horses and chariots were in style.

"She can carry four hundred kilos," GianPietro said proudly. "My wife, she say I love Delilah more than her."

"Delilah?" I tried to keep a straight face. "You named your truck Delilah?"

GianPietro grinned sheepishly and slid into the driver's seat.

"An appropriate name for a mistress," I said, climbing in beside him. "I bet Delilah doesn't nag you to take out the trash."

On the eastern edge of the castle, there was a long stone ramp that led up to the third tier. Residents who wanted to avoid the stairs drove up the ramp and jostled for the few parking spaces at the top. On holidays and weekends, the cars would pile up bumper to bumper, and God help you if you needed to get out the next morning. A stone archway a few feet away opened to a narrow path creating access to the interior apartments. GianPietro cruised up the ramp at full speed and headed for the archway.

"You're going through that thing?" I asked.

He changed gears and passed under the arch with barely an inch to spare on either side. "I have been here before," he reminded me.

We drove in as far as we could before the walkway ended abruptly in front of Leonia's front yard. She was outside in a flash. "*Non poi fare parcheggio qui!*" she called out, hands on hips and eyes blazing.

I got out of the truck.

"Anna!" I did not see you." She looked contrite. "I thought . . ." Her voice trailed off when she saw GianPietro get out.

"*Idraulico* to help me with a little plumbing problem. It will be only a few minutes," I promised her.

"What kind of problem?"

"Stopped up toilet."

"Stopped up?" She raised an eyebrow.

"*Un* backup," I corrected myself.

"Ah, *sì.*" She nodded her head. "You need supplies?"

"All here." GianPietro opened the tiny door of the van and handed me a bucket, disinfectant, and rags. When I looked inside, I saw shelves of neatly arranged tools and supplies lining both sides.

"Nice," I said. "You made these shelves?"

GianPietro nodded, beaming with pride. He pulled out a substantial-looking black cord with a knob attached to a metal crank. "*Serpente,*" he said.

"*Serpente,*" I repeated. I knew what that was.

I keyed into the apartment and started climbing the staircase with GianPietro huffing and puffing behind me. "You've got to cut down on those cigs," I told him.

"So my wife tell me . . . don't you start."

I tried another approach. "What will happen to Delilah if you aren't here anymore?"

GianPietro considered the question seriously. "She will find another. *Le Donne* are . . . *come si dice . . .*"

"Fickle?" I offered.

"*Sì,* fickle. They go where the money is."

I wanted to take issue with that statement, but I had a toilet to unclog. As we approached the bathroom, the stench hit us full on. The stagnant water had receded, but the stain still marked the side of the tub and the base of the walls.

"Where did the water go?" I asked, not sure I wanted to know. I visualized the ceiling below us collapsing at some future point. Probably the day after I left for San Diego.

"It drain in this hole." GianPietro pointed to an opening cut into the tile floor. "It go outside."

Thank God for that.

"You clean and I work." Gian Pietro brandished the snake and inserted it into the one area that had not drained. I averted my eyes.

I started scrubbing every surface in sight: tub, sink, walls, trying to tune out the ghastly sounds the snake was making.

"*Porca maseria!*" GianPietro screamed, the first of a continuous string of expletives that only increased in severity as the minutes passed.

"*Leccaculo!*"

I pretended not to hear, but that word—literally, "lick my ass"— had me doubled over with laughter. "Watch your language," I called out. "There's a lady present."

A few more minutes passed, GianPietro and the snake fighting it out in a ferocious battle. A loud *Cazzo!* rang out, followed by the sound of water going down the drain. GianPietro proudly held up the blackened end of the *serpente*. *"Vinto!* We win!"

Just in time. The swearing had escalated into subject matter my delicate ears were not meant to hear. GianPietro stepped into the hallway and lit up a cigarette like a man who had just experienced a particularly good roll in the hay. "You mind if I smoke?"

I noticed he posed the question *after* he lit up. My first impulse was to order him outside, but then I realized I risked upsetting the only plumber I knew in Italy. "Not a problem," I replied.

GianPietro helped me finish cleaning up, and we headed downstairs. "Nice place," he said, looking around. "You need *servizio* down here."

"Servizio?"

"A toilet and sink, very small. You have no *bagno* on this floor. Come in handy when . . ."

"Yes, I get it. Where would you put it?"

"Over there." He gestured to the northwest corner. Plumbing from upstairs on same wall."

"Would you be interested in building one for me?"

He regarded me thoughtfully. "You have *soldi* for this?"

"Sì, I have *soldi.*"

We walked to the truck in silence. "What do I owe you?" I asked, watching GianPietro back up Delilah a few feet and make a tight turn to face the way we had come.

"Quaranta euros."

"Forty euros?" I couldn't believe my ears. It was a fraction of what a plumber would have charged me back in the US.

GianPietro raised an eyebrow. "Too much?"

I was about to say, "Too little," but that might've been a dangerous precedent to set, especially if he was going to do more work for me. "Don't show all your cards at once," my mom used to say.

"Thirty-five euros and I treat you to a caffè at Il Ponte."

"Deal." GianPietro smiled, and we raced down the ramp into town.

I sat back against the polished leather seats of the tiny *Ape* and pondered my next move. "Can I call you "GP"? GianPietro is quite a mouthful."

"Call me what you like. Just pay me on time." He laughed.

I whipped out my pocketbook and counted out the bills. "GP, how do you feel about building me a kitchen?"

Chapter 8

Skeletons

MY CELLPHONE was vibrating. I reached inside my bag and looked at the screen. *Tino.* He must be up from his nap. Just the thought of him in Lala Land while I was scrubbing excrement off walls made my blood boil.

"Sleep well?" I said sweetly.

"Where are you?" the voice on the other end sounded cranky.

"GP and I are at the bar having a couple of drinks." I winked at my companion.

"At the bar? Who's GP?" He sounded anxious. "What about the apartment?"

"My new best friend and I are celebrating a victory. We needed serious sustenance after unstopping the *backup.*"

"What?"

"Inside joke. I'll tell you all the gory details when I get back."

"When is that going to be? I've been fielding questions from Agostino for the last hour about our plans for the evening. Do I tell him about our dinner with SJ?"

"We're headed up there now." I hung up and watched GP snuff out a butt seconds before it burnt his fingers. I waved the smoke away from my face. "That's your third cigarette, GP."

"I see you like to nag." He had just taken out another and was ready to light it. "Maybe I think again about working for you."

"I'm just trying to keep you alive now that we will be working together. I wouldn't want you to drop dead before the kitchen's finished."

⁕⌒⁕

By 3:00 p.m., the November chill had taken hold in the valley. The sun was ceding its dominance, and clouds were gathering at the edges of the mountains, waiting for nightfall. Weather in Italy always seemed as dramatic and volatile as its people—warm and inviting one minute and dark and threatening the next. I had learned to dress in layers and always carry an umbrella.

We sped through town, stopping only for a flock of sheep slowly making their way home. The bells around their necks made a comforting sound in the quiet of the late afternoon. Dinnertime came early for the beasts in the countryside.

After the last little lamb had crossed the road, GP's Ape roared up the hill and turned into the villa.

"Do you know the man who lives over there?" I pointed to SJ's pile of stone that had now come into view.

"*Sì*, Santo Urbino's son. He run the kitchen at Urbino Tartufo Headquarters."

"You mean the modern complex off SS395."

GP nodded. "He make all the recipes and try them out for customers . . . so they can see how to cook with the truffle. He used to give big parties at his place for the investors with soldi."

"No more?"

"He retire. Now he make wine and grappa. Very good grappa. Everything he do, he do well."

"A private man, yes? Do you know him personally?"

"Private, *sì*. I only say *buongiorno* when I go there."

"You go to SJ's villa?"

"To fix plumbing." GP gave me a sly look. "Even rich people's toilets have backup. "

GianPietro dropped me off near the service entrance, and I headed for the kitchen. In a place the size of Villa Urbino, it was the only room where you were sure to find another human being.

"Where have you been?" Agostino was bent over a long counter, rolling out pieces of dough on wax paper. He didn't even look up.

"Miss me?"

"Not in the least. Nice and quiet here all day, but your brother has been pestering me as to your whereabouts."

I wanted to laugh out loud. Tino had said just the opposite. I watched Agostino gently cut the dough into thin slices. "What are you making?"

"*Strangozzi*. Pasta rolled like rope, a regional favorite in Umbria. Here, I show you how to do it." Agostino took a sliver of dough and rolled it between his fingers. "It takes someone with a delicate touch. I'm sure you will have no trouble getting the hang of it." He handed me a cutting board with a dozen strips on it.

Agostino's comment was innocent enough, so why was I blushing again? I stared at the strips of dough and sighed. A nice soft bed and an hour of shut-eye had been my preferred plan. After all, I had gotten up at four, signed papers making me a homeowner, and scrubbed a *very* dirty bathroom. I think I was entitled to a little downtime. I would roll a few pieces just to be polite, I told myself, and take off.

"So, Tino tells me you are visiting SJ, your cousin, tonight." Agostino moved another cutting board next to mine and started rolling. "He is making you dinner?"

Cousin. Agostino thinks SJ is Santo's son.

"You are lucky to be invited to dinner. He is a great chef. Even though we are neighbors, I have never been invited."

"Have you ever invited him here?"

"Never." The way Agostino said it, I knew I had touched a nerve.

"Agostino, am I missing something? It sounds like you don't like him very much. Why?"

Agostino put down the dough and looked me in the eye. "It goes back a long way... something that happen between our families before I was born. I understand you have just discovered a family member you never knew about, but these families live here for generations. They have loved, hated, and grieved together. Drama like you would not believe. Like you Americans say, there is some serious shit lying around here, so be careful where you step."

While I wasn't exactly surprised by that comment, this was not the Agostino I thought I knew. I turned to face him. "I would hope that when I throw a party in my new home, *both* of you will come."

The spaghetti western was back on, Morricone's music swelling to a crescendo. The standoff lasted less than a minute before a twinkle came back into Agostino's eye.

"Miracles do happen . . . even in Scheggino."

I went back to rolling my dough. Agostino wiped his fingers on a towel and tucked an errant lock of hair behind my ear. He left his hand there for a moment. I glanced up quickly, and he smiled. There was a tender look in his eyes.

"I am sure buying a house can be a tiring business. Even though I would enjoy your company, I think a *pennichella* might be more what you need."

I looked up. "Does *pennichella* mean *nap* by any chance?"

"It does." He handed me the towel. "Time for me to show you where you will sleep tonight. I have chosen *Zia* Marina's room. She was my favorite aunt."

Marina Urbino's room was a refreshing change from the old-fashioned décor of the villa. Ivory linen drapes lined the old casement windows, and an armoire, a dresser, and several chairs of white-washed

Scandinavian wood were the only pieces of furniture in the room. There was a freshness about everything, a combination of sophistication and simplicity existing in perfect harmony.

"Did your aunt decorate the room?" I asked Agostino after we had keyed in. "It's absolutely lovely."

"She did. Everything to do with homemaking come naturally to her."

Was it a long time ago that she passed?" I asked gently.

"She die in 1975, when she was sixty-four years old." Agostino's eyes took on a far-away look as if a window to his past had suddenly opened. "We used to walk the road that runs along the river, below the villa, and pick the wild asparagus in spring. She knew the names of all the herbs and flowers that grow near its banks. Then we come back and cook something wonderful with what we find. Did you know *funghi* grow down there? Morels. They have the most flavor. I think it was because of her that I discover my love to cook. I still miss her." He paused for a moment as if remembering something sad. "I was just a boy when she die."

"She was young. What did she die of?"

Agostino did not answer right away, and when he did, his voice was full of emotion. "A broken heart."

I waited for him to tell me more, but he was silent. The faraway look was back.

I walked over to a wall on which hung a series of black and white pictures from the past. I saw Villa Urbino in its heyday, when it was a home, not a hotel. There was a portrait of an Italian beauty, with black hair and a glorious smile, holding a baby. "Is this Marina . . . and her child?"

Agostino was watching me warily, as if he felt my questions were those of a curious stranger rather than a caring friend. "She is with her daughter, Giulia," he finally said.

"What happened to Giulia? There is no room with her name on it."

Agostino's eyes had a steely look in them. "Maybe you should ask SJ that question."

Chapter 9

Forgiveness

I TURNED, catching my reflection in the full-length mirror. The silk dress flared gently like a soft blue cloud as it came to rest just above my ankles. My hair was caught up in a French twist, tendrils of curls cascading down my neck, half concealing oval shaped diamond earrings. I had spent more time than usual applying makeup: foundation, mascara, eye concealer … a lot of eye concealer. The overall effect was not entirely without merit, I decided … *even for a woman of a certain age …*

I reached into my suitcase and pulled out a velvet jewelry case. Inside, the cameo locket glistened on the golden chain. My mother had given it to me right before she died. "Find its owner and you will find the secret to our past," she had said. Now I knew who that person was. My grandfather's long, lost love, Agatha Altarocca. Tonight, I would wear it in her honor.

It was only 5:00 p.m., but I felt like I had not slept in days. The anticipated nap had been eclipsed by an attack of nerves soon after Agostino left the room. He had been cold, and even bitter, when SJ's name came up. Clearly, my host harbored a grudge against my uncle for something that happened years ago, something he didn't want to talk about. *In bocca al lupo.* Here I was, again, in a feud where my family was inextricably linked.

Tino did not answer my knock, so I walked through the pool area to the main salons and the kitchen beyond. As I opened the French doors, I heard voices.

"It will be interesting to meet him," I heard Tino say. "To learn about a lost relative is exciting stuff. I will be sure and tell you all about it . . . if we ever get there. We should have left thirty minutes ago."

"Sorry. It took a little longer than usual to get the desired result," I said walking into the kitchen.

Agostino turned, and I saw his clear gray eyes travel slowly down my body and back up. When they stopped at my eyes, I felt a shiver go up my spine.

"*Bellissima,* Signora." Agostino gave me a mock bow. "How do you say in English? You clean up good?"

I laughed, "You mean from what I looked like this morning? I can safely say you saw me at my worst. Anything would be an improvement. Thanks for the compliment though."

Tino rolled his eyes. "I hate to break up the love fest, but can we go now?"

"That's right, *chefs* don't like to be kept waiting," Agostino said with sarcasm.

"Just as you wouldn't if he were coming here," I shot back. *Fat chance that will ever happen.* I reached for my coat and started for the door. "Don't wait up. We have a lot of catching up to do." I smiled sweetly. "Shall I give him your best?"

"You may tell him I look forward to being invited to dinner at Paradiso Vinto someday."

"Paradiso Vinto?"

"The name of your relative's villa. You did not know? Agatha named it."

"Paradiso Vinto," I repeated. "Paradise Won."

"Great name," Tino said. "From the outside alone, I can tell a lot of hard work and ingenuity went into building that place. Sounds like she was proud of it."

"It came with a price . . . the price of her innocence," I said.

"Maybe that's why it felt like a victory." I fingered the locket around my neck. "In my opinion, she paid dearly for that success."

"Actions rarely come without a price," Agostino said gently. "Sometimes we have to accept the consequences even if we can't control them."

"And forgive," I cut in. "Don't discount the value of forgiveness. Don't forget, Agatha forgave the family of her assailant."

Agostino nodded. "Forgiveness is the one thing we hold back . . . as punishment for what has been done to us. I have been guilty of that in my life."

"It is a step in the right direction if you can admit it," I said.

Our eyes met, and a moment of understanding passed between us. The admission of his failing and my acknowledgement of his struggle restored our faith in each other. I, for one, was not going to let a past I had no control over affect a friendship I was beginning to cherish.

"Now go, both of you, before the chef decides you have insulted him and refuses to serve you. All I have to offer is *fegato di pollo*."

"I know what *fegato* is," Tino said, "Our mother served it as punishment when we were bad. Liver. And *pollo* is chicken, so I guess we'd better get over there in a hurry!"

⁓

Tino and I drove up the Roman road to the cemetery and turned left. The path that led to Paradiso Vinto was just beyond it, lined on either side with rows of cypress trees.

"What is going on between you two?" Tino asked as we drew up to the small parking area to the left of the villa. "There is definitely some chemistry. I just can't tell what kind. It feels like angry flirting."

"You mean Agostino and me? We're just sparring. Surely, you haven't forgotten my natural inclination for stirring up trouble?"

"How could I forget? You chose to stay in the mouth of the wolf instead of that really safe, boring, Il Ponte place in town."

"How can we get to the truth if we're way down there? There is some rift between Agostino and SJ that involves Agostino's great aunt, Marina. It happened ages ago. I'm hoping to get to the bottom of it tonight."

"Leave me out of your interrogation, please. I'm here to meet my uncle, enjoy some great food and wine, and admire the view. I take it there is one."

"Incredible. You will love this place, I guarantee."

Twilight had already sharpened the edges of the mountains casting shadows on the clay tile roofs of several cottages grouped around a courtyard at the rear of the villa. As Tino and I got out of the car, we could see a spotlighted dome, like an ancient Roman *basilica*, rising from the center of the main house. Fairy lights glittered through the trees, and a rustic wooden portico entwined with flowers covered the footpath where we walked. At the end of the walkway, a circular patio spread out in front of a massive arched entrance.

"Nice car," a voice called out. Looking closer, I saw an old man sitting quietly on a bench. He rose slowly, pointing with his cane as he walked toward us. "Maserati GranCabrio, 2015, if I'm not mistaken . . ."

Tino strode forward to meet him. "Good eye. I am Tino, your . . . uh . . ."

"Nephew, I think," the old man said and held out his hand. They both laughed.

I stepped into the light. "I sure am glad Tino brought that car along. Spares me a lot of tedious introductions. Tino raced cars when he was younger so you have already made points."

"NASCAR?" SJ asked.

"Formula 1," Tino answered. "Those were the days. When I valued thrill over living to a ripe old age. Now I just rent high-performance cars on trips to Europe."

"Maturity has its rewards," SJ countered.

"Yeah," Tino responded with a laugh. "Like a nice boring life."

"Many would argue with that statement," I broke in. "Traveling around Italy in a Maserati sounds pretty exciting to me. Even if the guy in the driver's seat happens to be my brother."

"I envy you, Tino. If I were ten years younger, I'd hop in the back seat and join you," SJ said.

"Never too late. Just give me the word." Tino slapped SJ on the back. "There are a few places I'd still like to visit."

I turned to SJ. "May I offer our excuses for being late? Making myself presentable takes longer these days."

"The effort was well worth it." SJ smiled, his eyes on the locket. A tear escaped and roll down his face. He brushed it away and smiled. "I'm sorry. It is just that the way you are dressed tonight—the elegant way you carry yourself—you remind me so much of my mother, Agatha."

"My posture is the result of a lifetime of ballet classes, I'm afraid." I was embarrassed, but touched.

Tino stepped in. "Anna was quite the ballerina in her day."

In her day . . . love hearing *that.* "It was a long time ago, SJ. In the stone age."

SJ seemed to sense my irritation. "If we keep talking about age, it will be a very dreary evening. I try to avoid the subject whenever possible." He took my arm, and the three of us walked up the steps to the villa. "I have a wonderful meal planned for tonight. A regional delicacy. *Trippa e zampa alla Marchigiana.*"

"Which translates to?" I asked, shooting Tino a warning look.

"Tripe and calf's foot."

Chapter 10

Paradiso Vinto

THE MOMENT we crossed the threshold, the magic of Agatha Altarocca's sanctuary enveloped us. Walking across the black and white marbled foyer, we entered the main living space. The room was enormous, but the décor felt intimate, enticing us to relax and stretch out in armchairs and on the long, modular sofas. Against the white-washed stone walls, slabs of travertine, serving as side boards, rested on pieces of clear glass as if they were suspended in mid-air. Iron shapes with lights functioned as floor lamps, and sculptures resembling human figures blended artfully into corners. A massive stone fireplace with a flue that stood off center from the great room bisected the open space around it. From where I stood, the kitchen and dining areas could be seen, lining the south wall. The main living space was a giant room where everything was at one's fingertips or easily visible.

Tino stood in the middle of the dome, looking up. "How does all this stand up? It reminds me of the Pantheon in Rome. Except for the fireplace, there are no support beams."

"I am impressed you noticed," SJ said. "It is called cross vaulting." He pointed to the middle of the ceiling. "If you notice, the exterior arches of the villa all intersect here, in the dome of the living room. The concept behind the Pantheon. My mother studied architecture, through books, of course. She did not have the benefit of a college education. She believed the technical achievements of early Rome helped pave the way for modern architectural design.

I looked up at the vaulted space. "Don't they have a lot of earthquakes in Italy?"

SJ laughed. "The Pantheon was built in 150 AD and the last time I checked, it was still standing. I'd rather take my chances here, than in one of those cinderblock contraptions your famous Frank Lloyd Wright built. Not that he didn't have talent—his designs were good— he just used the wrong materials."

I knew Tino was an ardent fan of the American architect. Time to switch subjects. "I see you share your mother's love of beautiful things, whatever materials they are made of. And yet, you decided to become a chef."

"I try never to compete with the best," SJ replied. "I chose another line of work to avoid the inevitable comparisons with my mother. The Urbino Truffle Foundation has high expectations, and they are notorious task masters, not to mention critical as hell."

SJ walked to the opposite end of the great room where a wall of sliding glass doors illuminated the fast-approaching darkness. "This is my only contribution to my mother's vision." He unlatched one end, and in seconds, the space opened up to an expansive balcony over-looking the Nera River.

"Masterful," I breathed.

"In 1941, when Agatha built Paradiso Vinto, the concept of indoor-outdoor living had not yet taken hold, nor did the technology exist for the accordion door."

"Agatha would have loved the idea," I told him. "Even if she didn't come up with it herself."

SJ laughed. "After much discussion on the matter, no doubt. The woman always wins, as they say."

"That's because she is always right," I reminded him.

"For the sake of our friendship, I will not disagree. Come, we must eat."

SJ led the way into the dining area. The opposite side of the fireplace was also serviceable, heating the kitchen and dining rooms and creating a warm, comforting atmosphere. "Do you ever use it to cook?" I pointed to the cavernous hole where a pile of fragrant wood crackled and burned.

"But of course. *Spiedini di maiale*, kebabs of roasted pork . . . and pizza. Have you had Umbrian pizza yet?"

"Yes! At the Valcasana Restaurant in town. Wonderful, like baked flat bread, not thick crusted like the Americans make."

"Wait until you taste mine! So light and flaky it doesn't compete with the toppings. That is the way to make authentic pizza."

I glanced at Tino. *Why aren't we having that tonight* was written all over his face.

The kitchen was another enormous space with a long wooden table that served as an island, its rustic appearance contrasting sharply with the modern appliances. Open shelving with wrought-iron brackets lined the unpainted stone walls and, underneath them, black soapstone countertops displayed a variety of cooking utensils.

"*Flavia! Dove stai? Mangiamo adesso,*" SJ called out. Almost immediately a small middle-aged woman came out of a pantry door, carrying a tray of meats and cheeses and placed them on the table.

"This is Flavia, my niece and *maestra della casa.*"

Tino and I nodded at the tiny woman, and I extended my hand. "*Sono felice de fare la tua conoscenza,*" I stammered.

Flavia gave me a quick surprised glance and then looked away. Her "*piacere*" was barely audible.

"Wait a second," I said, turning to SJ. "Flavia is your niece?"

"From my mother's side of the family," SJ said. "You remember, Agatha came from humble beginnings. She was just a servant girl working at Villa Urbino when she met your grandfather. She had three siblings, a sister, and two brothers back in her village of *Norcia.*

Flavia is the granddaughter of Agatha's brother. She speaks almost no English, but I suspect she understands more than she lets on."

Flavia looked down and smiled.

The two spoke together in an indecipherable dialect. Flavia then excused herself and went back to the pantry. A few minutes later we heard an outside door close.

"Does Flavia live with you?" I asked.

"She has her own little place in San Anatolia, the next village over. Sometimes, when I entertain guests for dinner, she stays in one of the cottages out back."

"Will she be joining us for dinner?"

I'm afraid not." SJ chuckled. "You saw her look. She is worried you are here to claim my inheritance when I die. Newly discovered relatives are always regarded with suspicion by family members in these villages."

"Especially American relatives," I added. "Rest assured, SJ. We are not interested in your money."

"Hey, speak for yourself," Tino cut in. "This place of yours would make a cozy little *pied-à-terre*."

SJ laughed. "When I met Anna in the cemetery, by chance, three months ago, I knew your family's intentions were honorable. I would never have invited her to my home if I thought otherwise."

"What you may not know, SJ, is our mother, Virginia, created an empire of her own. She was a schoolteacher, but real estate was her passion. She and my father saved and sacrificed to achieve success. We are the beneficiaries."

SJ nodded his approval. "Well said and worthy of a *nipotina* of an Urbino. We continue as caretakers of that hard won success. To squander it would be an injustice. Like my antipasto, here." SJ brought out small plates and forks and set them beside the tray. "Good Italian sausage and cheese should not go to waste while we talk. This"—he skewered something white and laid it on Tino's plate—"is called *strutto*. You Americans call it lard."

"You eat lard as an appetizer?" Tino's voice sounded strained.

"It is full of flavor. Try it."

Tino looked at the soft, glistening pile. He looked like he was going to be sick. I forked two slices onto my plate and started eating. I knew someone had to save face. When trying regional delicacies in a foreign country, it is considered rude if you don't at least make an attempt. As I chewed, the fat released its juices, and the flavors of wild pig, earthy and robust, filled my mouth.

"Delicious!" I pronounced, giving Tino a challenging smile. "Your turn."

Tino took a deep breath like he was facing an army of barbarians. "Okay, here goes . . ." He bit down and began chewing. A minute went by, and then his eyes lit up. "Tastes like *fritzole!* Mom used to fry up chunks of pork fat when we were kids. They were my favorite!"

We sampled rounds of sausage and cheeses I had never heard of. The most aromatic SJ saved for last.

"*Taleggio* from Lombardy. It tastes better than it smells."

Tino smiled and popped a chunk into his mouth without batting an eye. "I love stinky cheese."

In the dining room, we sat down at the sleek wooden table that resembled a redwood tree sliced in half. Gleaming silverware caught the light of the spider-like chandelier above us as Tino and I raised our glasses. "*Saluti, Zio!*" I said. "We are honored!" Together, gathered around the table laden with food, we drank the fruity Barbera d'Alba wine with the camaraderie of a family reunited.

Trippa e zampa alla Marchegiana turned out to be just like a dish Spirito used to make, and the pig trotters cooked with carrot and cabbage reminded me of meals eaten at my grandparents' house in San Diego when I was a child.

"No truffles?" Tino asked, sopping up the sauce on his plate with soft chunks of focaccia bread.

"This time of year, there is only the white truffle in Emilia-Romagna. Our truffle, the Diamante Nero, is harvested in late February. In March, the Urbino Truffle Foundation sponsors a festival here. We make a giant omelet with truffles for the entire town. A waffle iron seven meters long is placed in the area near the river where they have the rafting. Booths, food, entertainment. People come from all the nearby villages. You must plan to be here."

"I will be, SJ. You can count on it," I said.

Chapter 11

Questions and Answers

AFTER THE meal, SJ rose from the table and walked to a sideboard laden with amber bottles. "Time for the *digestive*, Italy's version of the nightcap."

I rose quickly to help with the glasses, and Tino began clearing the table. SJ turned to looked at him. "Thank you, Tino. Flavia will appreciate the help."

"I wash dishes too," Tino offered.

"Flavia has her own way of doing things. It is best to let her wash up. When I try, I get yelled at."

* * *

"Tino, Anna, come join me." SJ walked to the modern sectional in the living room, holding a bottle and three glasses, and sat down. "I have a feeling, after more than a hundred years of shared family history, your sister is about to ask me some serious questions. It might interest you to know I have a few of my own."

Tino sat down and poured himself a large glass of the *Grappa del Re*. "Sometimes questions have answers you don't want to hear. You go first."

SJ filled my glass, and his, and settled in. "Anna, when your grandfather, Spirito, married your grandmother, Marianna, did he tell her about his troubled past here? The murder of Armando Urbino?"

"Marianna knew about it. My grandfather called it a crime of passion, a duel over a woman. The reason for the murder, Armando's assault on Agatha, was only hinted at. As you can imagine, the whole subject was difficult for Spirito."

SJ nodded. "For my family too, of course. Did Marianna know about my brother, Santo? Spirito did not know Santo was his child until he came back in 1923 and met him. Did Spirito tell Marianna he had a child in Italy?"

"Marianna found a clipping of a newspaper photo that Spirito had saved, which showed Agatha and Santo together. She saw the resemblance and put it together."

SJ had something on his mind, I could tell, something he needed to ask me. "Did Marianna know that Spirito had been unfaithful, that he and my mother had been intimate on that visit in 1923?"

"I suspect she did. Once, when she was near the end of her life, we talked about infidelity. It had played a part in her side of the family as well. I remember saying, 'I'm glad *Nonno* Spirito never did anything like that.' She looked at me, a very telling look, and did not respond."

I paused and took SJ's hand. "My grandfather's one act of infidelity resulted in your birth. I know Agatha never regretted it. How can any of us?"

"Thank you. We sometimes do things with our hearts, not our consciences. Agatha and Spirito's love was real, and it lasted their whole lives." A tear slid down the old man's cheek, and he fell silent.

"Is it my turn?" I asked gently.

"One more question." SJ's eyes were intent. "If what you say is true, that Marianna knew about the affair, she must have forgiven him. After all, they stayed together."

I remembered, as a child, watching my grandmother caring for Spirito in those last years after his dementia had set in. "Yes, she forgave him. I suppose all of us have things we need someone to forgive us for," I said softly.

SJ nodded. "I know I do."

Tino spoke up. "This is all ancient history. Like Agostino said, why bring it up now?"

SJ sat up, fully alert. "You have been discussing me with Agostino?"

"To be clear," I hastily intervened, "Agostino said relationships in this town between families have overlapped for centuries. 'Drama like you wouldn't believe' I think he said."

"It is true." SJ's features hardened. "Ancient feuds can reignite from a single spark at any given moment. That is why we keep to our own territory."

"Agostino also said we hold back forgiveness to punish those who have hurt us. SJ, I do not know what has happened between you two but extending the olive branch might be a step in the right direction. I got the sense that Agostino would be open to it." I also got the sense that I had plunged headlong into a torrent of family shit, barefoot. The floodgates had opened, I might as well go for broke. "I take it Agostino's side of the family doesn't know your true identity?" I said. "He called you our *cousin*, not our *uncle*. He doesn't know?"

SJ's affable manner had turned wary. "Only you and Flavia know Agatha was my mother and not my grandmother. And Dr. Sabatini. He delivered me."

"Our great aunt's husband," I said. "The doctor who helped everyone."

Tino spoke up. "Why, after all this time, are you still keeping your identity a secret?"

"My mother knew she was pregnant six weeks after she and Spirito had been intimate in 1923. A woman without a husband, and who became pregnant, was a great scandal in those days, especially a woman like Agatha, who was well known and respected. Since aborting the child was not a consideration, she had little choice but to tell Santo, then seventeen, about her condition. He immediately suggested he marry his fiancée, Lidia, and that they raise me as their own. Lidia's condition could be faked with a period of confinement, and Agatha could stay out of the public eye until the child was born. It was a brilliant plan, and it worked. No one suspected that I was not Santo and Lidia's child. The problem was, as I grew up, my parentage could not be revealed without embarrassment and endless speculation ... all of it directed at my mother. I couldn't stand to let that happen. Now, it has become established history and difficult to alter."

I nodded my head. "Understood. In his lifetime, Dr. Sabatini never betrayed your secret, not even to his wife, and neither will we. We are honored that you chose to share it with us."

SJ sank back down into the sofa. He looked like he had aged right before our eyes. "I am old, too old, to hold onto feelings of anger and resentment that no longer seem worth fighting about. Agostino is right. Forgiveness should not be withheld to remind others of their failings. Our families have both been guilty of hurting each other. I am ready for it to end."

SJ stood and motioned for us to join him. Together we walked out to the balcony and looked toward Villa Urbino. I could see its proud lines, outlined by floodlights against the black expanse of the mountains. It looked like a fortress so strong it could withstand anything God or nature could throw at it.

But human nature was a force that could not be measured by the strength of brick and mortar. I knew the people within Villa Urbino and Paradiso Vinto had been vulnerable to ridicule and shame. Gossip could be cruel. In a town the size of Scheggino, it was the community that would make the final judgment on the character of its inhabitants, and because the Urbinos held themselves to a higher standard, they would be judged more harshly. It was a standard they had created and fought hard to maintain, but the burden weighed heavily on the shoulders of the living.

SJ turned to me. "Agatha's story does not end here. I am not proud of what I am about to tell you, but you and Tino deserve to know the truth."

SJ led us from the balcony into the living room. He gestured for us to sit down.

"There is another story that you need to hear if you are to fully understand why Agostino and I keep our distance. It involves his aunt, Marina Urbino. What has he told you about her?"

"He said she died of a broken heart."

SJ's voice faltered.. "I am the one responsible for that."

I was instantly alarmed. "I had no idea. Please, if this is too much for you . . ." I tried to reach out to comfort him, but he gently pushed me away.

"I have been carrying this around with me for more than half a century. It is time someone else in the family shared the burden."

PART II

Italy 1943

Chapter 12

Damage Control

FROM HER balcony, Agatha Altarocca looked north, toward the emerald-green mantle of the Vallo di Nera. It was the end of June, and summer had officially arrived. She had been looking for signs since the beginning of the month: hints of color, wild primrose, and Cynthia lining the banks of the Nera. A few weeks later, as if the earth were gathering its strength from beneath the ground, shoots of farro covered the fields with a faint tinge of green. Scanning the quiet valley with the morning fog hanging in the hollows, Agatha could hardly believe the country was at war.

A truck raced by on the old Roman road above her, and she glanced at the Royal Italian insignia on its side. The army still maintained a presence, but the tide was turning. Hitler and the German Army were losing ground, the allies already overrunning Sicily and moving north. With Mussolini's body swinging in the wind, the *partigiani* had sent a message to their countrymen that the reign of fascism was over. Scheggino was holding on to the deluded belief that they could make a comeback, that another Mussolini might emerge to rally the movement and return Italy to a position of power, but no one believed it. Soldiers in their dark green uniforms still crowded the *piazza*, eating and drinking in the bars and restaurants, but their talk about the rise of the Third Reich and victory had a false ring to it.

Agatha felt strangely removed. Ironically, her family's financial situation had improved during Mussolini's reign. Her brothers and sisters and their families had jobs, there was food on the table, and the future looked bright. Now, with the prospect of Italy losing the war and the hard times that were sure to follow, that future was uncertain. The Urbino Truffle Foundation had not suffered. Even in wartime, people coveted the fragrant lumps of fungus. Government officials who could afford them served the delicacy as a symbol of their elite status, and wealthy aristocrats, oblivious to the depleted rations of the working class, continued to indulge. Agatha knew, too, where the glass jars filled with truffles were hidden. The Urbino clan had buried them below Claudio's villa where the German army could not find them. The jars were corked and sealed with a special kind of mastic to prevent the mold that occurred when air got in. Someday, when the war was over and people could afford to buy, the Urbinos would cash in.

Agatha's work went on: designing new showrooms across Europe and, when time would allow, an occasional refresh of a businessman's villa. Moriano Fortuny, the fabric mogul, had contacted her to decorate his residence in Venice again. The last time had been in 1935, before the war. Rich clients grew tired of their décor so quickly Agatha could barely keep up, and trends that were hot a few years ago were suddenly passé. Out with the old and in with the new, she thought—the new these days being Baroque-style hand-painted ceilings and velvet couches. Mariano had commissioned her to create a whole new color scheme for his rooms: new fabric on furniture, window treatments, and walls, using his trademark designs, of course. She was due to travel to Venice in less than a week to begin work. She was honored to be chosen—Moriano was considered a genius throughout the designer world—but now was not a good time. Construction had been completed six months ago on Paradiso Vinto and she had just begun to settle in and enjoy her new home. The garden beneath her window was flourishing, and there was another three months of good weather to look forward to. The last thing Agatha wanted to do was leave.

Her eye caught a movement, and she looked down. Someone was in the garden . . . no—two people—SJ and Giulia, Marina's daughter from Villa Urbino. Agatha stepped back from the balcony, out of sight, and watched them.

Giulia ran through the clipped yews ahead of SJ, laughing, and looking back as if daring him to follow her. When they reached the edge of the cliff, SJ grabbed her wrist and pulled her to him. He held her face and kissed her, his mouth insistent and devouring. Giulia resisted, pushing her arms against him. His kiss became gentler, his lips moving to her chin, then her neck, until Giulia stopped resisting and wrapped her arms around him.

Agatha retreated into the house and closed the door to the balcony. She sank into a chair and covered her face with her hands.

She was still sitting there, a glazed expression on her face, when Lidia and Santo walked into the room. She looked up. "Something has happened. I saw SJ and Giulia together this morning behaving like lovers. They didn't know I was watching. If SJ finds out who his real father is . . ." Agatha's voice trailed off, and she looked at Santo.

Santo and Lidia hurried over to her and pulled up two armchairs. The couple had just arrived from Rome, planning to stay at Paradiso Vinto while Agatha was in Venice. Their faces were anxious, especially Lidia's.

Agatha continued, "I don't know how far it has gone with Giulia, but it has to stop. Right now, SJ thinks they are second cousins. If he finds out he is not related to her, he might pursue marriage. Lidia, you know your father will never allow it."

Lidia spoke up. "Are you sure it wasn't just a little harmless flirting? He's only nineteen. You know what boys are like at that age."

"If you saw what I saw, you would know it was not harmless flirting. It is only a matter of time. Even now, we may be too late." Agatha turned to face her son and his wife. "I think it is time to tell Claudio who SJ's real father is. It would resolve that other little problem as well." Agatha looked at Lidia knowingly.

"No!" Santo stood, his voice thundering through the room. "Absolutely not! I will not allow your reputation to suffer because of SJ's dalliances. He has no idea the pain this will cause our family."

"It is not his fault that we never told him the truth."

Santo's face was livid. "Do you want the gossip and the speculation to start up again? Don't tell me you've forgotten how they ridiculed you when I was born. I heard the stories growing up, too." Santo stopped when he saw Agatha's face.

"I guess I wasn't the only one who suffered. I am so sorry." Her eyes filled with tears.

Santo walked over to his mother and took her hand. "I don't want to see you go through that again. If we tell Claudio, he will tell Olivia. It will get out."

Agatha sighed. "After all these years, who cares?"

Santo looked at her. "I care. Claudio does not need this scandal either. He has a business to run and a reputation to uphold. The Urbino Truffle Foundation has been good to us, and now it is time to return the favor. If I have to override you on this, mother, I will. SJ is going with you to Venice. No arguments. He needs to get away from her, and Venice is the perfect place to distract him."

Agatha could hear SJ's step coming down the hall.

"Tell him now," Santo told her. "And be firm."

"SJ, come in here please. I'd like a word with you," She called out.

SJ entered the room and embraced the two seated next to Agatha. "Papa, Mama, I didn't know you were here."

Santo retrieved another chair and gestured to SJ to sit. "Your grandmother has a surprise for you," he began.

Agatha smiled, taking SJ's hands in her own. "As you know, I am leaving for Venice in a few days. I want you to come with me."

The room was quiet.

"I cannot go," SJ said simply. He held his grandmother's gaze with a defiance that surprised her. "I am working on hybrid plants in the greenhouse, and they cannot be left unattended."

Nice try, Agatha couldn't help thinking. She was going to have to come up with an equally good reason he had to accompany her. "My associate, the one who travels with me, and carries my supplies, has informed me that his wife is ill, and he cannot leave her. You will be his replacement. I think you will enjoy it. We will be staying at the Palazzo Pesaro Orfei, Moriano's private residence."

Agatha watched the young man, hoping he was weighing the benefits of her offer. The Palazzo Orfei was known worldwide for its stunning gothic architecture and furnishings. Only the most privileged of the Venetian elite were invited to go there, and very few were allowed to stay overnight. The class of people he would meet, the parties and young women frequenting the *palazzo*—all of it—would be an opportunity most men SJ's age would not want to pass up. She hoped SJ was thinking the same thing.

SJ turned to his grandmother. "I'm sorry, you will have to get someone else. I absolutely cannot go with you now."

Agatha rarely had to lay down the law with her sons, but it looked like, this time, she had no choice. Before she could speak, Santo walked over to SJ and stood over him. "You are *absolutely* going, and as you are still under your grandmother's supervision, you are not in a position to refuse. Pack your things and make the necessary arrangements. The groundskeeper, can look after your plants. You will be leaving at the end of the week."

SJ stared at their faces. Then, without saying a word, he stood up and walked out of the room.

SJ was furious. If he didn't know better, he'd think his grandmother was trying to get him away from Paradiso Vinto. He thought suddenly of Giulia. Maybe they had been seen together this morning when they were near the cliffs. Why was his grandmother so worried about them having feelings for each other? Second cousins marrying was not uncommon, especially in rural towns, and the two families had been close for as long as he could remember. He knew Giulia's family had been a big part of his grandmother's young life, helping her give birth to Santo, setting her up in Spello where she would be safe from prying eyes. Agatha's success and her rise within the Urbino Truffle Foundation had been made possible because of that help. The two families were joined at the hip. Feelings on both sides ran deep, even if not all of them were good.

SJ knew he had to see Giulia to tell her he was leaving for Venice in three days. Making sure no one saw him, SJ walked to the north end of the property and slipped through a little-used service entrance that led to the river. SJ had discovered the path last year when the house was under construction. Running parallel to the river, below the villa, an enchanted forest grew. Wildflowers and orchids flourished in quiet seclusion near the water's edge, and against the cliff, there were caves where a person could curl up and listen to the sound of rushing water.

He remembered the first time he had seen her: a vision of blithe innocence, still unaware of her emerging sexuality. It had been a hot, humid day in early May, and Giulia was climbing down the steep slope than ran below Villa Urbino to the river. Graceful as a nymph, her mane of dark hair wet against the edges of her face and the damp cloth of her dress clinging to her figure, she seemed like something out of a dream. There was a childlike eagerness in her movements as she negotiated the loose stones along the path that seemed at odds with the parted, sensual lips, the firm round breasts, and gently swelling hips. He watched her, transfixed, as she reached out to gather wildflowers and herbs and stopped to smell their scent before placing them in the basket she had brought with her. Intent on her task, Giulia had not noticed the dazed young man standing among the profusion of green. She was halfway into the river, picking the orchids that hung over the water, when SJ stepped out of the shadows.

"What will your mother say when she sees you? You are covered in mud."

Giulia turned quickly in the direction of the voice, ready to scream, but when she saw SJ, she smiled. "I know who you are. Agatha's grandson. How do you know about my favorite place?"

"Your favorite place? This is *my* place. I'm sure I discovered it before you."

"I don't think so. I've been coming here since I was five. *You* just moved in." Giulia was laughing, her eyes warm and taunting as if they were already aware of the power they had over him. SJ felt them looking into his soul and capturing his heart.

"Let me show you something only *I* know about." Giulia grabbed his hand, happy to share her magical fairy land with a new friend.

That was the beginning of it. Friendship on one side and a hidden growing passion on the other. Then, one month ago, as they became drenched in a sudden downpour and huddled together for warmth, everything changed. It was a late spring shower, gentle drops seeping through the steaming branches of the trees and covering them with moisture. He felt her nipples harden against his chest, felt the soft curve of her neck when he reached up to caress it. Suddenly, their lips and hands were touching, exploring, tasting. SJ felt heat rising up through his body, the rush of pleasure from his loins, and without thinking, he pressed himself against her. Her eyes widened as she felt him and she pushed him away. She covered her mouth with her hand.

"What are we doing?" She whispered.

"Enjoying each other," SJ said. "Is there anything wrong with that?"

"Aren't we related or something?" Giulia stammered, "Your mother, Lidia, is my mom's cousin. Doesn't that make us *second* cousins?"

"Sounds about right," SJ said vaguely, his attention more focused on the dewy softness of her skin than family blood lines. He could feel the heat of her body through the thin dress as he reached for her again. This time Giulia did not push him away.

SJ's thoughts were on that first kiss as he climbed down to the grotto, the secret hiding place where they always met. Giulia was not there. Devastated, he sat at the hollowed-out entrance and waited. *A month in Venice*. Normally he would have been excited to go, such a great city, sensual and alive, a visual feast. Now, it seemed like torture. Just the thought of being away from Giulia, not being able to touch her, made him crazy.

"I knew you'd be here." Giulia was standing at the entrance to the grotto. "They said you were packing, that you were leaving for Venice." Giulia's eyes bored into his, anxious and searching.

"I came here to tell you. How did you find out?"

"Uncle Santo told me. I saw their car from my window and rode my bike over to your house. Something is wrong, SJ. I can tell. Santo was not happy to see me."

SJ put his arms protectively around her. "I think they know we've been seeing each other."

Her body stiffened. "And they don't approve. None of your family approves."

"They are afraid, always afraid of gossip or their blasted reputation. It feels like there is some secret between our two families that no one wants to talk about. It makes me sick." SJ was bitter.

Giulia stared at him. "Why don't they want us to be together? You will be twenty in March, and I am eighteen next month. That is a normal age to get married . . ." Giulia's voice waivered. "I know we haven't talked about it but I thought . . ."

"Of course, my God, I can hardly keep my hands off you. I want you with me . . . I want us to have a life together. This waiting is torture for me."

Giulia's embrace tightened. "For me too."

SJ drew her closer. He knew they were both on fire.

"Make love to me," she whispered.

God, how he was tempted. How many times had he fantasized about undressing her here, deep in the anonymity of the forest, both of them slaves to the instincts of nature? He thought about what her naked body would look like as he mounted her on a bed of sycamore leaves, her flesh white against the green, her eyes bright with desire. As if she were sharing the same dream, Giulia pressed against him . . . he pulsated against her hip . . .

Suddenly he pulled away. "If we make love now, it will only be harder for us when I leave."

A soft moan escaped her lips. "I don't care. I want you now . . ." She pulled at her blouse, ripping it, as if constrained by its tightness. SJ stopped her, caressing her cheek with the back of his hand. "When I come back, I will ask your mother for permission to marry you."

Her breath caught, and she laughed softly. Suddenly her dark eyes were taunting him. "Is this a proposal of marriage?"

SJ blushed. "I . . . yes . . . I mean . . . will you . . . ?"

Before he could utter another word, Giulia put a finger to his lips. "I accept."

She kissed him then, tenderly, savoring the moment for the weeks ahead. Her lips moved to his ear, her voice already sounding proprietary. "Just come back safely and keep your hands off those Venetian tarts."

Chapter 13

An American in Venice

RICK ZONIN finished the last flaky bite of his *cornetto con mascarpone* and sighed with pleasure. He wiped his mouth with a napkin, took a sip of his cappuccino, and signaled the waiter for a check. At forty-five years old, the Italian American painter from Redondo Beach liked to think he had sampled all the sensual delights of his favorite city at least twice. Even in the midst of war, Venice was the epicenter of decadence and indulging in its many pleasures an imperative to good living. A freshly baked pastry in the early hours of the morning was one of them. He rose, paid his bill, and started down the narrow, cobbled walkway toward the Palazzo Pesaro Orfei.

Everywhere he looked, the threat of German occupation was imminent. The streets and canals were deserted, and except for military personnel, the crowds of tourists decorating the bars and restaurants were nowhere to be seen. Despite his zest for life and his belief in the inherent goodness of people, Rick could sense the wave of antisemitism sweeping the city. It lapped at the edges of the canals and seeped furtively into alleyways. It hung in the very air he breathed, like a virus, perpetrated by the powerful force of the Nazi party waiting in the wings. For Rick, the artist, it felt like all the light and beauty of the city had gone undercover, waiting for the horror of war to pass.

Rick scanned the canal, watching the sun dot the water like gold from a miner's pan. Even after fifteen years, Rick still couldn't believe he was here. The credit for his transformation from a California beach bum who liked to paint to serious muralist belonged to Rick's mentor, the brilliant Venetian painter Fausto Tasca.

Rick had met Fausto in the summer of 1927 while working on the murals for the Trust and Savings Bank in Los Angeles. Fausto, already an established name on the west coast, needed an assistant, someone to carry supplies, prepare colors, and wash brushes.

Rick's father, Sandro Zonino, an immigrant brick layer from northern Italy, insisted his son apply for the job. Sandro had left his country in 1901, along with many others in Europe, looking for a better life. At Ellis Island, when the officer couldn't pronounce his first name, Sandro shortened it, dropped the 'o' in the last name, and became Sam Zonin. Sometimes a few letters change everything.

Sam was worried his twenty-five-year-old freewheeling son was wasting his life away. Surfing Redondo's waves and flirting with the half-naked women who frequented the bars lining the waterfront was not a career.

"When I was your age," Sam had said in his still broken English, "I was already apprenticed to a *muratore*, making the bricks for chimneys. In my little town, young people were expected to contribute to the household. Maybe I make a mistake bringing our family here to America. I wanted a better life for you, but not like this . . . on the beach all day. You want to be an artist? Then go work for one."

The job was demeaning at first, lugging buckets and mixing paint, the smell of turpentine everywhere, but between trips to replenish supplies, Rick watched the artist work. He marveled at Fausto's talent, the way he could capture the essence of a scene from a single black-and-white photo and bring it to life. Rick began to appreciate the opportunity to work with a master.

Fausto saw the young man's interest, encouraging him to paint the backgrounds for more detailed sequences that Fausto would fill in later. It was during those long, hot days, working side by side, that Fausto told his budding protégé about his beloved city of Venice.

"Why did you leave?" Rick asked.

"An Italian American priest from California offered me a commission I couldn't refuse, painting an entire church in San Diego, a small town near the Mexican border. I booked passage to America and never looked back." Fausto dipped his brush into a pot of turpentine and swirled it onto his palette. "That commission marked the beginning of my career and the relationship with the Urbinos—the family who owned a diner and traded meals for portraits. I will always cherish that memory."

"It sounds like you became good friends with them," Rick said, sweeping his brush across an empty panel with a wash of color.

"I did. I had breakfast there first thing every morning. Many times I was the only customer. You can get to know someone pretty well over a plate of sausage and eggs."

A month later, when the bank mural was finished, a letter came from Father Rabagliati. Could Fausto come down for a couple of weeks and do some touch up work and paint the stained-glass windows in the sacristy? The artist asked Rick if he wanted to come along. He would pay him out of his own salary, and San Diego, with its pristine beaches, promised warm weather and friendly people. "Wait until you meet the Urbinos," Fausto told Rick. "Spirito serves the best rib-eyes in town."

Father Rabagliati greeted them with open arms when they walked into Our Lady of the Rosary Church on Colombia Street, but there was more work than he had mentioned in his letter. In addition to the sacristy windows, there was an entire apse to be painted. The two weeks Father had allotted was not going to be enough time for one artist to complete the work. Fausto allowed Rick free rein in painting the apse. "Make it your own," he said. Rick created a concept, chose a color scheme, and began a series of scenes depicting Christ as shepherd leading the people to salvation. It was dramatic and modern, and Father Rabagliati loved it.

"Have you thought of spending a year in Italy?" Fausto asked Rick one day during lunch at the Urbino family diner.

"You must see Florence," Spirito said, laying two juicy steaks in front of them. "The best art in the world is there."

"But Venice has the gondolas . . . and the play of light on the canals," Fausto reminded him.

"Come with me," Rick suggested. "You can show me everything."

Fausto shook his head. "That time has passed. I have a wife and son . . . my life is here. But *you* must go . . . *now* . . . before it is too late."

The following spring, Rick said goodbye to his family and set sail for the city that all artists dream of and only a lucky few get to experience.

During the fifteen years after his arrival, Rick paid his dues, painting backbreaking frescoes on church ceilings and murals for the old Venetian families whose money still held sway in this town. When the artists hanging out at the bar near the *Accademia di Belle Arti* started calling him "Il Zonino," Rick laughed at the irony of it all. He knew his father would have been proud.

Crossing the footbridge to the back entrance of the Palazzo Pesaro Orfei, he saw a woman and a young man disembark from the private Fortuny gondola. Servants were transporting luggage from the boat to the palazzo, and by the number of suitcases, Rick judged the guests were planning to stay awhile. Then it clicked. The woman must be the designer Moriano had talked about and the boy, now weighed down with fabric and leather cylinders, must be her assistant. Not relishing the prospect of lengthy introductions, the artist slipped unnoticed through the palazzo's service entrance.

"Bring the fabric, swatches, everything, up here!" Someone bellowed from the second floor.

Moriano, Rick thought. He could hear the irritation in the designer's voice as it resonated through the vaulted stone rooms and the clatter of servants' footsteps as they traveled up and down the stairs in response. Rick sighed. The peace and quiet he had enjoyed while working on the murals these last two months were over. With the arrival of the woman and her assistant, Moriano's production was about to take center stage.

"Zonino! *Dove stai*? Where are you?" The level of Moriano's voice had risen.

"*Qui, Signore* Fortuny. I have been here all morning."

Moriano appeared at the railing and glared down at the artist. "Don't lie to me. I just heard you come in. Your breakfast lasted longer than usual, I see."

Rick didn't even try to explain that he had been soaking up the sights and smells of Venice on a glorious day in July. Moriano couldn't care less. The only thing his boss understood was work. Earthly pleasures, apart from the feel of silks and satins, had no place in his world.

"I was looking at the colors of the canal . . . for the murals. They need to be right."

"Yes, yes. That is why I need you up here. La Signora Altarocca is here with her samples. They need to match the hues of the murals."

Rick climbed the stairs, shaking his head. *This could be a problem.* If the designer was set on a fabric that clashed with his murals, he would have to adjust the colors. With the current cost of silk and satin thread, it was not going to be the other way around.

Rick walked into the master bedroom, brushing off his rumpled jacket and shoving paint-stained fingers deep inside his pockets. He hoped he wouldn't have to shake hands.

"Signora Altarocca," Moriano said and looked at Agatha. "This is the esteemed artist I have hired to paint the murals. Il Zonino trained with the great Fausto Tasca. He is known all over Venezia as a master of color."

"*Piacere,* Signora." Rick took in the woman's luscious curves and Botticelli-like features. Painting her, he mused, would be a pleasure.

"And this is her grandson, Signore Urbino," Moriano added.

"Please call me SJ," the young man insisted.

Rick nodded and kept his hands in his pockets. The woman looked too young to be a grandmother, and the boy looked vaguely familiar, but he couldn't place him. Unusual, he thought, since he almost never forgot a face.

Like a benevolent benefactor, Moriano clasped his hands together and gazed fondly at the two artists. "We need to choose the perfect combination of shades where murals and fabrics blend so smoothly that one is surprised by their originality but not blinded by it. I will be back in one hour to see what you have come up with." With a *buona fortuna* and a dramatic flourish of his hand, Moriano was gone.

Agatha laughed softly. "How well do you work under pressure, Signore Zonino?"

"I prefer it, actually, "Rick answered. "Provided I get to make all the decisions."

SJ spoke up. "It is obvious, *Signore,* that you have not worked with my grandmother before."

"Even an artist such as your grandmother knows perfection when she sees it." Rick gestured confidently to the four walls of the bedroom. I'm sure she will have no problem finding shades to complement my murals."

Agatha walked the room, taking in the painted panorama of the

Venetian city come to life. Rick had created a *trompe l'oeil* where the walls reflected the scene beyond the windows. Like a mirror to the outside world, green-gold water lapped against multicolored patinas of ancient stone, and bridges curved over the canals. On the north wall, there were far-off glimpses of Isola Giudecca and, to the south, the cupola of Santa Maria Maggiore gilded by a setting sun.

After she had studied all four walls, Agatha turned to face the artist. "Perfection doesn't exist, thank God. If it did, what would we have left to create? You, however, have come as close to capturing the beauty of the city as no one else. I have a feeling we will have no trouble working together."

Spreading out her supplies and squares of swatches on the table, Agatha began making her selections. Rick, with his unerring eye, followed the line of her Botticelli-like features as she bent over the shimmering silken fabric.

Early the following morning, SJ boarded the Fortuny gondola heading for the factory on Fondamenta San Biagio in the Isola Giudecca. The red brick building had been acquired by Moriano in 1919, when his business grew too large for the workspace in the palazzo. Originally a convent, the factory-like building was transformed by the designer into a manufacturing laboratory with offices and a showroom where clients could view firsthand the Fortuny collection.

Once the laboratory was up and running, Moriano went looking for women willing to be trained to work the looms. With the lack of job opportunities for Jews on the mainland, housekeepers and laundresses were grateful for the opportunity to learn and rewarded the designer with quality workmanship. In return, he gave them permanent employment and a decent living wage. The methods and designs used in production were kept under wraps and a code of honor developed among the employees never to reveal trade secrets.

SJ had been sent by his mother to pick up the rolls of fabric selected from the swatches and bring them back to begin the long, tedious process of cutting, nailing, and upholstering. SJ told the gondolier to wait dockside, let himself into the service entrance, and found the offices on the first floor. Both the showroom and adjacent offices were exquisitely outfitted with panels of Fortuny silk on the walls, chairs, and sofas. Revolving samples the size of rugs lined one wall where clients could view all the designs at a glance.

Even at this early hour, the room was crowded. SJ noticed several men, presumably designers, looking through the panels and speaking to one another in hushed tones. He strode past them toward the elegant woman behind the desk dressed in a tailored silk jacket, white blouse, and pencil skirt. She was deep in conversation with a distinguished older gentleman sitting across from her.

The minute she caught sight of SJ, she rose and put up a hand. "These offices are off limits to the public."

"I am here to collect Signora Altarocca's materials," SJ said.

The woman's eyes widened. "Just a moment." She said something to the client and motioned for SJ to follow her.

They wound their way up the staircase to the manufacturing laboratory located on the second floor. The huge room was manned by women bent over their looms, the shuttles clicking back and forth in a constant whirring rhythm. Panels of finished fabric hung on polls suspended from the rafters where the weavers were working.

"All this is the signora's." The woman pointed to sacks of furniture batting, a dozen boxes of upholstery nails, and twenty rolls of fabric wrapped in layers of tissue.

SJ stared at the pile in front of him. "I could use some help getting all this to the gondola."

The woman eyed him coldly. "I'm afraid no one can be spared this morning."

SJ could hear the irritation in her voice as though she were thinking, *That's your job. Why would the assistant need assisting?*

It was obvious he had overstepped. He considered telling her he was the designer's grandson and they would have found people to carry the supplies, but it wasn't his style to demand preferential treatment.

"Then I can handle it," SJ assured the woman. "Not to worry." With a quick nod and a relieved look, she hurried back down the stairs.

⁌ ⌒ ⁍

Meanwhile, Rick was entering the Palazzo Pesaro Orfei, expecting Moriano to appear any minute and berate him for being late. There was only silence. He made his way up to the master bedroom to see his murals in the early morning light.

"Ah, you are finally here," Agatha exclaimed. "I think I have found the perfect fabric for *les fauteuils* and *chaise longue*. I have already sent SJ to the factory to collect the needed fabric and supplies. There is just a hint of blue to accent the sky, and there are splashes of gold to highlight the sunlight on the rooftops. What do you think?" Agatha came toward him with an armful of swatches, her eyes alive and shining.

Rick examined the material and held it up to the light. "It brings out the blue of your eyes, and for that reason, it is the perfect choice."

Agatha wagged her finger at him. "If it weren't for your reputation with the Venetian ladies, I might believe you. This is not the time to be sidetracked. We have work to do before SJ returns with the supplies."

Rick was disappointed. It would seem Signora Altarocca was all work and no play. "And where is our favorite designer this morning?" he asked her. "I am surprised he is not here, hovering over your every move."

Agatha looked up. "He is creating another gown for Henrietta to wear at Christian Dior's Tiepolo Ball. You will not see him today."

Rick had almost met Henrietta once, the year he first arrived in Venice. He had been one of a dozen craftsman hired by Moriano Fortuny and his wife, Henrietta Negrin, to paint faux marbling on the many columns adorning the foyer of the Palazzo Pesaro Orfei. The entire residence was being refreshed, and all the artists, including himself, hoped to stand out enough to be allowed to paint a ceiling or two in the designer's private quarters.

That was fifteen years ago. Even then, at fifty, Moriano had been a task master—no detail overlooked and no deadline unmet. After giving instructions to the team of artists, he would stride up the wrought-iron staircase and sequester himself in the cutting room off his bedroom. Henrietta, his muse, was often called in to model his latest creations.

Rick remembered the morning he had climbed the stairs to ask the designer a question. The door to the cutting room was ajar, and as he approached, he saw the nude body of Henrietta Negrin spotlighted by the amber light of the arched windows. She was standing motionless, head lifted, and eyes closed, while Moriano draped her with cloth. Her gorgeous features and snow-white flesh, looked like a chiaroscuro painting come to life. The diaphanous cloud of fabric caressed her breasts and cascaded to the dark place between her legs. For Rick, a man in his prime, the scene was both sensual and heartbreaking. He watched as Moriano arranged the fabric over his wife's naked body, completely oblivious to her beauty.

"What a waste," Rick muttered under his breath, remembering the sense of irony he had felt that day. For a painter, there was no comparison between the sensuality of living flesh and a piece of fabric.

"*Signore Zonino!*" A voice called him, and his gaze refocused on Agatha.

"*Scusi*, Signora, the gold fabric . . . may I see it against the mural?"

Together, they walked toward the light and held up the swatches.

Just before noon, SJ entered the foyer of the Fortuny palazzo looking for help bringing in the supplies from the gondola. The place seemed deserted. With a sigh, he went back outside and began unloading.

Even though he appreciated the creative process of seeing the rooms transformed, he couldn't help wishing he was back in Scheggino. It had only been a week, and he was missing Giulia more than he ever thought possible. The beautiful young ladies of Venice he had met were only interested in parading around in their finery and dreaming up excuses to entice rich young men into their beds. He had listened to their conversations as he passed by, their keen eyes sweeping over him while they chattered in their little groups.

Even with a war on, the Venetian elite's primary focus was on sensual pleasure. Sex was casual, and men and women coupled without worrying about their reputation . . . or their health. SJ could only imagine the diseases running rampant in this decadent city. When he thought of his unpretentious Giulia gathering wildflowers instead of suitors, his heart ached. If his grandmother thought the pleasures of Venice could make him forget her, she was mistaken. If anything, seeing how different Giulia was from these shallow young women made him realize how lucky he was to have found her. He couldn't wait to go home and hold her in his arms.

He was halfway up the stairs when he heard voices. Laughter and the sound of wine being poured into glasses echoed down the hall. His mother and the painter must be taking a break.

An assortment of cold meats and cheeses lay on top of the muslin cloth, spread picnic-style on the floor.

"Where did all this come from?" Agatha held out her glass to be filled. "You brought it with you?"

"One has to be prepared when working for Moriano," Rick said. Sometimes I cannot leave until after midnight. I have learned to keep my knapsack full of food."

"And the wine?"

"Let us just say I know where the wine cellar is, and you looked like you could use some refreshment."

"You are resourceful as well as observant." Agatha gave him a special smile as she reached for a round of mozzarella.

Rick sat on the floor next to her and filled his glass. "If I may be allowed to say, Signora, you look *much* too young to be a grandmother."

"And with that blonde hair and your American accent, *you* look like a transplant from Los Angeles." Agatha was still smiling but her eyes looked wary.

"You're close. I grew up in Redondo Beach."

"Is that where you met Fausto?"

Rick nodded and took a sip of his wine. "He gave me my first commission—painting an apse in a church in San Diego."

Agatha's eyes widened. "San Diego," she repeated.

"Friendly town," Rick continued. "We went down to complete some work Fausto had done earlier for the church. We ate at this diner every day for lunch. The owner was a great guy . . . had a wife and daughter . . ."

Agatha downed half her glass of wine.

Rick reached for the bottle and topped off the glass. "I have been thinking . . . SJ reminds me of someone. Who is his father?"

"He is my son Santo's boy," she answered quickly.

"And Santo's father?"

Agatha flashed him a suspicious look. "Why do you want to know?"

"I pride myself on never forgetting a face. SJ looks remarkably like the man who owned the diner. His name was Spirito Urbino."

Agatha's breath caught.

Spirito had not talked about his wife and child that day in Spello when they lay in each other's arms. Their presence had come between them afterward . . . after the passion had been spent. Even though she had made her choice long ago, hearing Rick describe Spirito's life in America, she felt a pang of jealousy. Her heart still ached for the love she had lost. And now . . . what were the odds that this man had known Spirito? It was a coincidence she would never have believed possible.

"Did you know Spirito?" Rick asked.

"I, yes, I knew him . . . so long ago . . . when we were young. It is a long, sad story, one I have tried hard to forget."

"I know the story," Rick said quietly.

Agatha looked at him in disbelief. "How . . . ?"

"Fausto told me how he would come into the diner, early for breakfast, before going to work at the church. There was no one in the restaurant at that hour, and he and Spirito would talk. Fausto said he always felt Spirito needed to unburden himself."

"What do you know?" Agatha's voice was strained.

"I know he had a great love, a passion for a woman he could never forget . . . so great it made him unfaithful to his wife."

"SJ is his son, too, isn't he?" Rick asked gently.

Agatha was silent a long time before she spoke. "When Spirito came back in 1923, for the reading of his uncle's will, he came to Spello looking for me. Nine months later, I gave birth to SJ."

A clatter, as if something had been dropped, echoed in the hallway. A moment later, footsteps receded down the stairs.

"SJ!" Agatha shouted, scrambling to her feet and following her son as he ran through the foyer and out into the street.

When she reached him, SJ was standing over the canal, retching.

Agatha tried to touch his arm, but he pushed her away.

"I can't believe it." He wiped his mouth with the back of his sleeve. "How could you . . . he was married . . . it's disgusting."

Agatha saw a look in her son's eyes she had never seen before. Instead of caving in, she stood up straight and faced him. He deserved to know the truth.

"It didn't feel that way."

"How did it *feel*?" SJ sneered at her.

"Like we were caught in a moment between two worlds . . . his and mine . . . in a place where we could recapture the love that had been denied us. Armando's brutal act had changed our lives forever." Agatha's voice was strained and tight. She was trying to hold herself together. "In that moment, it was as if the past had never happened, and we were free to love again. You are too young to know what I am talking about. Perhaps, someday, you will understand how love can make you do things you never thought possible. This is a great shock to you, I realize. It will take time to absorb, and I will help you as much as I can."

Agatha looked at her son, her eyes begging him to forgive her.

SJ turned from his mother's penetrating gaze and looked out over the canal and the play of sunlight on the water. "I understand better than you think. I'm not a child anymore. I always thought you had gotten over your feelings for Santo's father . . . especially since he had created a life for himself in America. I never considered you still cared for him enough to . . . it's just such a shock, that's all."

Agatha sighed. "Only later, much later, did I realize there would be consequences."

"And I was one of them."

Agatha took both her son's hands and looked at him squarely in the eyes. "A consequence I thank God for every day of my life. That is why I have no regrets."

Chapter 14

Pheromones

"GIULIA, DO you like the pink or the gold?" Marina grabbed a length of chiffon from the bolt and drew it out. "The pink works with your skin tone, but the gold brings out the flecks of color in your eyes."

Marina waited for Giulia's answer. Her daughter was slouched in a patio chair, her glazed stare showing not the slightest bit of enthusiasm. Her great aunt Gabriella and her cousin Lydia were seated nearby in the courtyard of Villa Urbino. A pitcher of warm orange juice and plates of half-eaten pastries baked in the late afternoon sun.

Marina sighed. "Your birthday is two weeks away, and you haven't even chosen the material for your gown. Gabriella can't make the dress until you pick the fabric. This is your coming out party . . . the chance for the village to see what a grown-up young lady you've become."

"Breeding time," Gabriella muttered sarcastically.

Giulia sat up. "What do you mean by that?"

Gabriella glanced at Marina and Lidia's shocked faces. She obviously had some explaining to do.

"When a girl comes of age, a party is given to introduce her to society and, in particular, to all the eligible men in the region. One of them will be chosen by the family to be her husband."

Giulia laughed. "Zia, what era are you living in? Maybe that was true in your day but now we choose for ourselves. No one does it *for* us. Besides, I already know who I'm going to marry."

Gabriella snorted. "Unless it is Nello, the gardener, I have no idea who that would be. You never socialize . . . always down by the river, playing like a child."

Marina smiled indulgently at her daughter. "A classmate's brother in Spoleto, or Perugia, perhaps?"

Giulia's eyes sparkled. "He lives much closer than that."

Lidia was on her feet. "I think the gold, to go with your dark hair. We will find a matching comb to sweep it back with." She gathered up the bolt and handed it to her niece. "Now go, you and Gabriella. It is not too early to begin cutting out the dress."

After they had left, Lidia pulled her chair closer to Marina's.

"Do you know who the young man is that Giulia mentioned?"

Marina waved her hand dismissively. "She was just trying to get a rise out of Gabriella. Giulia doesn't have any male friends. She prefers plants to people."

Lidia chose her words carefully. "What about SJ? Don't they spend time together?"

"SJ? Your son? They are like brother and sister."

"I wouldn't be too sure," Lidia replied. "They are both of that age when they become aware of the opposite sex." Lidia paused for a moment and said, more quietly, "Have you told Giulia who her father is?"

Marina stiffened. "No, I haven't, and I'm not sure I'm going to . . . not that it's any of your business," she added.

Lidia was unfazed by the remark. "What have you told her about him?"

"That he is dead . . . killed in an accident shortly after she was born."

"I'm not sure that was wise . . . she might find out the truth someday." Lidia deliberated continuing but decided necessity demanded it. "What if something has developed between Giulia and SJ? Feelings that are not those of a brother and sister?"

Marina's eyes widened. "What makes you think . . . ?"

"You might as well know. Agatha saw them together when they thought no one was watching." Lidia looked at Marina intently. "It has to stop. Now. SJ and Agatha are returning from Venice next week. He is not to see Giulia before the party. Santo and I will come up with some excuse why he cannot attend. Santo is concerned about the scandal it will bring to our families . . . and to the foundation."

An hour later, Marina sat on the edge of her bed. Ever since she had heard the news about Giulia and SJ, she hadn't been able to think of anything else. Why hadn't she noticed it before? They were so similar. . .almost the same age . . .both loving nature and the outdoors. She had been naïve to think a sexual attraction couldn't develop . . . especially since it had happened to her. Marina rose from the bed and looked at herself in the full-length mirror. No matter how difficult it would be, she knew she must save her daughter from making the same mistakes she made . . . if it wasn't already too late.

Marco Urbino put down the pencil and looked up. The sound of the typewriter stopped, and from the opposite side of the desk, a pair of warm brown eyes smiled back at him. He felt a stirring in his loins when he thought of what had gone on earlier, on their lunch break, at the tiny flat the foundation owned on Porto Consolare. Tonight, he would tell his boss, Santo, that he and his secretary needed to work late . . . again. He knew he had to be careful; he was being groomed to run the flagship store in New York and someday head the entire Urbino Truffle Foundation. If Santo found out, he would not only fire him but also tell his father about the affair. God only knew how Claudio would react. The scandal would rock the empire his father had worked so hard to build.

He knew it was wrong. He should have stopped it the first night they stayed late working on the New York campaign. They both felt the attraction, the pull of a force they could not control . . . When he reached across the desk and kissed her, a world that had been dull and colorless became suddenly brilliant and beautiful and full of promise. There was no going back.

"Are we crazy to be doing this?" Marina said, resting her hands on his hips, her body between him and the desk. The last employee had left an hour ago.

"Crazy in love," Marco answered.

"But we're both only sixteen . . . if your father and Olivia find out . . ."

"They won't. I'll make sure of that," Marco said, pulling her to him. Marina snuggled closer and wrapped her arms around him.

A few minutes later, Marco's pants were around his ankles, and Marina was sitting on top of his desk, her legs wrapped around him. Their lips were locked and their hands were everywhere.

"What the fuck are you doing?" Santo shouted. He was standing in the open doorway to the back room.

Uttering a cry, Marco lifted Marina off him. He pushed her into a corner and pulled up his trousers. "I'll handle this. Don't say a word," he told her. He faced his boss. "I can explain . . ."

"Marco, how could you?" Santo said, backing away, a look of disgust on his face. He turned and ran out of the room.

Marco raced after him.

"Please don't tell my parents," Marco pleaded as he caught up with the figure clattering down the outside staircase. He shivered in the night air, dried sweat turning cold underneath his flimsy shirt. "We will be dead meat, both of us."

Santo whirled on him. "You should have thought of that before you got involved. Marina is your first cousin; any kind of sexual relationship is highly inappropriate. This has got to end . . .

immediately. I can't believe you could do this to the foundation and our families..."

Marco broke in, "It ends tonight. I promise. Just don't tell anyone... please." He was crying now, silent tears of humiliation running down his cheeks.

Through his tears, Marco saw a range of emotions cross Santo's face: rage, disgust, even pity. *What a romantic fool he must think I am, risking my relationship with my family and my future for love.* Marco knew his boss would never allow passion to rule his life. For Santo, duty and reputation always came first.

<hr>

A week later, Marco sat quietly, his arms folded and his eyes on the floor; the blood red walls of Santo and Lidia's palazzo reflecting the heated atmosphere inside the room. Santo stood next to a woman swathed in a shawl, her face grim.

Agatha looked flushed and bloated, Marco observed, nothing like the svelte elegant figure he had always known. It had been more than a few months since he'd last seen her. Perhaps she was ill.

"I have taken the liberty to confide in my mother regarding your situation," Santo began. "She is the only one who knows." Santo turned his palms up by way of explanation. "I needed her advice."

A baby was crying in one of the rooms, and Agatha turned sharply in the direction of the sound.

Santo's hand rested gently on her shoulder. "Lidia can handle it," he said softly.

Agatha nodded and sat back.

"We have come up with a way for you to extricate yourself from this situation. Given your impulsive nature, and your apparent ardor, we want to protect you from doing something foolish in the future." Santo's voice was firm, brooking no argument. "Olivia and Claudio have a distant relative living here in Spello... Simona is the widow of a nobleman, a descendant of the Savoias. She has expressed an interest in marrying again."

Marco paled. He could see where this was headed.

"How old is she?"

Agatha shot him a scathing look but remained silent.

"I hardly think you are in a position to ask that," Santo replied. "Let us just say she is older than what you may be used to."

Marco felt his face grow hot. They were going to marry him off to some rich old widow, and he could do nothing to stop it. A stifled sob escaped his lips, and he dropped his head.

Agatha's voice broke the silence. "Even though it may seem that way to you now, we are not being unnecessarily cold-hearted. You chose to violate a code of propriety that makes it impossible for those around you to remain unaffected by scandal. What happens to you now is the price you must pay for those actions. This scenario will protect not only your livelihood but also the reputation of the woman you have implicated. If nothing else, think of what it will do to *her* if the nature of your relationship becomes known. If people find out that Marina had intimate relations with her cousin, it would ruin her life. If you care in the least for Marina, you will break it off and agree to marry the *duchessa*."

"And if I don't?"

"You will find that people will turn against you, and the life you and Marina now enjoy will cease to exist."

After Marco left, Lidia entered the room and handed a fitful infant to her mother-in-law. Agatha opened her shawl and guided the baby's mouth to her breast.

Lidia sat down in the chair Marco had vacated. "You were both pretty hard on him. All my brother did was fall in love with the wrong person."

Agatha was quick to respond. "Falling in love always has

consequences. That is why it is important to use prudence and restraint."

Lidia's face registered surprise. "With all due respect, you, of all people, should understand that in matters of the heart, even the most virtuous can fall short of those intentions."

Agatha looked down at the infant suckling her breast and then at her son's wife. "You are right. I had to learn the hard way . . . twice."

Chapter 15

Family Secrets

FROM THE balcony of Paradiso Vinto, SJ could see the outline of Villa Urbino rising out of the early morning mist. He had returned from Venice a week ago and hadn't seen Giulia even once. Every day he had wound his way down to their secret spot below the two villas and sat by the river waiting for her. She had not come.

Yesterday, he coerced Nello to walk over to the villa with him on a pretext of needing extra containers for his seedlings. He had been turned away at the gate and told Giulia was not accepting any visitors.

"What is going on?" he asked his friend. "Why can't I see her?"

"There is going to be a party tomorrow, Giulia's eighteenth birthday. Maybe she is too busy."

"A party? I don't know why I haven't heard about it. I'm sure our family is invited. I'll go ask fath—" SJ stopped. "I mean Santo . . ."

SJ walked off before he saw the gardener's puzzled look.

SJ searched out his brother and found him upstairs in the little office adjacent to the bedroom he and Lidia used when they were in town. "What am I supposed to call you now?" SJ said. "I am so confused."

Santo looked up from his paperwork. "We go on as before . . . to the rest of the world. No one needs to know outside of Lidia and our mother that you are not my son. To say otherwise at this point would make us all look ridiculous . . . like we were covering up something we were ashamed of."

SJ looked confused. "But by hiding the fact, you were acting like you *were* ashamed."

"It wasn't my . . . our . . . intent. I was thinking of what people would say about our mother if the truth came out—two bastard children—even if the father is the same man."

SJ's face turned red, and he looked away. "I still can't believe it. All those years thinking you and Lidia were my parents." SJ looked at his brother." How did you find out Spirito was your father?"

Santo didn't answer right away. "I was only seven when I heard the story."

"Who told you?"

"I overheard Claudio talking to our mother one day when they thought I couldn't hear." Santo dropped his voice. "This is between us, you understand?"

SJ nodded. Part of him didn't want to hear it but another part felt he had a right to . . . so much had been withheld already.

"In the summer of 1914, mother and I were still living at Villa Urbino under the care and protection of Angelo and Mariella," Santo began. "They were getting older. Eight years had passed since Armando's death, and Angelo was getting ready to pass the management of the farm on to the surviving son. Angelo's nephew, Claudio, had assumed control of the truffle foundation by then and married Olivia. The twins, Lidia and Marco, were six, a year younger than me.

"Our mother was getting more and more involved with the foundation, designing the packaging logos and all the artwork for the advertising campaigns, but Claudio wanted more. He had bought land up the road from the village and was envisioning a brand-new facility where there would be room to process and distribute the truffles all from the same location. He wanted Agatha to help him design it.

"One morning, I was kicking a soccer ball around in the

courtyard of the old office complex. I could hear Claudio and Mama talking inside.

"Claudio was complimenting her work, saying something like, 'I don't know what I would do without you.'

"I remember looking in the doorway and seeing him put his hand under Mama's chin and look at her differently . . . not like a business partner. Even though I was only seven, I could tell he was in love with her."

SJ started to protest. "But he was married . . . with children . . ."

"It was only a gesture," Santo replied. "But I knew what it meant. What Claudio said next confirmed it. He said, 'If it had not been for *that field hand*, things might have been different between us.'

"I remember Mama pulling away from him. 'Is that what you think of Spirito? A field hand who seduced a poor servant girl?'

"Claudio tried to apologize. 'I didn't mean it that way. I just meant if it weren't for your situation we would have been free to marry, to build a life together with *our* children.'

"I held the soccer ball and crept closer.

"'By *situation*, I guess you mean Santo,' Mama said.

"Claudio's voice changed. It was no longer tender. 'My plans have always been to develop this company into a global entity,' he said. 'It would have been difficult to explain the presence of a field hand's son to the rest of the world.'

"'Yes, it would have.' Mama's voice sounded cold. 'That *field hand's son* adores you, I hope you know. All he talks about is working for you one day.'"

"That same day, when we were alone, I asked Mama why she didn't marry Claudio. That was when she told me about my real father . . . *our* father. She said there was only one man she would ever love but he lived in America and could not be with us."

SJ looked at his brother. "And that man was Spirito Urbino. That's where I get my name, isn't it? I never knew what the *J* stood for."

"Agatha came up with it," Santo said. "I always thought it was her way of keeping our father's name from being spoken ... so the association between you and him would remain a secret. Maybe the word *junior* was something she learned when she traveled to America. I really never asked her. Anyway, it stuck ... and I'm afraid you're stuck with it now, too." Santo smiled at his little joke and looked at his brother. "Are things a little clearer, now?"

SJ was silent for a moment. "I realize that it is the names, not the relationships, that have changed. If anything, what I know now reinforces what I have always felt. With you and Lidia so often in Rome on business, Agatha seemed more of a mother to me than a grandmother."

Santo looked hurt. "You are saying, then, that you thought of me as a distant parent?"

SJ nodded his head.

Santo put a hand on SJ's arm. "I would like to close that gap ... even if it is only as a brother. I hope it is not too late."

SJ smiled. "It's not too late. There is one thing though ... since this has to remain a secret, I am worried about slipping up tomorrow night."

Santo appeared puzzled. "Tomorrow night?"

"Giulia's eighteenth birthday party. I wouldn't want to say the wrong thing and get us all in trouble."

"We will not be attending." The voice came from the open door on the other side of the room. Agatha had been listening to the conversation.

SJ whirled to face her. "What do you mean we will not be

attending? This is a big event in Giulia's life. She will never forgive me . . . us . . . if we are not there."

Santo started to speak but Agatha held up her hand. "No, Santo. As his mother, I need to be the one to say this."

Agatha gripped the arm of a chair as if to steel herself. "I know what has been going on between you two. I saw you together a month ago, before we left for Venice. Have you been intimate with her?"

SJ tried to push past her, but she grabbed his shoulders and held him. "Tell me the truth."

"You have no right." SJ wrenched himself away from her grasp and headed for the door.

"She could be pregnant," Agatha called out after him.

SJ slowly turned around. "And what would be so bad about that? Did you forget? We aren't related."

"There are reasons a union can never take place between you and Giulia," Agatha said gently. "And they have nothing to do with you."

"Jesus," SJ cried out in exasperation. "Will someone tell me what is so goddamned wrong with us loving each other? If you don't level with me, I will take her away from here and never come back."

"It's time he knew," Santo told his mother.

Agatha set her lips together and nodded.

Chapter 16

They Can't Tell Us What to Do

SJ HEARD music playing. As he leaned out of the window of his bedroom, the faint sound of violins carried across the fields from Villa Urbino. *Sounds like a live quartet. Gabriella's choice, no doubt. Giulia would have preferred the Andrews Sisters.* His heart ached at the thought of her celebrating this important night without him. Did she know why he wasn't there? Probably not. Her family would have made up some story.

Suddenly the music changed. He could hear a waltz beginning, followed by a burst of applause. He pictured Giulia walking slowly down the staircase in full view of her guests and taking the hand of some lucky young man as he whisked her onto the dance floor. A wave of jealousy washed over him.

SJ rushed to the bedroom door and turned the handle. *Locked. Leave it to the Italians to create hardware that could lock someone in as well as out. Probably designed by some protective father to keep his daughter from joining her lover in the middle of the night.* The windows, on the other hand, were still operable. He walked over to the casements and cranked one open as far as it would go. He could squeeze through if he took off his belt and held his breath. He looked through the branches of the sycamore tree scraping the house to the ground below. It was a long way down if he fell, but he wasn't thinking about that. He was thinking about seeing Giulia and holding her in his arms. Before climbing onto the sill, he grabbed a sheet of notepaper and scribbled a few words: "Meet me in the old laundry room. I need to see you. SJ."

Folding it up, he stuffed it into his pants. He ran a hand through his hair and took a quick look at himself in the dresser mirror. He had looked better.

He climbed along the arms of the tree, careful not to make a sound, until he found the crotch with his foot. Taking a deep breath, he jumped. As soon as he hit the ground, he stood up, brushed himself off and listened. Apart from the first notes of another waltz there was only silence. He crossed the property line between the two villas, the fields of farro waving like silver feathers in the moonlight. Skirting the entrance, he made his way to the servants' wing, keeping an eye out for any guards that had been hired to protect the grounds. It was during parties like this, when everyone was distracted, that robberies happened. A bullet to the back was not part of his plan for the evening.

Passing through the service entrance, SJ saw servants hurrying back and forth from the dining room to the scullery, their arms holding trays of dirty dishes and cutlery. He looked at their faces to see if he recognized someone who could pass a note to Giulia.

"SJ," a voice called out, "why aren't you out there with the guests?"

SJ turned to see one of the older servants. Aldo had been with the Urbino family for as long as SJ could remember.

"I . . . uh . . . well, it's hard to explain, Aldo. Say, could you do me a huge favor and pass this note to Giulia? It's important."

Aldo took the tiny square of paper and put it in his breast pocket. "Sure thing. Anything you want me to say to her?"

"Just make sure she gets it. And, Aldo, don't tell anyone about it . . . okay?"

"Not a word." The older man grinned and slapped SJ on the back.

"You young people gotta have *some* fun. She sure looks pretty tonight. You seen her?"

"Not yet. Thanks, my man. I owe you."

SJ slipped back out and headed for the laundry room.

Moonlight shone through the only window illuminating the ancient stone floor. A dampness hung in the air as if the steaming moisture of decades of wet clothes still clung to the walls. On one side, two washing machines rested underneath shelving full of laundry and cleaning supplies, and in the center, neatly folded tablecloths and towels were piled atop a long trestle table. An old wooden bench lay half-hidden underneath. SJ pulled it out and sat down.

On the way over to the villa, he formulated a plan. He was going to tell Giulia everything . . . his true identity . . . what he had been told about their families . . . and let her decide. If she agreed, they would run away together, far away where no one would ever find them.

"Where's my present?" Giulia stood in the doorway, the moon's rays lighting her gorgeous curves like a spotlight. She looked like a vision from another world.

SJ looked at her helplessly. "My God, you are beautiful."

The dress she was wearing shimmered like sunlight, the strapless bodice of silk organza revealing bare shoulders and a hint of cleavage. From her tiny waist, a cloud of honey colored chiffon cascaded down to her ankles in a multitude of layers.

"What did you bring me?" Giulia asked again, tauntingly.

"I . . . didn't . . ." SJ felt suddenly uneasy . . . like he was on the edge of a precipice and afraid to look down. "We need to talk. I have something to tell you."

Without taking her eyes off his, Giulia wriggled out of her dress and kicked it away. "Tell me later."

SJ's gaze traveled from her firm breasts to her hips, then to the lace panties and the barely concealed triangle between her legs. A sudden shot of fire began deep in his loins and crept up through his body.

As she walked toward him, his resolve weakened. The girl he had fallen in love with that day in the forest had become a woman . . . a woman who wanted him. At that moment, their passion for each other meant more to him than anything else . . . even the wishes and demands of his family. They came together, their bodies on fire, and their kiss a confirmation of what they were both anxious to explore. He felt her naked flesh hot against his chest, her breath quick and insistent as she pressed herself into him.

"This is our time," she whispered. "We have waited long enough. They can't tell us what to do now."

In one movement his arm cleared everything off the table, and he lifted her onto it. He spread her legs, his body hovering over hers. He looked down at a flushed face and eyes that were wild with desire.

"Are you sure you want to do this?" he said, his voice barely a whisper.

"More than anything in the world," she whispered.

As their passion escalated, everything else seemed to fade into oblivion. Restraint and consequence gave way to a sensual pleasure they had never known before. It became the only thing that mattered.

"I can't hold back," he gasped.

"I'm there too," she answered. In the next moment, they climaxed together, their breath and the heat of their bodies steaming in the dampness.

⸪ ⌒ ⸪

A cry like that of a wounded animal in pain rang out in the moonlit room. The couple on the table looked up and saw the agonized face of Marina in the doorway. In an instant, Marina was across the room, wrenching the lovers apart. SJ scrambled off the table and pulled up his pants before retreating into a corner of the room. Marina uttered another cry when she saw Giulia's ripped panties.

Giulia's gaze traveled to the blood on her thighs and then to her mother's face. "You're too late, Mama." Her eyes glinted defiantly. "I guess I'm not your perfect little girl anymore."

Marina covered her daughter with a towel and turned in SJ's direction.

"Get out."

Before SJ could make a move, Giulia put a hand up. "No. He stays. Let's make one thing clear: We both wanted this. We are both of age, Mama. We want to marry and spend the rest of our lives together."

Marina's chilling laugh bounced off the damp walls. "Is that what you think is going to happen? It wasn't my intention for you to find out this way but now you leave me no choice."

"Find out what?" Giulia asked.

"Who your father is."

"My father? You told me he died when I was born." Giulia looked at SJ. "Do you know what she's talking about?"

SJ was silent.

Marina looked at her daughter. "When your father and I met, we were both sixteen. We were too young to know what we were doing but we were so in love that nothing . . . and no one . . . could keep us apart. We kept it a secret for as long as we could."

"Why did you have to keep it a secret?" Giulia's eyes were wary. "Who was he?"

Marina said the words she had not dared to say for so long. "Your father is Lidia's brother, Marco Urbino."

Giulia's face turned white.

Marina glanced over at SJ. "You know what that makes you and my daughter. You are first cousins, just like Marco and me. I don't think I have to tell you how that kind of inbreeding is looked at by the rest of the world. First Marco and me and now both of you."

"We didn't know . . . SJ couldn't have known . . ."

"What makes you so sure he didn't know?" Marina sneered.

"If he knew, he would never have . . ." Giulia turned to SJ for support.

A stillness hung in the room as she waited for his answer.

"I didn't know . . . until last night when Santo told me. I swear." SJ's eyes were desperate. "That's why I came here tonight, to tell you."

Giulia's eyes were wild. "You *knew* and you still fucked me?" she screamed.

SJ took a step forward. "Let me explain . . . there was a reason . . ."

"Marina rushed at him, her eyes blazing. "Get out. I never want to see your face here again. As far as this family is concerned, you cease to exist."

It was midnight when SJ climbed back into his room. He lay on the bed, fully dressed, staring at the ceiling. How had it gone so terribly wrong? His original intention had been to see Giulia alone, tell her that they were not related, and suggest elopement. Even after Giulia found out who her father was, he felt sure she would still want to marry him.

And then he had seen her . . . like an apparition in the moonlight . . . half angel and half devil, taunting him, making him forget about everything except making love to her.

He had lost himself . . . they had lost themselves . . . and now they would have to live with the consequences for the rest of their lives.

Marina was only protecting her daughter when she banished him, he reasoned. It was what any mother would do. Then he remembered the way Giulia had looked at him . . . like he had deceived her intentionally.

Why hadn't he told them then, of his true identity? Get it out in the open? Then he thought of his mother. He didn't want to be the one responsible for revealing her secret. He could trust Giulia not to talk, but he could not trust Marina. When people found out about his mother's indiscretions, no matter how many years had passed, they would ridicule her . . . and Santo for trying to "fix" them.

A knock and the sound of a doorknob turning brought him back to reality.

Santo strode into the room, his face anxious. "Get up. Something has happened to Giulia. She's missing."

Chapter 17

Consequences

IT WAS THREE in the morning, and the guests had finally gone home. Aldo was washing the last of the dishes in the scullery.

He glanced out the window. The floodlights cast an eerie glow on the figure of a woman dressed in trousers and a warm jacket. There was a duffel bag stuffed into the basket of her bicycle. Aldo put down the towel and rushed outside.

"What are you doing? Where are you going?"

"Aldo, I am meeting SJ, but you cannot not tell anyone in my family, especially my mother. Not if you care about my happiness."

Aldo put a finger to the side of his nose. "I will never tell, I promise. But you cannot go like this . . . it is too dangerous. Let me get the fiat. You are lucky, I just put gas in it.

He pushed the little car a short distance away from the villa before starting it. Giulia waited for him outside the gate, along the road that led past the cemetery.

"I will never forget this," she said, blowing him a kiss before heading up the hill, past the village of Saint Anatolia, toward the highway.

<hr>

The headlights of the Cinquecento barely illuminated the old Roman road in front of her. Dawn was two hours away, and by that time, she hoped to be in Spello. Her eyes, swollen from crying, scanned the side roads looking for police cars hidden underneath the shadows of the trees.

"Watch out for *Carabinieri*," Aldo had said. "If they see a woman driving alone, they will stop you and send you home . . . unmolested if you are lucky."

Dear Aldo. Without him, she never would have made her escape.

Giulia thought about how much her life had changed in just a few hours. The image of SJ cowering in the corner of the laundry room while her mother berated him flashed before her. He had tried to tell her about her father, but she had been too focused on her own pleasure to listen. She realized now what had happened had been her fault as well as his. Speeding toward Spello, her tiny car but a speck in the vast darkness around her, the reality of what she had done set in. She knew with a sinking heart that SJ was lost to her. The dream of a life together surrounded by a loving family was over. She fought back the hysteria that hovered on the edge of her consciousness and tried to formulate a plan for her future. It was too late to undo the damage, but if she ran away, maybe each of them could save what was left of their lives.

Finding her father and asking him to help her was her only chance.

"He married someone Lidia's side of the family knew . . . a Duchessa Sabauda, I think," her mother had said when Giulia begged for information. "He lives in Spello, in the Villa Fidelia. It is a grand estate, much grander than ours."

Giulia knew where it was. "Does he know about me?"

"I don't know. After our families found out about us, we never saw each other again. I was already six weeks pregnant."

Giulia couldn't help but be appalled at how her mother and Marco had behaved. Then she thought about what had happened on the laundry room table.

"You've had no contact with him in almost eighteen years?"

"None. His wife wouldn't allow it. She keeps him on a tight leash." Marina's voice had a bitter edge to it that comes with a lifetime of resentment.

Hours later, the sky was turning from black to blue as Giulia drove up to a high stone wall surrounding a vast estate. There was an old chapel right off the *Via Centrale* and an opening next to it big enough for a car to go through. Beyond it, a serpentine cobblestone driveway wound toward a three-story building at the top of the hill. She passed a sentry station, but at that hour, there was no one to stop her from driving right up to the entrance. She stopped the car and looked up at the villa still shaded by the pre-dawn sky. No one would be expecting her, and there was every possibility she would be turned away before she even uttered a word. If that happened, she had no idea where she would go.

Shoulders squared and chin held high, she walked up the steps and rang the doorbell.

Giulia waited a minute and rang again. All was silent behind the massive wooden door. Figuring that the servants were probably the only ones up and that they were in the back of the house, she was about to ring again when there was a turn in the lock and the door opened. A tall, gaunt man peered down at her, his black service coat slightly askew and his few gray hairs standing straight out on either side of his head. He looked like he had gotten dressed in a hurry. He took in Giulia's traveling clothes, her duffel bag, and the vintage Fiat out front.

"May I help you?"

Giulia took a deep breath. "I am here to see Signore Marco Urbino."

"And you are?" The man's face had an irritated look, like he had already been waiting too long for a satisfactory answer.

"I am a relative."

The man's irritation was growing. "Without proper identification, I'm afraid that is impossible." He made a move to shut the door.

Giulia stuck her foot out and stopped it. "I think he will want to see me."

An eyebrow lifted.. "Your name, please?"

Giulia stood up straight and looked him right in the eye. "My name is Giulia Albani Urbino."

Both eyebrows went up this time, and he motioned for her to enter. "Wait here." He pointed to an antique chair against the wall and turned to go up the stairs. She noticed he took them two at a time and didn't look back.

Giulia wondered if the servant knew that Marco was her father . . . maybe in this household, unlike in her own, there were no secrets. She took a moment to examine her surroundings. The foyer was a large room with an impressive curving staircase at one end and arched doorways leading to other parts of the house on either side of it. An ornate round table rested in the middle, topped by an urn of fresh flowers.

Giulia looked at her watch. Ten minutes had gone by. Then twenty. Finally, thirty minutes later, she looked up to see a cadaver-thin figure of a woman slowly descending the stairs. Her black silk dress rustled as she moved with an elegance borne of good breeding and fancy finishing schools. As the woman drew near her, Giulia instinctively rose and curtseyed.

"An honor to meet you, Duchessa Sabauda. The woman gave Giulia a slight nod of acknowledgement.

"I see you know who *I* am." Her beady eyes, like two onyx stones, glinted underneath creased lids. "Now, tell me who *you* are."

Giulia made a split-second decision to tell the truth.

"I am Marco Urbino's daughter, Giulia Albani Urbino."

The *duchessa* flinched as if she had been struck. A moment passed. Then she started laughing.

"Well, you have guts . . . I'll say that much for you. What do you want?"

"I want to see my father."

The *duchessa* didn't flinch this time, Giulia noticed. This could only mean she was already on her guard.

Managing a tight smile, Duchessa Sabauda led Giulia across the foyer through one of the arched doorways. A servant hovered in the background. "Maria, this young lady is famished. Would you serve us breakfast in the morning room at once?"

Giulia discreetly observed the opulent décor and expensive furnishings as she passed through a formal dining room. The *duchessa* pointed to a photo resting on a grand piano.

"My relative, Giovanna di Savoia's wedding reception was held here in 1930. She married Tsar Boris of Bulgaria. That man on her right is a young Benito Mussolini."

"Giovanna di Savoia," Giulia repeated. "Isn't that . . . ?"

"The daughter of Victor Emmanuel III, the former King of Italy."

"You are related to her?" Giulia was awestruck.

"By marriage. My family, the Sabaudas, are Sardinian, but my first husband, Duke Eugenio Amedeo Aosta, was a cousin of Victor Emmanuel III. Eugenio was the acknowledged offspring of Amedeo I, King of Spain, even though his mother was not the queen. I still keep my title, even after Amedeo's death, but now I use my maiden surname." The *duchessa* looked at Giulia. "It is all a bit confusing, I know.. Ah, here we are. The Morning Room is where my husband and I have breakfast every day. He should be joining us soon." The *duchessa* smoothed her skirt and gestured for Giulia to be seated. "Please sit down."

The table was already prepared with slices of *panettone* and a platter of fresh fruit. When another servant appeared with a pitcher of coffee, the *duchessa* took the pot and waved her away. "That will be all. Cream and sugar, Giulia?"

With a curtsey, both servants left the room.

As soon as they were alone, La Duchessa Sabauda dropped the consummate hostess act.

"You want to tell me, after eighteen years, why you decided to show up?"

"I only found out ten hours ago."

The *duchessa* laughed mockingly. "Even if that is true, you think you can just waltz in here and make demands? Who do you think you are?"

Giulia felt a cold, harsh reality set in. When she had set out that morning, there had been no time to think things through. Her only thought had been to see her father and beg him for help. She realized now that her father could do nothing without this woman's approval. "What I am about to tell you may be too shocking," Giulia said.

"Try me."

Giulia had no choice but to tell her everything, right down to the little part about Marina finding her straddling SJ on the laundry room table.

"That's when she told me about my father," Giulia continued. "The last thing my mother wanted was for me to make the same mistake she did . . . which was falling in love with the wrong person. I guess I disappointed her."

"Why did you leave? You would have gotten over each other in time. You are both young enough."

"If I'd stayed, I would have made love to him again . . . there was no way I could have resisted." Giulia should have stopped there, but she didn't. "That is why your husband, and my mother, could never see each other again."

Giulia's last words seemed to hit the *duchessa* hard.

Her hands fluttered to her throat, and the flinty eyes were suddenly vulnerable. "I saved him from disgrace. I saved all of you. She was his first cousin *and* pregnant. He would have been finished."

"The decision my father was forced to make is the one I am making now . . . by choice."

Tears formed at the corners of the *duchessa's* eyes. Perhaps Giulia had insulted her by suggesting Marco had been forced into marriage. Marina tried to soften the blow. "For many reasons, I will never go back."

It took less than a minute for the *duchessa* to compose her features. The tears were gone, and her face was once more an impenetrable mask. "Although I sympathize with your unfortunate situation, I do not see how I . . . we . . . can help you."

Giulia sensed that if she showed any sign of weakness, she would be escorted out the door. This woman respected strength. She had no choice but to play her trump card.

"I'm guessing my family's sordid little tale will not sit well with your Savoia relatives, especially the part that concerns your husband."

Giulia heard the mocking laughter again.

"If I didn't know better, I'd think you were trying to threaten me. You forget where I come from. My family has weathered far worse scandals than this in the last five hundred years: murder, poisoning, and incarceration, to name a few. This is but a blip on the horizon."

Giulia's heart sank. Her strategy had failed. The *duchessa* had called her bluff.

"I'm sorry you feel that way. I won't take any more of your time." Giulia rose to leave.

"Simona, please!"

Giulia turned in the direction of the pleading voice. A man stood at the edge of the room, his eyes focused on the *duchessa*. He looked to be in his mid-thirties, but already, the burden of life seemed to weigh heavily on his bent shoulders. An expensive suit hung on his spare frame, and the once lustrous hair was thin and tinged with gray. He had the saddest eyes Giulia had ever seen.

"Marco, there you are." The *duchessa's* voice sounded shrill and artificial. "We have a surprise visitor. This is . . ."

"I know who she is." Marco crossed the room as Giulia rose to meet him. "I would recognize you anywhere."

Giulia briefly envisioned her father's arms reaching for her, all the years of separation vanishing in a heartfelt embrace. The moment passed. Marco offered his hand, and Giulia grasped it.

Simona spoke up. "This young lady has told me she intends to spread a lovely little tale about incest among the Urbinos if we don't help her."

Marco's shoulders drew inward another inch. "I'm sure there is something we can do . . ."

"Well, she can't stay here. That's for sure."

"What about La Principessa Elena? Couldn't they find a family to take her in?" Marco asked.

"In Turin?" Simona seemed to be thinking out loud, "far enough away . . ."

"A lady's assistant or nanny, perhaps?" Marco began.

"or scullery maid," Simona finished.

Giulia stood by silently as two strangers, one of them her father, decided her fate. She had flung herself on their mercy by coming here, and she knew she would have to accept whatever plans they made for her.

The *duchessa* stood up, her eyes leveled on her guest. "We will help you find a place to stay, under one condition."

Giulia waited.

"You are not to breathe a word to anyone about Marco's past or who you really are, and we never want to see you or hear from you again. If you violate this command, you will be out on the streets in seconds. Is that understood?"

Giulia looked at her father. Tears streamed down his face. "Understood," she replied.

Chapter 18

Without a Trace

SANTO SAT at one end of the utility table in the kitchen of Villa Urbino. Marina and a contrite Aldo sat at the other.

"I think she went to meet SJ . . . to elope. I knew they were in love . . . I was only trying to help."

Marina's face was anxious, and her hands picked nervously at invisible lint on her skirt. "You are a romantic fool, Aldo. Because of you . . ."

Santo intervened. "Without his help, she might have been picked up by the Police or a stranger prowling the roads at night. Either scenario would have been worse. At least she has a car. Did she tell you where she was going, Aldo?"

The old man shook his head. "'I will never forget this' was all she said."

Santo thought for a minute. "Marina, did you two talk last night . . . uh . . . after SJ left?"

"She wanted to know about her father."

"Did you tell her where the *duchessa* and Marco are living?"

"I did." Marina looked up suddenly. "Do you think she went to Villa Fidelia?"

"It's possible. She could get some answers to her questions and have time to make a plan. That is, if she could make it past the door." Santo rose and prepared to leave. "In any case, we will go there and find out."

"We?"

"SJ and I." Marina started to protest, and he held up a hand. "If you ever want to see your daughter again, you had better let me handle this. SJ is the only person who has a chance of getting through to her now."

SJ stared out the window as Santo's Lancia sped along Via Centrale. The little walled villages came and went, Campello sul Clitunno, Trevi, Montefalco, clustered on the hillsides like barnacles on the hull of a gigantic ship. As the first rays of the morning sun burst over the mountains, SJ visualized the villagers waking up, fires being lit in the *caminos,* and slabs of porchetta sizzling on racks of iron. He knew their lives were hard, with endless chores and back breaking days in the fields, but it was simple and uncomplicated. Thinking about the uncertain future that lay ahead of him, he would have traded places with any one of them.

Santo's voice brought him back to reality. "I was the one who brought Marco and the *duchessa* together. Claudio and Olivia knew the family of a rich young widow who was childless. Her family was desperate for an heir to keep the blood line alive."

"What blood line was that?" SJ asked.

Santo hesitated. "Simona was from a noble family in Sardinia. That's all I know. Agatha and I thought Marco, being a much younger man, was bound to give her a slew of children."

Santo slowed the car and turned off the main road toward Spello. "Of course, that was before we found out Simona Sabauda had a dirty little secret of her own. She had been caught *in flagrante delicto* with a young nobleman's wife, and her reputation was ruined. It seemed her tastes ran more toward women than men."

"Good God. Didn't her first husband know?"

"He was fifteen years older. Rumor had it he liked to watch."

SJ grimaced. "Sounds decadent. Poor Marco. He probably had

no idea what he was getting into."

SJ was silent for a while, thinking. "Tell me, Santo, what would have been so terrible about Marco and Marina staying together? In Sicily, first cousins marry all the time. It is even encouraged."

"That is a different culture. Let us just say they have reasons why they keep their clans together. Here, on the mainland, we view cousins marrying differently. The Church frowns on it, just like intimacy outside of marriage . . . even though people do it. Then there was the age thing. Marina was sixteen when the affair started. They were both underage *and* first cousins. It would have gone badly for them. With the information we had at the time, Agatha and I did what we thought was best for both families."

"*And* the foundation," SJ said bitterly.

"The foundation has given our mother . . . and both of us . . . the opportunity for a good life. You have never been poor or hungry. Just remember where your loyalties lie. Our mother would suffer greatly if you told the truth about her past and who you really are.

"If it weren't for the foundation, I could have told Giulia we were not related. It would have changed everything between us."

Santo's voice became irritated. "There is something that you, because of your youth, do not understand. My father-in-law's business has reached the level of success where the eyes of the world are always on him. The rich and the powerful, and those associated with them, are judged more harshly than people who are less important. Do you understand what this means?"

"I'm beginning to," SJ said, letting the words sink in. "This isn't just about our mother, is it? You are an important part of the foundation now. I think you are afraid my behavior will reflect badly on *you*."

"It's not just me. Lidia will be affected too. When people find out about her faking the pregnancy. She will be talked about . . . and judged."

SJ put his head in his hands. "God, what a mess our families have made of everything. No wonder Giulia ran away."

Santo was silent.

"What will happen to her now?" SJ asked.

"Giulia? It depends on the Duchessa Sabauda. She calls the shots in that household, I suspect. If Giulia plays her cards right, there could be a future for her with them. Perhaps that is why she chose to go there."

"Are you saying there's a chance she will *not* come back with us?"

"It might be better if she didn't." Santo glanced at his brother. "Could the two of you keep away from each other if she came back?"

SJ sighed. "I'd be lying if I said yes. Maybe I'm only speaking for myself, but staying away would be torture." Even now, when he thought of her naked body underneath him, he felt a stab of heat coming from his groin. He stifled a groan and crossed his legs. "What are we doing here then?" He asked.

"If Giulia agrees, and it's a long shot, I will help the two of you find a way to be together . . . even if it means you have to leave us."

"What do you mean, leave you?"

"There are places you can go where you will be safe from prying eyes. Sicily, Malta . . . I will support you until you both can get on your feet," Santo said gently.

"Would I be able to tell her, then, that we are not related?"

"If you were far away, yes."

SJ lay back against the seat and closed his eyes. His mind drifted.

They were walking hand in hand. On either side of the dirt road, tufts of tropical-looking plants reached out to touch them. Suddenly the foliage gave way to a sandy beach and a narrow wooden boardwalk. Directly ahead, the tourmaline sea shimmered in the hot sun. "Shall we go for a swim?" SJ looked at his bride. She looked back at him and smiled. They kicked off their shoes and ran toward the water.

"We're here."

SJ opened his eyes. The sandy beach was gone. Ahead was a high wall surrounding a piece of property that looked as big as an entire city.

Villa Fidelia.

"How do we get in?" SJ said, noticing the armed guard just outside the sentry box. "This place looks like the Quirinale in Rome."

"How about the old-fashioned way?"

"Which is?"

"Going right up to the guy with the gun and telling him who we are. The Urbinos from Scheggino," Santo said.

"Do you have a backup plan in case that name doesn't sufficiently impress him?"

"I'll think of something."

The Lancia turned into the driveway, and within seconds, the guard stepped into the road.

"Name please?" the man muttered, a cigarette hanging off his lower lip.

"Santo and Spirito Urbino. Relatives of Claudio and Olivia, and executives with the Urbino Truffle Foundation. We are here with a two-kilo supply for the *duchessa*."

"Truffles?" The man threw away the butt and lowered his gun.

"I'm really not supposed to do this but would you like some samples? We had an excellent crop this year." Santo reached into the backseat and pulled out a white box. The perfume was unmistakable.

"*Grazie.* My wife will be in heaven," the guard said, accepting the gift, "*Strangozzi con tartufo* is her favorite. Please, go right on through."

As they drove by, the man had put his gun down and was opening the box.

SJ was dumbfounded. "Do you always carry truffles with you?"

"Only when I think a bribe might be necessary."

"Do you really have two kilos back there?" SJ was examining the back seat.

"I wish I did." Santo pulled up to the entrance and looked at the massive wooden door. "If the *duchessa* is a fan, it might have helped our cause."

"What's the game plan?"

"It all depends on Giulia . . . and the *duchessa,*" Santo said.

Before they even got out of the car, the front door opened. A thin, fastidiously dressed servant stood in the doorway.

"How did you get past the guard?" The man did not look happy.

Santo appeared unruffled. "We told him who we are, and he let us through."

"That idiot. I told the *duchessa* we should fire him." The man eyed his guests suspiciously. "And who *are* you?"

"We would prefer to disclose that information when we are safely inside and given proper nourishment," Santo said coolly. "It is way past breakfast."

Without waiting for an answer, Santo walked into the villa. SJ was right behind him.

Once inside, everything changed. The *duchessa* and Marco were waiting for them in the foyer.

SJ took in the imperious-looking woman in the black silk dress and the man standing next to her. Marco looked like a whipped dog.

"So, you got yourself in the door. Now, what do you want?" Simona's eyes were hard.

Santo held out his hand. "Wonderful to meet you again, Simona. The last time we met, you were much more gracious." He turned to Marco. "My wife sends her regards. She misses you."

Marco gave a slight nod.

Santo turned to SJ. "This is my . . . uh . . . son, SJ."

The *duchessa* did not shake hands nor did Marco. They barely looked at him.

Santo addressed his hosts: "This is not a social call, as you may have guessed. We are looking for my niece. She has gone missing, and we thought she might have come here." Santo looked at Marco. "You see, she learned a short while ago that you are her real father. As you might imagine, the news upset her greatly, and she took off in the middle of the night with a somewhat old and unreliable car. Have either of you seen her?"

"How dare you come here pushing your way into my . . . our . . . home," Simona hissed. "Even if she did come here, we did not ask her to. You have no right to intrude on us like this."

"This charade has gone on long enough," SJ broke in. "Where is Giulia?"

The *duchessa* faced SJ defiantly, like the victor in a hard-won battle. "You are too late, young man. She left of her own free will. I offered her an opportunity for a new life, and she accepted."

"In exchange for what?"

"For keeping her mouth shut," Simona said simply. "And you will do the same if you care what happens to her."

SJ's fists balled up, and Santo quickly stepped between them.

"How long ago did she leave?" Santo asked.

"More than two hours ago. She was safely escorted by one of my most trusted servants. Do not ask where she has gone because we will never tell you."

Marco's shoulders sagged. "Let her go, Santo. You will not find her now."

"Why did you send her away?" SJ blurted out. "What kind of threat could Giulia pose for you? If it's your family's reputation you are trying to protect, don't make her suffer for it."

Duchessa Sabauda looked at SJ. "You have no idea the lengths I will go to protect a dynasty from scandal. One thing is clear. You have lost Giulia. The sooner you accept this and go on with your life, the better."

Italy 2015

Chapter 19

The Adventure

A COOL breeze blew in through the open accordion doors of Villa Paradiso as I put down my empty grappa glass.

"And I thought *our* family was dramatic."

Tino shot me a *how can you be so insensitive* look.

"Bad joke. Sorry, SJ," I said.

SJ grunted. "No, you're right. Seventy years later, it does sound a bit like an Italian melodrama starring Al Pacino."

"Or Glenn Close," I offered. "That *duchessa* could be Cruella de Vil's sister. Was she for real?"

"Oh, yes. Very real."

"What happened to her?"

"She lived into her eighties. Died at Villa Fidelia in 1987."

"And Marco?" Tino asked.

"He was fifteen years younger. I don't know what happened to him."

A silence hung in the air.

"What about Giulia?" I finally asked.

SJ poured the last bit of liquid into his glass from the decanter. He leaned his head back and downed it in one gulp.

"I realize now that Giulia was my one great love. *Il mio fulmine.*"

"*Fulmine?*" Tino looked puzzled.

"Thunderbolt," I explained. "You know, like in *The Godfather*? When an Italian man gets blindsided by love and becomes a complete idiot."

"Like our grandfather when he met Agatha?" Tino asked.

SJ sighed. "Yes. Italian men seem to be prone to this particular affliction."

"Even men who are half Italian," Tino said.

"I should have tried harder to find her, but those first couple of years Santo watched me like a hawk. My brother was paranoid about not only Agatha's reputation, but also his own . . . and the man he worked for, Claudio Urbino. Santo's obsession with success meant he could never allow himself to falter or make a mistake; to let himself be governed by his emotions would mean losing control. He lived his entire life that way, and it affected us all.

"As time went by, I began to see that Giulia had made a choice, and I needed to respect that. By then, she had surely built a life for herself, and I no longer had a place in it. Even if I did find her, and she was married, dredging up the past would have been worse for her than for me. I let her go, just like the *duchessa* advised me to, and got on with my life."

"It must have been all the more tragic that she never knew you were not related. Do you think it would have made a difference?"

"I believe if we had gotten there in time, I could have convinced her to run away with me. That part hurts the most . . . that I was too late."

Suddenly, a light bulb went on in my head.

"Why is it too late?" I said. "Look, SJ, I may be hallucinating from all that grappa, but have you considered trying again? To locate her, I mean? It is different now . . . you have . . ."

"One foot in the grave, I think you Americans say. Even though it sounds tempting, how do I know she is . . . ?"

"Still alive? Pardon me for being so blunt, but because of her age . . . she would be around ninety now . . . the chances are slim. If you can accept that fact, then you have nothing to lose by trying to find her." I put a hand on SJ's arm. "Humor me, okay? Flash forward, *many* years from now, to the end of your life."

Tino started to protest.

"Wait, hear me out. I play this game with myself sometimes . . . when you are lying there, contemplating your life . . . are you content with the way it turned out? What about the unrealized dreams, the things you never told someone, the emotions you hid away because you were too afraid to confront them? I am asking you this now, SJ, because you still have time . . . are you brave enough to think about your death now? And if so, what are the things you will regret *not* having done?"

SJ stared at me. "That's easy. Not making the effort to find out what happened to Giulia."

"Even after seventy years?"

SJ nodded. "Even after seventy years."

"Then do it! It just so happens you have two energetic relatives who are free for the next week to go on an adventure . . . and they just happen to have the perfect car for a family road trip."

Tino held up a hand. "Before anyone gets too excited, no car of mine is going anywhere without a fully disclosed destination and a road map to get there. You don't even have a clue where she is." He looked at SJ. "Or do you?"

"There are a number of possibilities. I wouldn't be surprised if Agostino knows something."

"Agostino?" I perked up. "Why would he know?"

"When he was a boy, he was very close to Marina. I would see them together in the village often. They looked like mother and son."

"So, you think Marina knew where her daughter was?"

"It's possible. I don't think they ever saw each other again, but they might have corresponded.""

Another light bulb went on.

"SJ, if what you say is true, would you consider inviting Agostino to come along? He may be able to open doors that remain shut to us."

SJ's face hardened. "No. For two reasons. One, Agostino and I have not spoken to each other in years, and now you know why. Marina never wanted to lay eyes on me after Giulia left. I was a painful reminder of why her daughter ran away."

"What's the second reason?"

"To my knowledge, Agostino has never learned my true identity. No one from his side of the family ever told him . . . Can you see the three of us hanging around him for a week without blowing my cover?"

"Blowing your cover!" I was getting exasperated now. "You make it sound like you are in a witness protection program! This is 2015. You and Agostino are just two old and cranky bachelors rattling around in your drafty mansions. Sorry to sound indelicate, SJ, but all those people you think you need to protect are resting peacefully in the cemetery on the hill. I can't believe you are still quaking in your boots that someone is going to find out that your mother had two children by a man she adored . . . even if she never married him. Times have changed. Nowadays, she would more than likely be looked at as a woman who never settled for anything but true love."

SJ smiled. "You remind me of someone," he said, "someone who never took 'no' for an answer."

"Who was that?"

"My Giulia." SJ sat for a long time in silence. "Maybe you're right. The charade of the Urbino family feud has played itself out. It's time to re-evaluate. Let me think about this. No leaking our prospective plan until I give you the green light."

"And when will that be? Tino and I are only here for ten days . . ."

SJ interrupted me. "Enough! I need a good night's sleep first . . . and that begins right now. I will be in touch tomorrow."

"Does that mean *you* are going to ask Agostino?" I pushed. "Maybe it would be better if I approached the subject first."

"Maybe it would be better if you left that decision up to me," SJ said. "Good night."

It was almost midnight when Tino and I left the villa. A full moon hung in the dark sky, lighting the way to the parking lot, and as we passed the cluster of guest cottages, I saw a single lamp still burning. In the valley below, the lights of the village twinkled. "It all looks so peaceful and calm down there," I said.

"Looks can be deceiving." Tino chuckled. "I bet there is a shitload of drama going on inside those little houses."

Approaching the Maserati, Tino opened the car doors with a flick of his remote, and we got in. "I guess I should be eternally grateful to you for including me in another of your harebrained escapades but I suspect what you really want is a car and a driver." He turned the key in the ignition, and the car roared to life.

"A *really good* car and driver," I assured him.

"Okay, okay. I get it. Do you actually think Agostino is going to go along with this? He might find the idea about as enticing as a kick in the nuts."

"I've been thinking about that. The opportunity to chauffeur us in a late-model sports car might be an incentive."

Tino turned off the motor. "Oh, no. Not on your life. If I'm going to go along with this, *I* will be the one and only driver."

"Turin is over six hundred kilometers from here. You might need to take a break once in a while."

"I have the stamina of a bull. I can go forever."

"Fine. We will see if you have the bladder of a bull. Now, before we get to Agostino's we need to agree on one thing. It's not midnight yet and he may be awake. We will talk about this tomorrow morning when our heads are clear. Agreed?"

"Agreed. Maybe by that time we will be sober enough to rethink the entire thing."

We drove up the cypress-lined dirt road to the cemetery and cut across the Roman road to Villa Urbino's iron gates. They were shut tight.

"*Damn*. We will have to use the intercom. I was hoping to sneak in without waking him up."

Tino laughed. "Midnight is still the shank of the evening for Italians. I'm sure he's still prowling around."

I pushed the button and waited. Almost immediately it buzzed back, and the gates slowly opened.

"That was quick," I said.

"Almost like he was sitting up waiting for us," Tino said. "I bet he can't wait to hear how our evening went."

"Remember. No hinting at our plan until tomorrow. We need to present this as a spur of the moment idea."

Tino looked confused. "Didn't SJ say he was going to do the presenting?"

"Yeah, but it was my idea."

"You just can't help stirring up trouble, can you?"

We drove to the parking space at the southern end of the villa where the servants' quarters used to be. As we passed the old laundry room, I gave it a quick glance. Suddenly, I had a whole new appreciation for the part it had played in the Urbino family history.

"*Buona sera.*" A voice broke through the stillness. "Did you have a nice evening?"

Agostino came out of the shadows and walked toward us. He looked at his watch. "Almost midnight. You lose track of the time?"

"How sweet of you to wait up for us," I said.

"I always check property at night when I have guests . . . to make sure they make it home safe."

"It shows what an excellent host you are," Tino said. "I don't know about you all, but my grappa high is plummeting. If you'll excuse me . . ."

Agostino looked disappointed. "I was hoping for a *recap*—as you Americans call it—a review of what you ate for dinner."

"Tomorrow, Agostino," I promised him. "We also have something we would like to discuss with you. A proposal."

Tino shot me a *what-the-hell-are-you-saying?* look.

"A proposal?" Agostino asked.

"Tomorrow, you will know everything. Breakfast at eight?"

Chapter 20

The Proposal

IF I'D HAD any idea what it would feel like to run three miles at dawn with a grappa-induced hangover, I would have stayed in bed. Not that two more hours of sleep would have made any difference. Somehow, I managed a feat any woman in similar circumstances would appreciate. I showered, dressed, and put on makeup without once judging what I saw in the mirror. At 8:05 a.m., I knocked on Tino's door.

"Don't tell me," I said when he opened the door and saw my face. "You don't look much better."

We walked through the pool area leading to the dining room's double French doors. All I wanted to do was spit out the proposal before I lost my nerve, and then I was going straight back to bed.

Agostino had assumed his usual morning position... legs propped up on the table with *Il Messaggero* open to the sports section.

"Scrambled eggs con tripe?" He grinned.

I felt my stomach lurch, and Tino groaned.

"Just black coffee," we both said at the same time.

As soon as two steaming mugs appeared before us, I launched into my well-rehearsed pitch about our plans to embark on SJ's last-gasp adventure. I was barely past the first sentence when Agostino stopped me. *"Basta!* I have heard enough."

"But I haven't even gotten to the good part yet," I protested.

"Not interested," he replied, reaching for the paper and

positioning it right in front of his face for emphasis.

I sat back, utterly deflated.

A second later, Agostino put down his paper and looked at me. There was an unmistakable twinkle in his eye. "It maybe interest you that I had an unexpected phone call this morning."

I could barely muster up a tepid, "Who was it?"

"Your relative from next door."

I sat up. "SJ? He called you?"

"Seven o'clock. Surprise the hell out of me. Want to guess what he say?"

I tried not to get my hopes up. "I can't imagine."

Agostino laughed. "It looks like I must clear my calendar for a week. SJ wants me to go with him to Turin." He waited a good minute before he added, "And he wants both of you to come too."

"Yes!" I pumped my fist and danced around the room. Before I knew it, I had my arms around Agostino's neck. I planted a big kiss on the top of his head.

He turned bright red.

"And how are we getting there?" Tino had his arms crossed and was eyeing Agostino coolly. "*Flying*, by any chance?"

"SJ say you offer your car as transportation."

"He did, did he? And did he say who was going to do the driving?"

"He say we take turns."

"No, no, and no. Only I drive or the trip is off." Tino's voice thundered with an authority that discouraged further discussion.

"No problem," Agostino said. He looked crushed.

"Okay," I broke in. "I'm glad we got *that* important detail settled. Now, can we get on to the real reason for the trip? What did SJ tell you?"

"He say something about a 'game' he has been playing, a game that has made him realize things must change between our families. I want that too. He has something important to say to me tonight, and I am ready to hear it."

My cellphone buzzed, and I picked it up. "Hi, SJ. We were just talking about you. Tonight? Let me ask." I looked at Agostino. "SJ wants to know what you're making for dinner."

Agostino chuckled and took the phone.

"*Minestre di passatelli d'Urbino* to start, then *spiedini misti Spoletini* ... and for dessert"—Agostino winked at us—"you will surprise us. *Va bene?*"

He handed the phone back to me.

"I didn't understand a word of that." Tino glared at us suspiciously. "I didn't hear *tripe,* did I?"

"All regional dishes. You will love it," Agostino assured him.

"Why can't we just have pizza?" Tino grumbled.

While Agostino was busy checking his supply of ingredients and jotting down items to buy at the *alimentari,* I stumbled off to my room and climbed into bed. I could only imagine how much drinking we were going to do tonight, and I needed to sleep off the rest of my hangover before I started another one.

I had just drifted off when I heard someone pounding on the door.

"Signora? You there?"

GP! I leaped out of bed and swung the door open.

GP was standing there in a pair of overalls with pant legs rolled up to his knees, striped socks, and the dirtiest work boots I had ever seen. He had a pipe wrench in one hand and a *serpente* in the other.

I had a horrible thought. "Did my apartment have another backup?"

"Not yet." GP grinned and treated me to a mouthful of tobacco.

"Are you chewing tobacco now, too?"

"You tell me to quit smoking."

I shook my head. *Hopeless.*

"Did Agostino have a plumbing problem?"

"*Sì.* I work this morning on garbage disposal and sink drain. He say it will get a lot of use tonight." He looked at my wrinkled T-shirt and leggings. "We need to pick out tile for kitchen. You ready to go now?"

The minute I heard "now," my head started throbbing. "I thought businesses closed from 1:00 to 4:00 p.m. in Italy."

"Eurobusiness never close."

"Eurobusiness? What's that?"

"A store that sell everything. Tile, furniture, even sinks. Cheap."

I looked at my watch. It wasn't even noon yet, and my head felt like it was going to bust open. "Can we do this tomorrow?"

GP paused to consider this. "Okay. Tomorrow. I meet you here *alle sette.*"

"Seven . . . in the morning?" *Jesus, doesn't this guy eat breakfast?*

GP's eyes narrowed. "You change your mind about me?" He took out a pinch of tobacco, popped it into his mouth, and started to walk away.

"No, no." I ran after him. "Seven is fine."

"Good. We look at *frigo e forno* too."

Frigo and *forno. Sounds like two characters from Middle Earth.*

"Sounds good, GP."

He hesitated a moment as if he wanted to ask me something.

"I will bring my credit card. Not to worry."

He looked relieved. "*Bene. Domani, alora.*"

"Domani. Can we stop at the bar first for cappuccino?" Before he had time to say no, I added, "My treat."

GP nodded and held up two fingers. "*Due minuti.*"

"Two minutes," I promised him. I closed the door and sighed. It was dawning on me how naïve I was. Homeownership was a lot more work than I thought.

Before climbing back into bed, I walked around the room, taking a closer look at the pictures on the wall. Yesterday, with Agostino, they had held only a passing interest … sepia faces from another time. Now, after hearing SJ's story, I looked at them differently. They were flesh-and-blood people who made mistakes and were vulnerable. There was the photo of Marina and Gabriella as children in the garden where the pool and cabana now stood. Then the one of Marina, smiling, with a dark-haired Giulia in her arms. They both looked so happy, so sure they would always be together. Beneath it, I noticed a picture I hadn't seen before of an older Marina holding the hand of a small boy. The way he was looking up at her, like a son with his mother, I was sure it was Agostino. No wonder there had been such bitterness between the two families; if Marina had told Agostino about SJ's part in the disappearance of her daughter, it would have destroyed any chance of a reconciliation. It was time to bring this saga out in the open and hear both sides of the story … I just hoped there was enough *Grappa del Re* on hand to smooth over the rough spots.

With a few hours to spare before dinner, Tino and I decided to walk to the cemetery. It was high time to pay the relatives a visit.

We met by the kitchen entrance and started up the hill that led to the *villetto* and the old Roman road. From there, it was just a short hike to the burial grounds.

"Did you see Agostino? I feel bad we're not helping."

"I think he wants to be in charge," Tino said. "When I saw him an hour ago, he had a grocery list a mile long and was headed to the market in Spoleto. It's going to be a feast. I heard some squealing and the sound of an axe a while back."

I grimaced. "Any idea what *spiedini* means?"

"No, but I get the feeling it involves at least one animal carcass."

Up ahead, the walls of cemetery came into view.

"I came here, once," Tino said, "with Mom and Dad in '95. He pushed open the iron gate, and we walked among the graves to the back of the cemetery. Here's the Urbino grave." He pointed to a modest marble plaque with five names on it. "Our great grandfather Francesco, our great aunt Assunta, her husband and her daughter, Teresina."

"And Dr. Sabatini." I read the inscription under his name: "*Beneficando Sempre Tutti.*"

"Meaning?"

"He never turned anyone away regardless of whether they could pay. The man who admired Mussolini but lived like a socialist."

"Wasn't he the one who delivered SJ in secret?"

"He was."

Tino's brow furrowed. "There is something I've always wondered about. Including Assunta's spouse, there are five names on this headstone and only one plot of ground. How do they all fit in here?"

"The Italians have an ingenious consolidation system when it comes to their dead. I call it the bone box."

"How do you know this?"

"Brunetta told me when I asked her the same question. As soon as a person decomposes, they put their bones in a container to make room for the newer additions.

"You mean they put all the bones together?" Tino looked horrorstruck.

"Well, it makes sense. There isn't enough room here for six coffins, and in Italy, real estate for the dead is scarce."

"Why aren't they just cremated?"

"It's happening more and more, but there is still a stigma among Catholics about cremation. They believe bodies must remain intact so the soul can go to heaven."

Tino shook his head in disgust. "I seem to remember that macabre detail from catechism class. If I croak here, you promise to send me back to the States, right?"

"And if *I* croak here, I want to be buried over there." I pointed to the three miniature palazzos with the name Urbino over the top. "That's where Santo, Lidia, and Agatha are buried."

Tino peered inside the window of the small, locked door.

"Looks like they have their own sarcophagi. No sharing space for that crowd. Is this where SJ will be buried?"

I nodded. "There's a block of marble between Agatha and Santo with no name on it."

"Nice digs." Tino looked around. "Where is Agostino's side of the family?"

I led him to the opposite part of the cemetery where a group of less ostentatious memorials stood. There were two buildings side by side with only a rusty iron grate separating the living from the dead. I read the names on the first one. "There are five tombs in here. Agostino's great grandparents, Angela and Mariella, and Agostino's father and mother." I looked closer to read the date on a very old block of marble: "Armando Urbino. Born 1885. Died 1906."

Tino sucked in his breath and whispered, "That's the one who raped Agatha . . ."

"And got a bullet in his head by our grandfather. 'Spirito's Revenge.'"

Tino started looking around. "Where is Marina's grave?"

The second stone enclosure was newer and had a substantial steel gate protecting the entrance. I peered through the bars. It appeared to have six crypts in it.

"Marina is here," I told Tino. "And what looks like her parents and another man. "Maybe Gabriella's husband? Then there are two empty places."

Tino read the inscription as he peered over my shoulder: "Marina Albani Urbino. Born 1907. Died 1975."

"The two empty graves," I said, "might be for Gabriella and. . . ?"

"Agostino," Tino whispered ominously.

I nodded. "There are no more spaces, though. Why didn't the family figure Agostino would be needing a space for a wife?"

Tino's eyes widened. "If he does get married, he'd better tell her about the burial situation. She might want to make sure she dies first . . . early bird gets the crypt . . . so to speak . . ."

"Or maybe, if he dies before her, they will just squish her in on top of him."

"Ugh!" Tino made a face. This place is starting to give me the creeps. Let's get out of here."

Chapter 21

The Reunion

IT WAS early evening before I could summon the courage to look at my face in the mirror. My hangover was gone but the tell-tale ravages of last night's debauchery remained. The streaks of red, stretching across my eyeballs, could be remedied with drops, and concealer would help the purple craters under my eyes. But what about my *hair*? The ball cap I had been wearing all day had plastered it against my head, and whatever had escaped was sticking out like a frizzled halo. I looked at my watch. I had one hour to transform myself into someone who didn't resemble a raging alcoholic or a homeless person, and I was going to need every minute of it. I peeled off my T-shirt, kicked off my sneakers, and headed for the shower.

Forty-five minutes later, I surveyed my handiwork. Rather than try to tame my unruly locks with hair product and a flat iron, I decided to go for the Sophia Loren look. I flung my hair up and down a few times, scrunched it a few more, and let it do its thing. After applying the slutty looking eyeliner and mascara Italian women are so fond of, I strung big gold hoops through my ears. The red spaghetti-strap sheath came next. I slipped it on and adjusted the plunging neckline. It was painfully obvious where the Sophia Loren similarity ended. My puppies bore no resemblance to that quintessential Italian beauty's pair of St. Bernard's. *Oh, well. No one is perfect.*

Staring at myself in the mirror, I wondered why was I doing all this primping, anyway. Ever since I had come to Villa Urbino, feelings

I thought had died with menopause were resurfacing. What the hell was going on? I was fifty-nine years old, for Christ's sake. Suddenly it hit me. The owner of Villa Urbino was responsible for this ridiculous behavior.

There was something about Agostino that set him apart from the usual assortment of men I had dated in the past. I had always gravitated to successful men who avoided both domesticity *and* intimacy—a subconscious choice, no doubt, for a woman who wasn't ready to commit herself. A preoccupation with our careers always provided an excuse for not getting too close. Agostino was different. He loved to cook, balance a budget, and cater to the needs of a hotel full of guests . . . in short, all the things I had considered unnecessary for a career in the performing arts. Always on the road shuttling from one ballet company to another, I had never mastered the domestic skills he excelled in nor experienced the joy he seemed to take in pleasing others. As a performer, I had only been interested in myself.

As far as his essence as a man, Agostino seemed comfortable in his skin. He was not afraid to speak his mind if he disagreed with something, but he was quick to accept an apology or welcome a change of heart if he was convinced of its sincerity. The way he was ready to wipe away years of acrimony between his family and SJ's showed me he was a person who could surmount a long-standing grudge and admit that no one . . . and that included himself . . . was perfect.

The only red flag seemed to be our age difference. I knew he was younger than me. But how much younger? He had said he was just a boy when Marina died in 1975, but I couldn't remember if he had mentioned his age. What if I was wrong about his possible feelings for me? I could just see myself sneaking up to his bachelor pad in a sexy negligee only to find he wasn't interested in older women.

For about a nanosecond, I considered changing into something more befitting my age … like a baggy caftan and flat shoes. The nanosecond passed. I slipped on my four-inch heels, gave my miniature poodles a hike, and walked out the door.

The minute I stepped into the dining room, I heard a deafening clatter followed by cries of "*cazzo!*" and "*stupido, che fai!*" It sounded like Agostino and SJ. Without breaking my stride, I headed for the kitchen.

When I walked in, both men were on all fours, scrambling to pick up a dozen spear-sized iron skewers that were scattered all over the floor. They were laughing hysterically. At least they weren't lying in a pool of blood with stab wounds sticking out of their chests. My eye traveled to the counter where I saw a half-empty bottle of grappa and two glasses.

"I thought Agostino was cooking and SJ was making the dessert," I said.

Without looking up, Agostino called back, "We decide to collaborate."

That set them off into another gale of laughter.

"You know, Agostino," I countered, hands on my hips, "two chefs in a kitchen, drinking grappa, is never a good idea … especially in a kitchen as small as yours."

Agostino swiveled around, a challenging expression on his face. Then his jaw dropped. He sat back on his heels and whistled.

"*Scopabile!*"

SJ socked him in the arm and looked at me. "Sorry, a reflex action. Just trying to defend my kin's honor."

Now I was curious. "*Scopabile*," I repeated, "What does it mean?"

The two men were silent.

"I hope it is a compliment." I smiled brightly.

"Compliment, *sì, per sicuro*." Agostino looked uncomfortable.

"I know that word." Tino had walked in from the dining room

and was looking over my shoulder at the two men. "I learned it the first time I set foot in Italy. I was nineteen and just beginning a summer college extension program. A beautiful lady on the street said it to me as I walked by. It was the beginning of a short but *highly* informative course in human relations."

The other two men chuckled in appreciation as they picked up the skewers. Tino refilled their glasses.

"We sterilize them. Not to worry," Agostino said when he saw my face.

Tino started opening cabinets looking for another bottle. "Ah. Well stocked, I see." He took out two, uncorked one, and poured.

"Whoa." I waved away the offered glass . . . Maybe later. I'm still recovering from last night."

"Tail of the Dog. Like you Americans say," Agostino grinned.

"I never understood that expression," SJ said.

"First of all, it's '*hair* of the dog,' not tail," I explained. "It means a little bad can make something good."

"I could not agree more. SJ, come, we make a toast. To a reunion many long years overdue. Bottoms up and down the thatch!"

I choked, and Tino knocked back his glass.

"I'll drink to that!" he said.

Despite the shaky start, once we sat down to eat, the meal took center stage.

"*Primo piatto. Minestre di passatelli d'Urbino*," Agostino announced as he brought out a large steaming pot and began ladling a thick, green soup into bowls.

Tino stared at it. "What exactly is this?"

I rolled my eyes. Not again.

Agostino fished out a lumpy white ball and plopped it into Tino's bowl. "Consommé with meat dumplings. They are made with ground meat, spinach, breadcrumbs, and eggs and butter. You squeeze it through a gadget, like your colander, and add it to broth."

Tino picked up a spoon and dug in.

"I like to know what something is before I eat it," he said between mouthfuls. "No offense intended."

"None is taken but, sometimes, you have to trust the chef."

SJ uncorked the first of three bottles of wine he had chosen for our meal and poured. "Compliments, Agostino! I have not eaten this dish in ages. It comes from Urbino, in the mountains of Le Marche. Our ancestors originally came from that town before they moved here. *Minestre di passatelli* goes back as far as the fifteenth century."

Agostino beamed. "Eat up! Next we have kebabs *a la Spoletini*."

It felt like a production with Agostino as chef, waiter, and master of ceremonies all rolled into one. I couldn't take my eyes off him.

After our consommé, he spirited away the bowls and came back wheeling a cart with a tray of sizzling kebabs and deposited two on each of our plates.

"We have pork, chicken livers, and lamb with layer of pancetta between. A little sage, rosemary, and salt. It sit for six hours and then bake for fifteen *minuti*."

"If there is a heaven, it can't be any better than this," I said, sopping up the last of the pan juices with focaccia bread. "I am stuffed already."

"But we have the dessert. SJ has made something especially for Tino. He tell me you always want pizza."

Tino frowned. "For dessert?"

"Pizza *dolce*," SJ said, wiping his mouth with a napkin and preparing to leave the table. "Freshly made in *questo* momento." He made a slight bow and disappeared into the kitchen.

"Let's go watch," I said.

SJ peeled back the cloth from the deep cake pan, where the

dough had rested for an hour, and began brushing the top with beaten egg.

"The dough is made with lemon rind, oil, egg yolk and sweet white wine." He turned the oven up high and shoved it in. "In thirty minutes, it will be done. It is best not to open the oven until then. Come, let us go back and sit. I have something I want to tell Agostino."

I had a feeling I knew what *that* was. I only hoped it was news our host was ready to hear. The trip we were about to take depended on it.

We all sat down and waited.

SJ cleared his throat. "I have my American relatives to thank for helping me come to my senses. Sometimes it takes an outsider to see the truth more clearly." SJ nodded to Tino and me and turned to Agostino. "To put it simply, our families have been estranged for too many years, and I want it to end. I accept full blame for what happened to Marina's daughter seventy years ago. There is a secret about my birth that has never been told. Not even Giulia knew, and if she had, I am convinced she would not have left. I was wrong to keep it a secret, but there was a reason." SJ took a deep breath. "Agatha Altarocca was not my grandmother. She was my mother. Santo and I had the same father, a man called . . ."

Agostino finished the sentence: "Spirito Urbino. I hope this doesn't shock you, but I suspect for some time this secret."

SJ's eyes widened. "How?"

"I was still a boy when I would see you and Santo together. I always thought you act more like brothers than father and son. And then your name, it is Spirito, after all. We knew Agatha loved someone, before Armando ruined it, and there was never another man in her life. It was not hard to put together."

"Do you think Marina knew, too?" SJ asked.

Agostino thought for a moment. "I don't know. It is possible. Whether she know or not, she wanted to believe *you* were the reason Giulia left. Otherwise, she would have to admit that it was because of what she did with Marco." Agostino paused before he spoke again.

"There is something I else I need to tell you, something I have struggled with for many years. Because of the mistakes my family made, I am sensitive to this *consanguineità* . . . the mixing of the blood. When I was older, after my aunt passed, I learned about Marina and Marco's love affair. It shocked and disgusted me. I adored my aunt, and I couldn't understand how someone so good could do such a thing. And then the same thing happen with you and Giulia. I promised myself, at an early age, that I would never make the same mistake. I realize now how wrong it was, blaming you for Marina's broken heart and Giulia's going away. It was easier for our family to point the finger at you so we didn't have to blame ourselves. I am guilty of that too." Agostino reached out and grasped SJ's hand. "One thing I *am* sure of, if Giulia knew who you really were, she would have found a way to come back to you."

SJ's eyes filled. "Thank you for that. If what you say is true, this trip is long overdue. This is my last chance to set the record straight and wipe away the residue of shame. I must try to find her. Will you join me?"

"It would give me great pleasure to accompany you," Agostino answered.

"Don't forget about us!" I chimed in. "You will need a car and driver."

SJ laughed and turned to me. "I wouldn't dream of leaving behind the person who is responsible for all this. It was your idea, after all."

"*Cazzo! La pizza!*" Agostino sprinted to the kitchen, grabbed a pot-holder, and hauled the pizza out. The crust was golden brown on the edges and bubbling. "It is not burned. I can't believe it!"

SJ walked in and started sprinkling it with powdered sugar. "Thirty minutes exactly. Tino, are you ready to sample a dessert the Urbinos have enjoyed for centuries?"

Chapter 22

Early Squirrels Get the Nuts

HE LOOKED into my eyes and pulled me to him. "Scopabile," he whispered. I felt his warm breath in my ear and a tingle up my spine. "You never told me what it means," I whispered back. He laughed and nuzzled my neck.

Somewhere, in the recesses of my brain, I heard pounding.

"Signora! You there?"

My eyes flew open, and I reached for the phone. Seven a.m. I had overslept.

"Be right there, GP!" I yelled, groping for the running clothes I had set out last night. "Almost ready!" I yelled again, tying my shoelaces and throwing on a jacket. I mentally reviewed the necessities I needed: underwear, sweatshirt, leggings, ball cap, phone . . . and purse. In seven minutes flat I was out the door.

"You have a bad night?" GP was looking at the circles under my eyes.

I forgot makeup! I quickly calculated the odds of meeting someone I knew at this hour and in a foreign country. It never fails that whenever you look your worst, you always run into someone you know, and they *always* look better than you do.

I dashed back into my room to retrieve my makeup bag and sunglasses.

"You *sure* you have everything?" GP asked sarcastically. "Why do women need so much stuff?"

"It's hard to explain, GP. We are complicated creatures."

We walked to the parking area where the Ape and Tino's Maserati were parked.

"That your car?" GP asked.

"Not mine. My brother's. He won't let me drive it."

"Smart man."

I slid into the front seat of the Ape. Spotless. GP may have looked like a mess, but he kept his truck in tip-top shape. Only the best for Delilah. I hoped he treated his wife as good as his mistress.

We drove past the open gates of Villa Urbino and down the road toward town. My need for caffeine was beginning to surface.

"*Due minuti* for cappuccino," I reminded him.

"Too late. You lost five minutes getting ready."

No coffee? For a whole day? My hands felt clammy, and my head started to throb.

We headed out of town on Via Acquasparta where the landscape changed from townhouses to countryside. There were large swatches of land divided into individual farms, each one inhabited by several generations living under one roof. Every few kilometers, a cluster of shops and cafes appeared along the road to serve the residents who lived there.

"How much farther?" I asked GP. We had only been driving for thirty minutes, and I was already in the early stages of caffeine withdrawal. We passed an open bar, where two old men were sitting outside, smoking.

"Stop here!" I screamed, lunging for the steering wheel and turning the car in the direction of the two men. GP slammed on his brakes and stopped the Ape inches from their feet. I got out and ran into the bar before he could back up.

"*Scusi,*" I said, barely registering the way the two men they were looking at me. Like I was demented or something.

I sucked down the first cappuccino in seconds and was ready to order another when GP walked in.

He saw the empty cup. "You talk about my cigarettes, but you are no better than me. Addicted to caffeine."

"Pick your poison," I snapped. "Booze, tobacco, or caffeine. We've all got our weaknesses."

GP grinned. "Why I have to pick? I like all three." He pulled out his pack and shook out a cigarette. "Have another cappuccino. I go outside to smoke."

"Whatever," I muttered. So much for my image of self-discipline and restraint. My vulnerability felt exposed and violated. I summoned the bartender and ordered a double-shot of espresso.

Two double cappuccinos and three cigarettes later, GP and I got back in the car.

"Look, GP," I began, "I realize we only met three days ago, but I already feel we understand each other's weaknesses better than some married couples I know. Let's come to an agreement. I won't count how many cigarettes you smoke if you don't remind me of my caffeine addiction. How does that sound?"

"It sound like you could be possible mistress material. Except," he patted the dashboard, "that job is already taken."

"Don't worry, I could never hope to compete with Delilah." I looked out across the fields running endlessly in all directions. The only structure in sight was a solitary warehouse with no windows and a glass door so filthy you couldn't even see through it. "Where is this store of yours?"

GP pulled into a gravel parking lot and cut the motor. "We are here."

I looked at the plain cement walls and pathetic landscaping out front. "It sure could use a little curb appeal."

"Curb appeal," GP repeated. "What is that?"

"When businesses fix their place up to attract buyers."

"Eurobusiness don't need to look pretty. People come because prices are cheap and they no have to go anywhere else."

"A one-stop shop," I suggested.

GP slapped his knee. "One-stop shop. Haha . . . that's a good one! We go inside, and I introduce you to the owner."

We pushed open the glass door and walked into a dingy cement foyer with a staircase going up to another level on the opposite side.

"What's up there?" I said, pointing to a railing and another filthy glass door.

"*Pranzo.*" GP clapped me on the back. "We eat lunch there after we shop."

It did not look like a place I wanted to set foot in, much less have a meal in, but I didn't want to act like a princess. I figured GP was doing enough for me, the least I could do was push around a salad to make him happy.

He pushed open the door that led to the store. The instant I was inside, I felt transported to another world. The merchandise was stacked in aisles too narrow to pass through, and there were shoppers everywhere. I had never seen so much stuff: light fixtures next to linens, toilets alongside pots and pans, and children's bikes competing for space with adult toys.

"Come. We go look at frigo e forno now." GP dragged me up a flight of stairs into another gigantic space packed with furniture and appliances. *Frigo* turned out to be a refrigerator, and *forno* was an oven, not to be confused with *stufa*, which was a stove.

"Not to worry," GP said when he saw my face. "Just point to what you want, and I will get you the best price." He examined a tag and snorted. "This not what you pay when you are with me!"

I chose the appliances I liked: a fridge, a range and oven combo, and a sink for the kitchen.

"*Servizio*," GP reminded me. I found the tiniest sink and cabinet I had ever seen. GP picked out the toilet.

In another room, I chose a mattress and box spring for each bedroom and a futon for the tiny third room. At this point, I had no idea how many guests would be joining me in the future, so I wanted to be prepared. Besides, the prices did not seem unreasonable compared to what I had seen back in the States. GP wrote everything down on a notepad and totaled it up. "Time to meet Luigi Scoiattolo, *the boss*," he said.

We walked to the far end of the second floor to a finger-stained door marked "*Privato*" and knocked.

"*Pronto*," a voice called from inside.

"GianPietro qui," GP called back.

A minute later, the door opened, and a pair of bright eyes stared back at me. From the size of his belly and the broken blood vessels in his nose, Signore Scoiattolo looked as if he lived life to the fullest, poisons included.

"This my new friend, Signora Wilson, from America. She buy a casa in Scheggino, and I help her put in kitchen." GP held out the notepad. "She like these things. You can give her the Scoiattolo discount?" GP said this in English, obviously for my benefit.

Luigi studied the pad and looked at me. "You come for *pranzo* later?" He pointed to the dingy-looking restaurant I had seen earlier. I had a feeling the extent of the discount depended on my answer.

"Of course." I nodded vigorously. "Looking forward to it."

Luigi scribbled a few words on the pad and handed it back to GP.

"Be sure to take her to look at the *piastrella*. Paolo will take good care of her."

"Who is Paolo?" I asked GP after Luigi had disappeared into his office.

"His brother own the stone shop in the back. We need tiles for the kitchen. We go there next, after we pay."

At the check-out counter, arrangements were made to transport the appliances to the apartment after the kitchen was completed. As I reached for my credit card, I glanced at the notepad. Luigi had written across the top: "30% off everything."

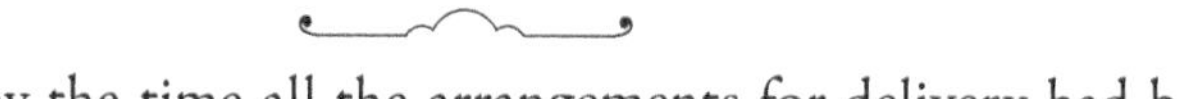

Paolo Scoiattolo looked nothing like his brother. Rail thin and wiry, he rubbed his hands together as he steered us toward the most expensive stone samples. My eyes bulged at the prices.

"Don't you have something less expensive? A veneer, perhaps?"

GP translated: "*Impiallacciatura.*"

Paolo's face fell. He pointed to a section of the store where slivers of stone in webbed sections were stacked. The prices were much more affordable.

"This is what I want!" I picked out a rosy travertine that matched the walls of the castle. I suddenly had an image of cabinets being hauled down the castle stairs in the middle of the night. "When this kitchen is installed, it cannot be removed, right?"

GP caught my drift. "*Molto permanente,*" he assured me.

"I'll take it!" I said.

The notepad came out, and GP began writing.

"The Scoiattolo discount will be applied here as well?" GP said in Italian, showing Paolo the bill.

With a resigned "*Sì,*" Paolo wrote, "30% off" next to the total.

It was noon by the time all the arrangements for delivery had been made. The parking lot was filling up, and customers were now joining us as we filed up the stairs to the restaurant.

"They only open for *pranzo,*" GP explained. "If we want a table, we must hurry."

The inside of Luigi's restaurant was another revelation. Long tables, lined end to end, filled the room. Along one wall, a glass case held platters of food, and servers in white caps and aprons stood ready to accommodate the line already beginning to form.

I eyeballed the crowd. These were not well-heeled pedestrians, whiling away a couple of hours on their way to somewhere else, or businessmen from nearby Spoleto, lunching with one eye on their cellphones. These were farmhands, masons, and car mechanics. They sat shoulder to shoulder, their plates piled high, shoveling in food to get them through the long hours still ahead. They talked with their mouths full, showing half-chewed food between their teeth, and wiped their mouths with the backs of their sleeves.

I remembered my mother's stories of my grandfather's diner in San Diego—the crowded tables, the hearty laughter, the appreciative comments of the workers when plates of homestyle food were placed in front of them. When it came to satisfying a hungry appetite, it didn't matter what country it was or what language was being spoken. Looking around me, I thought about all the tourist brochures I had read. If I was looking for the quintessential Italian experience, it didn't get any better than this.

When we got to the counter, the choices seemed endless. Platters of meat, fish, marinated vegetables, desserts.

"What are you going to have?" GP whispered. "You can't think about it too long, there are people behind you."

"Tell me what some of this is," I said. I felt like Tino.

"*Branciallini*, which is pork chop, *pollo arrabiatta*, chicken with anchovies, *coniglio*, rabbit, and *calamaretti*, a small lake fish . . ."

I looked behind me. Everyone was staring.

I turned to the server and pointed to GP. "I'll have what he's having."

As soon as we sat down, Luigi came over. He eyed our full plates and grinned. "I hope we see you here again soon."

I thought of the 30 percent Scoiattolo discount. "You can bet on it," I said.

Stuffed to the gills, we said goodbye to Luigi and waddled out to the car. I checked my phone: five messages, all from Tino. I quickly dialed his cell.

"Where are you?" He sounded irritated. "We are meeting with SJ at 2:00 p.m., remember?"

Shit. I hadn't showered since yesterday, or changed clothes, and I smelled like cuttlefish.

I looked at GP. "I have a meeting at Paradiso Vinto in thirty minutes, and I need to take a shower. Can you get me to Villa Urbino in fifteen?"

GP gave me a look Mario Andretti would have been proud of. "Watch me." He grinned.

GP raced to the onramp of the autostrada and put the pedal to the metal. I closed my eyes and said a Hail Mary as we roared through the tunnel and up the road to the villa. Fifteen minutes later, I was one minute into my two-minute shower and gurgling mouthwash.

I heard a knock. "Anna, you ready?" It was Agostino.

"Almost," I yelled, stepping out of the shower and reaching for my towel and makeup bag. *No way was I going to let him see me without mascara.*

"Meet us in the car," I heard him say as I zipped up my jeans and threw on a jacket. He sounded annoyed.

Another makeover record, I thought proudly as I hurried after them. Thirty minutes ago, I was eating anchovies with a bunch of car mechanics. I couldn't wait to tell the boys all about it.

When I got to the car, no one even looked at me.

"You're late," was all Tino said.

"Sorry. I was at Eurobusiness all day. Just let me tell you what I bought . . ."

"Eurobusiness!" Agostino looked back at me from the passenger seat. "Be careful, they sell oranges over there."

"What?" I said, "I didn't see any . . ."

Tino's shoulders were shaking.

"You know, merchandise that don't work," Agostino explained.

I heard a loud guffaw coming from the driver's seat. "*Lemons*. He means *lemons*." Tino banged his hand on the steering wheel and howled.

❧

The front door of Paradiso Vinto was open when we got there.

"First time for you?" I asked Agostino.

"First time." He looked at me and smiled. "I think I have you to thank for this."

My heart did a summersault.

SJ was the consummate host. Showing Agostino around, he seemed calm and relaxed. It was as if he had finally started living the life he had dreamed of, one with no lies, no pretense, just freedom to be himself. It felt good to see the transformation.

Grappa was poured, and we all gathered on the sectional to discuss the details of the trip.

Tino spoke first. "As much as I love your company, I hope this trip isn't a wild goose chase." He looked at Agostino's puzzled face and kept talking. "Do we have any information on Giulia's current whereabouts?"

Agostino took an envelope from his pocket and handed it to SJ. "I found this among Marina's things."

SJ opened it and took out a photo of a woman with curly black hair, brown eyes, and a Mona Lisa smile. He put his hand to his mouth and stifled a cry. "It is Giulia," he whispered. He read the date in the corner of the photo. "May second, 1959. Sixteen years after she left."

"So, you think Marina and Giulia corresponded?" I asked Agostino.

"This is the only letter I find."

SJ looked at the envelope. "If they did, it looks like it was one way only. There is no return address."

I leaned over to look at the glossy image. "Where was it taken? Can you tell?"

"May I see it?" Tino asked. SJ handed it over.

"There is an iron gate and a big building in the background. Wait, I see a plaque . . . and an address . . . Piazzetta Reale One."

I Googled it on my phone. "It's the address of the Galleria Sabauda. Originally the residence of the Savoia royal family." I read on. "In 1946, the Savoias sold it to the state." I looked up. "That was three years *after* Giulia's disappearance. Maybe she went there."

SJ looked doubtful. "It also could just be a photo she took on vacation. I do remember that, when Santo and I went to Villa Fidelia, Duchessa Sabauda said a servant had taken her somewhere we would never find her. Well, we may be a little late, but we are going to prove the *duchessa* wrong. Since this address is all we have to go on, we will tentatively use Turin as our final destination.

"Okay," Tino said. "Now that we know our destination, what about itinerary and accommodations? If I may make a suggestion . . .?"

"Yes, please!" I piped up.

Tino addressed the group. "My parents did a lot of traveling after they retired, and they developed a system. My dad would book their trip one year and Mom would book the next one. That way, everyone got to contribute and exercise their preferences. I suggest, at each stop, one of us picks the hotel."

"Love it," SJ said. "I get dibs on Bologna."

"Wait," I said. "We don't even have an itinerary."

"Yes we do," SJ shot back. "My trip, *my* itinerary. I hope you like it."

I sat back and crossed my arms. He had a point. This trip was for him. We were just along for the ride. "Can we hear it?"

"We drive from here to Florence. Lidia and Marco's mother, Olivia, came from a very wealthy family who still live in their original villa in Florence. The Francobaldis go back to the Seicento and were in the same profession as the Medicis."

"What profession was that?" Tino asked.

"Banking. Now they make wine … *very* expensive wine. The family still owns the Casa del Cortile, the palazzo Matteo Francobaldi bought in 1667. It is near the center of town on Via Curtatone. It's a longshot, but it's possible the current relatives know what happened to Giulia."

"I got dibs on Florence," I called out. "There is a great hotel near the American Embassy and the park called Hotel Executive on Via Curtatone. One of the Medicis lived there."

"Okay, done. Then we drive east to Bologna. I have stayed many times at the Hotel Corona d'Oro. Leonora and Julio, the owners, are old friends. Leonora's family used to live near the Francobaldis' summer residence in the Emilio Romagna. There might be a lead there, as well. Agatha was very close to Leonora's parents, and I often played with the Francobaldi kids when I was a child. After Bologna, we drive to Turin."

"I've got Turin," Tino said. "In my salad days, I used to stay at the Majestic, near the train station."

SJ's face looked grim. "Tino, I hate to tell you this, but that place is a dive now."

Tino looked embarrassed. "Well, it *was* in my salad days …"

"Salad days? What is that?" Agostino asked.

"Never mind. Some American expressions are impossible to

explain." Tino moved on quickly. "I did stay once at the Principessa di Piemonti. Very fancy . . ."

"Great choice," SJ said. "I don't know about you, but my hostel days are over. Once we get to Turin, everything is up in the air. We don't know what we will find . . . if anything. Are you all okay with that?"

Everyone nodded.

"Good. Each of you is responsible for booking the four of us on your given day at the hotels we mentioned. Three or four separate rooms, depending on if Anna and Tino want to share."

I held up a hand. "If it's all the same to you, Tino, my days of bunking with family members on road trips are over. I'm booking *four* separate rooms."

Tino looked relieved.

"And we need to leave tomorrow," I said. "Tino and I leave for the States in nine days, and I have things to take care of at the apartment before I go." I looked around the room. "Can we do it?"

"We can. Meet here"—SJ looked at me—"No, meet at Villa Urbino at 8:00 a.m. It will give Anna a little more time."

Tino stood and raised his glass. "I never thought I would say this, but the significance of Anna's macabre little game is becoming clear. I have always wanted to squire friends around the Italian countryside in a Maserati, and at our age, fulfilling our dreams should be a priority. To the Deathbed Game! May we play it every day for the rest of our lives."

Everyone raised their glasses. "To the Deathbed Game!"

Chapter 23

Road Trip

I WAS ready to go when Tino knocked on my door at 8:00 a.m.

"Agostino and SJ are waiting for us at the car," Tino said. "They aren't sure how long it is going to take."

I saw Agostino eyeing my carry-on as we walked up. "*Brava*. Only one bag." He nodded approvingly.

What I decided not to mention was that my *one bag* was packed to the gills and weighed a ton. Mostly shoes. A girl can never have too many shoes, not even on a road trip with three guys.

"The GranCabrio was not designed for four people *and* their luggage," Tino said. "Thank you for considering its small cargo space when you packed."

"A small sacrifice to make," Agostino replied, running his hand along the car's sleek curves.

"Indeed," SJ concurred as he slipped into the back seat.

Tino protested. "Wouldn't you be more comfortable in the front, SJ?"

"No, thanks. Then I'd have to navigate. Too much work. I just want to sit back and appreciate my surroundings."

"I will navigate," Agostino offered.

"That means no nodding off," Tino said. "Unless you want to end up in Ravenna. I have a tendency to get lost when I don't have a racing track to follow."

"Six eyes are better than two, bro," I called out from the back seat.

Ten minutes later, I was fast asleep.

I woke up when the car turned off the A1 onto a side road. I sat up and looked around. This was definitely not Florence. "Where are we?"

"I thought you might want to take a look at Villa Fidelia. Maybe have a cappuccino?" Tino said.

We all looked at each other. "What's the real reason?" I asked.

"I have to pee."

"I thought you said you had the bladder of a bull," I said.

"Testicles," Tino called out. "I said I had the *testicles* of a bull."

"Actually, I think you said *stamina*, but let's not quibble. Besides, I never say no to a cappuccino."

After stopping at the bar where *everyone* had a cappuccino, we drove north along Via Centrale until we saw the high stone wall surrounding Villa Fidelia. There were signs of neglect even from the street: dirty stucco walls, litter blown in from the highway, and overgrown landscaping.

"It looks like no one is living there. I wonder who owns it now." I whipped out my phone and Googled *Villa Fidelia*. "It's for sale! Only five million euros." I looked up the long driveway leading to the villa. "Anyone interested in taking a look?"

SJ shook his head. "I think it's best if we don't risk taking the car up there."

"I hadn't thought of that," Tino said. "On second thought, I'll wait here."

"Me too," SJ said.

Agostino opened his side, got out, and pushed back the seat. "Coming?"

Without waiting for an answer, he offered his hand and pulled me out.

"In case we come back running, with a pack of Dobermanns at our heels, you will be ready, right?" I looked back at the two men.

Tino waved me away. "You're on your own. I don't want to get my car scratched up."

Agostino laughed and took my hand. We ran up the cobblestone path toward the house like two kids playing hooky.

Inside the grounds, the property looked even more rundown. The gardens were so dry and overrun with weeds that the terraced levels that formed the east property line were barely visible. The caretaker's cottage, halfway up the road to the villa, was shut tight.

"This was once a knot garden." Agostino pointed to a mess of tangled greenery. "See the border of yews? The design inside is still there if you look close."

I was surprised. "It sounds like you have studied landscaping."

"I wanted to be landscape designer before my father die. Then everything change. Someone had to take over management of the villa, and I was the only heir."

"And your mother?" I asked gently.

"I never knew her. She die giving birth to me. I was raised by my grandmother, Gabriella, and my great aunt, Marina. My papa tried to be a farmer like his father, but he did not have the stamina. He was never a strong man."

"How old were you when he died?"

"Seventeen. That was the end of my schooling. After the funeral, I take a good look at our finances. If I did not want to sell, I had to come up with a plan. I look at our property and see potential . . . guests and wedding receptions make money."

"So, you turned your home into a hotel."

"It paid the bills. Nothing comes without sacrifice."

He pointed to a balcony and a cement railing jutting out from one of the upper terraces. "Maybe there is *esedra* up there. Sometimes there is a stairway to get to the top. Let's climb up to see."

Agostino motioned for me to follow him. On one side of the upper terrace, there was a set of stone stairs leading to a carved-out space. It looked like a patio with a few benches.

"L'esedre!" Agostino said. "I knew it!"

We climbed up the staircase to the patio. At the opposite end, a high ledge rose from the base of the balcony. It was shaped in a semicircle, like the apse of a church. At eye level, an oval window was cut into it, revealing a gorgeous panorama of the valley below.

Agostino gestured to the carved-out space in front. "This is the *esedra*. In English you call it . . . ?"

"An exedra," I said, reading from my phone. "A hidden space with a view and a seat. For lovers to neck in the old days . . . where no one could see them." I added.

Agostino laughed. "It say that?" He walked over to me and leaned over my shoulder.

I could feel his chest against my back and when his arm reached around me and rested on the rim of the oval window, I felt a quiver of fire run through me.

"Tino said your sister was the rock and you were the feather," Agostino started to say.

I glanced up at his face. His expression seemed to be a cross between tenderness and admiration.

"I see it different," he continued. "I see you as a woman who is not afraid to take a chance, to walk that path that many only dream about."

"The road less traveled," I whispered, half to myself. "Robert Frost, a great American poet once said, 'Two roads diverged in a wood and I took the one less traveled by. It has made all the difference.'"

"That is you." Agostino smiled down at me. His blue-gray eyes were warm and inviting. I wanted to dive in and lose myself in them.

Voices drifted up from somewhere down below. "Do you see that?" Agostino pointed to the rear of the villa. There was a truck we hadn't seen before and two men loading furniture into the back of it.

"Holy shit," I whispered. "Maybe someone bought the villa and those are the new owners."

"Or thieves in the act of ransacking the place. Andiamo." Agostino grabbed my hand again, and we started running down the stone steps. We ducked our heads and crawled along the rim of the first terrace to a line of trees shading the walkway. We kept an eye on the villa until we were near the street entrance and the opening in the wall. As soon as we saw the Maserati, we made a dash for it. The car door opened and we scrambled in. With a screech of tires, we were speeding down Via Centrale and onto the ramp leading to the autostrada.

"A clean getaway!" Agostino laughed, reaching behind him to give me a high five.

A few minutes past noon, we turned into the circular driveway of the Executive Hotel in Florence.

"This looks wonderful," SJ said, looking up at the nineteenth century façade. "How did you find it?"

"I booked a fleabag room down the way a couple of years ago and discovered it on my way back from a run in the park. Parco delle Cascine is right behind the hotel. This building belonged to Florentine royalty in the seventeenth century, and the awards for the Palio horse race were given out here. The loggia was built by the Grand Duke of Lorena. But more importantly," I informed everyone, "they have an elevator and you can have breakfast sent to your room."

"I'm ready for a nap," Tino said.

"I hate to be a spoil sport," SJ said gently. "But we are expected at the Casa del Cortile, the Francobaldis' palazzo, in two hours. The dress code is studied casual. That means your Gucci and Ferragamo labels need to be properly displayed but no bling." SJ studied his watch. "We meet in front of the hotel at 1:30 sharp."

"Stai attento! Molto prezioso!" Tino yelled.

SJ and I turned to see Tino holding up his hands in mock horror as a man came down the steps and started getting behind the wheel of the Maserati.

The car attendant grinned and held out his hand for the keys. "Not to worry, Signore. We take good care of her."

SJ laughed. "Your brother's Italian is improving daily." He watched the porters bringing up the bags. "That nap sounds like a good idea, Tino. I have a few years on all of you, don't forget."

I watched his bent figure slowly climb the stairs to the lobby. "I'll try to remember that," I called after him.

An hour and a half later, I walked down the marble staircase to the lobby. The three-mile run in the park had been just what my body needed after all that sitting. The hot bath with perfumed salts hadn't hurt either. I was wearing a slinky teal halter dress under my coat and a pair of four-inch heels. They hurt like hell but, in a city like Florence, comfort must *never* take precedence over style.

The three men came down a moment later, looking appropriately aristocratic. Agostino was wearing a white button-down shirt, unbuttoned to his pecs, and a leather jacket slung over one shoulder. His faded jeans clung to his body in all the right places. I bit my lip to stifle a groan.

The Maserati pulled up, and the young valet got out, dangling the keys in front of him. He had a big smile on his face. "You need someone to drive you? I get off work in fifteen minutes. *Very* reduced rates."

Tino snorted. I could just read his expression. *Nice try, ragazzo,*

but around the corner to the garage is all the driving you're going to do.
With a firm *"No, grazie,"* he held out his hand for the keys.

"So, how well do you know this filthy rich family?" Tino glanced at his passenger in the front seat. We had just crossed the Arno and were headed east on Via Santo Spirito.

"Not well," SJ replied. "Olivia was one of six children back in 1907, when she left home to marry Claudio. That was three generations ago. You can imagine how many relatives have been in the picture since then. The only real connection I had was playing with the Francobaldi kids at Leonora's parents' house eighty years ago."

I was listening to their conversation from the back seat. "I guess you couldn't just call them up and ask some questions, right?"

"You have to understand, with people like the Francobaldis, you don't walk up to the door and ring the bell. There is a whole social protocol that must be followed. They retain a layer of servants around them for protection. If you call them on the phone, for instance, it is not sufficient proof that you are who you say you are. There have been kidnappings of family members on more than one occasion in the last four hundred years. Long story short, I asked Leonora to contact a childhood friend who paved the way for us to have a private audience with the current resident.

"It seems like a roundabout way of doing things. After all, you are Olivia's grandson," Tino said.

"Stepgrandson," SJ reminded him.

"Right. I guess they don't know that you are not, in fact, related."

"No. I decided to withhold that piece of information until we get our foot in the door."

"Good idea," Tino said.

Up ahead, a large Renaissance-style building came into view."

Pull over," SJ told Tino. Before opening the car door, SJ turned around and addressed all of us. "Don't be surprised if this is a dead end. The current resident may be older than me and might not remember what he had for breakfast much less the whereabouts of a distant relative."

The front entrance to the Palazzo Francobaldi was a simple armored door crowned by an iron crest with the initials M.F. scrolled above it.

SJ pressed the intercom and said, *"Signore Spirito Urbino qui."*

An iron peep-hole cover shot up, and a baleful eye looked through it. *"Aspetti,"* the eye said.

A second later, I heard a distinctly American voice say, "For God's sake, Fabio, open the friggin' door!"

The door swung open, and a striking woman in her mid-forties stood there smiling at us. She was wearing a diaphanous purple caftan and leather sandals, her gray-blonde hair crowning her face in a halo of curls. She wore a silver encased quartz stone around her neck, and her earrings glistened like prisms from a Murano chandelier. Before SJ knew what was happening, she enveloped him in a warm hug. "Spirito, we finally meet!" Her eyes looked past him to the three of us standing there. "Who are your lovely friends?" She stepped back from the embrace and held out her hands to us. "Welcome. My name is Star."

SJ made the introductions, and our host led us through a long dark corridor, passing rooms full of antiques into a light-filled sitting room absent of furniture. There were candles and incense holders, and a profusion of brightly colored pillows were scattered all over the floor. On the opposite side of the room, French doors opened to a large, enclosed garden circling a Baroque wall fountain.

Star quickly retrieved a chair for SJ and gestured to the rest of us to sit. She plopped down on the floor and crossed her legs. As I sat down, her eyes swept over me. "You were a dancer, am I right? I would guess ballet by your well-developed sternum."

I nodded, surprised by the expert observation. Everyone else looked clueless.

"My mom wanted me to be a dancer," she continued. "I even studied at Rosella Hightower's studio in Cannes one summer. I never could get over the masochism of pointe shoes, so I gravitated to yoga. She waved her arm around the room. "My home is now a clinic for stress-related disorders. Today, the rooms are all occupied." She gestured to the garden. "There is a chakra yoga class going on right now."

"So, you run this by yourself?" SJ asked.

"Yes. Papa is in Tibet visiting the Dalai Lama . . . they are close friends . . . and mother is renovating our summer residence in Sorrento. She is turning it into a home for pregnant teenagers." Star looked at our stunned faces and laughed. "Perhaps a little family history is in order. The Francobaldis have always been bankers, their powerful alliances helping to further the cause of Mussolini's reign during World War II. In the sixties, Papa's parents wanted him to go to an American college, hoping he would benefit from the US's modern technology. He was expected to follow in his father's footsteps, but something unexpected happened. San Francisco, in the sixties, was the center of the peace movement that was sweeping the country, and my father got caught up in it. Majoring in political science, he saw how flawed the ideology of fascism was and became ashamed of his family's connection to it. He was at an anti-war demonstration in Berkeley when he met my mother. I was conceived in a fleabag hotel in Haight Ashbury . . . or so the legend goes. When he came back to Italy, with his bride, he was a changed man."

As she chattered away, it was obvious Star was only interested in hearing herself talk. Far from worrying about extracting information from her, our only problem seemed to be finding a way to escape.

SJ cut in. "Do you remember anything about my grandmother Olivia's son, Marco?"

"Oh yes, I saw him at Simona's funeral . . . I was fifteen at the time. That woman . . . God . . . what a bitch . . . I remember Marco was the only one *not* pretending he was sorry she died. He looked like a man who had just escaped a life sentence. I don't care who her first husband was. No one gets away with being that mean."

SJ sat up. "Who was Simona's first husband?"

"He was a cousin of Victor Emmanuel III, King of Italy. His name was Eugenio Amedeo Aosta of Savoia."

"The Savoias of Piazza Reale One, in Turin," SJ said slowly.

"Not anymore," Star said. "They have been in exile since 1948."

SJ was looking at Star with renewed interest. "Any idea what happened to Marco?"

Star looked surprised. "You don't know? Marco left for Capri the day after the funeral. We never heard from him again."

SJ had one more question. "Did you ever hear of a girl named Giulia?"

Star thought for a minute. "Never heard of her."

Even though it was not the answer we had hoped for, we could see an opportunity to escape open up. We all rose to go.

"Do you want to see the Francobaldi Chapel?" Star asked, getting to her feet. "It's in the basilica right behind us. The Basilica of Santo Spirito's property abuts our own, and there is a private back entrance the tourists don't know about."

It was hardly an invitation we could refuse. Star walked over to a cabinet, opened a drawer, and pulled out a ring of keys. As she led the way through the garden, her caftan billowing in the breeze, she nodded to the instructor and the group of ladies sitting cross-legged on mats.

"Breathe through this stretch," a calm, resonate voice said.

Star unlocked the heavy iron gate separating the properties and walked to a non-descript door that cut into the church. She unlocked it with another key and the door swung open.

"Our chapel is in transept number twelve, the one with the huge choir screen. Our family used to sit behind it to avoid being seen by the masses. I would accompany you, but I have to supervise the preparation of dinner this evening. Would you like to join us? We are having carrot and turnip mash, braised radicchio leaves, and gluten-free carob bars."

Agostino quickly stepped forward. "Thank you for the offer. It sounds delicious, but we have another engagement."

Chapter 24

Testing the Boundaries

"I THINK this is the sacristy," SJ said as we passed through the outside door into a deserted hallway. Ahead, we could see a door open to the main church. Our footsteps rang out on the stone pavement as we walked the horizontal transept, counting chapels until we reached number twelve. A gilded choir screen occupied one part of the chapel, and across the aisle there were several pews. I saw a figure bent over in prayer in one of them.

"That must be Matteo," Tino whispered pointing to a stone bier high up on the side wall. Underneath it was a large plaque.

"*Urbano VIII Pont Max MDCXLIV.*" I read out loud. "That means Pope Urban the Eighth dedicated this chapel in 1644."

"Looks like this family was hoping to buy their way into heaven," Tino said. "I just hope they weren't disappointed when they got to the pearly gates."

"Shhh." The man in the pew lifted his head and gave us a dirty look.

I glanced at the large oil painting of a Madonna and child above the altar. "This is wonderful."

SJ was studying the laminated description of the chapel. "Filippo Lippi's Madonna with Child with Saints." I heard a sharp intake of breath, and he grabbed my arm.

"It says here that the Sabauda family donated the artwork to the Francobaldis in 1925." SJ looked at us. "The duchess was a Sabauda."

"Or the *bitch* as Star calls her," Tino said with a chuckle. "Hey, any family that can give away a Lippi has to be pretty powerful . . . and have some serious bucks. It certainly looks like there was a strong connection between the *duchessa's* family and your stepmother's—strong enough to donate priceless paintings to them, anyway. Did you happen to ask Miss know-it-all where this *duchessa* is buried?"

"We could go back . . ." I suggested.

"And be stuck eating turnip mash for dinner? No way. Besides, I don't see how this will help us find Giulia." SJ's voice sounded tired.

I looked over at the old man. "Time to get some fresh air," I said, steering him toward the entrance of the church. As I passed an open door that led to another room, I stopped short. "I remember this church now. This is where the Michelangelo crucifix is displayed. Have you seen it, SJ?"

"Exquisite," he mumbled. "Not to be missed. If you have never seen it, go. I'll wait here." He slipped into a pew, leaned back, and closed his eyes.

"It'll only take a minute," I said, grabbing both men by the arm before anyone could object.

We stood outside the unadorned nave where the plain wooden crucifix, and the figure of Christ as a nude young man, was displayed. The effect was startling because it differed from the usual crucifixions one sees in churches throughout Italy. The figure was youthful, delicate, with skin carved so true to life that it looked like real flesh.

"Its sensuality seems at odds with the subject matter," Tino said. "What's the story?"

"Legend has it that when Michelangelo was a teenager, he often came to the convent hospital nearby to sketch the dead . . . to learn the anatomy. There was a young friend of his who died in the night and who became the model for the sculpture." I looked up at the clean lines of the young male torso. "In my opinion, it is the sensuality of the piece that makes it so riveting."

Tino nodded. "I agree. I'm just not so sure the Pope would."

"You might be surprised. The clergy loved Caravaggio's paintings of sensual boys. And don't forget the Sistine Chapel and the great penis cover-up."

"I'm sorry?" Tino looked puzzled. "The great penis cover-up? I'm not sure I heard about *that* Vatican scandal."

"A travesty is more like it," I said. "In 1599, Pope Pius IV commanded that all of Michelangelo's nudes be painted with drapery to cover their private parts. Thank God the artist had died the year before and didn't have to witness it. Then, when 1974 rolled around, Pope John Paul II ordered the drapery painted out. Penises were back in style!"

Agostino flung his hands up in exasperation. "It is so ridiculous, this obsession with the naked body. Why we always have to cover it up? I think it is beautiful!"

I pictured what was underneath that shirt and those form hugging jeans.

"Agostino, I think Michelangelo would have agreed with you . . . and so do I."

"Time to get SJ home. He looks beat." Tino said as we left the chapel and walked toward the figure sacked out in the pew. "I'll go get the car and meet you out front. I hope the hotel has room service because I have a feeling our uncle will not be joining us for dinner."

Tino pulled up to the front of the church just as we stepped out. The day had waned and there was a chill in the air.

"Don't let me ruin your evening. Just drop me off at the hotel and keep going," SJ said, getting into the car.

"What are you going to do for food? You have to eat, you know." I felt like an overprotective daughter with a difficult parent.

"The hotel has room service. I checked." SJ muttered, settling back in the seat.

After we drove west and turned into the driveway, a porter met SJ at the bottom of the stairs and helped him to the lobby.

"We forget he is ninety-two years old," I said to everyone in the car. "This trip is a big ordeal. I hope we aren't pushing him too hard."

"He is up for it," Tino observed. "He wants to do this, and he knows he can't do it alone."

"Dinner?" Agostino looked at Tino and me.

"Sure," Tino said. "Just let me take the Maserati to the garage. It's a few blocks away. Then we can find a restaurant on the way back to the hotel."

"You've been to the garage?" Agostino asked.

"Earlier, when everyone was napping. I wanted to see if the accommodations were acceptable for my—"

"Mistress?" I broke in.

Tino and Agostino grinned.

"I saw some pretty nice wheels in there. Two Ferraris and a Lamborghini. The American and French consulate are next door, so the clientele is strictly VIP."

Tino waved to the man in the booth. "That's also why there is an attendant twenty-four hours a day. For protection."

"From thieves?" I asked.

"No, from bombs. It does happen. Just read the papers."

I looked nervously around the underground space. "Meet you guys out front," I said, heading for the elevator.

***

"Tino looked at his watch. "I'm starved. I know it's only five o'clock. . . a little early for dinner by Italian standards. Will the restaurants be open at this hour?"

"In Florence, the restaurants are always open," Agostino assured him.

The two men strolled ahead down Via Curtatone as I stumbled along behind them. My feet were beginning to rebel from stiletto abuse.

The atmosphere was infectious. Good-looking waiters stood outside restaurants, beckoning people with their come-on lines: "We have the *bistecca alla Florentina*, prepared just how you like," they called out. "With American French fries!"

"American French fries." Tino laughed. "That's a good one."

"Empty table for two." I pointed as we passed a quaint bar, the amber glow lighting up the packed crowd inside.

We rushed in and pulled up an extra chair.

"Three Amaros," Agostino called to the waiter as we took our seats. "You will like the Amaro del Capo. Strong but sweet like nectar."

"Can't wait to try it . . . and I won't even ask what it's made of," Tino said.

"*Erbe*," Agostino said. "In English it mean?"

"Herbs," I answered. "Leave it to the Italians to make liquor out of weeds."

When the drinks arrived, Tino knocked back the glass in one swallow. "Well, I don't know about you all, but I'm having a blast . . . even though we don't know how it will end."

"Could be some drama in Turin," I said. "SJ may need our support."

"One thing I can't figure out," I continued. "Santo must have known the *duchessa's* parentage, and the fact that her first husband was a Savoia. Why didn't he ever disclose that information to his brother? It sounds like SJ didn't know."

"Maybe Santo did not want him to know," Agostino suggested.

"Because then SJ would have had a clue where to look for Giulia. Is that what you mean?" I asked.

Agostino nodded.

"I am beginning to understand Santo's fear of scandal," Tino remarked. "The Francobaldis and the Savoias are not families I'd like to have pissed off at me."

"Let us talk of something else, tonight." Agostino raised his glass and looked at me. "You are an Italian homeowner now! It is a brave step, not one many Americans take."

"I know there are challenges ahead," I said. "But there is no better way to be a part of the community than to own property."

Agostino shook his head. "Owning property is not enough. You need to spend time there . . . enough time to get to know the people, learn their customs and traditions. Otherwise, you will remain a stranger in their eyes."

Agostino was right. It would take more than an address to make Scheggino my home. I took a deep breath. "I can manage one month three times a year. How does that sound?"

Agostino smiled at me. "It will be a good start."

"Does this mean you will be celebrating your birthday milestone in Italy in July?" Tino asked.

I froze.

"Milestone?" Agostino looked puzzled.

I tried desperately to catch Tino's eye, but he wasn't looking.

"The big six-oh. You know . . . *sessanta*."

I rattled the glass during the last sentence, but it was too late. Everyone at the table, if not the entire bar, heard it. Agostino didn't bat an eye. I was grateful for that. I downed the Amaro and stood up. "I feel a headache coming on. See you back at the hotel."

Pushing through the crowd, I heard Tino's voice: "What did I say?"

By that time, I was too far away to hear Agostino's answer.

How could he? I knew Tino wasn't intentionally being dense. It just came with the territory of being male. They didn't think about age the same way women did. If a man took care of himself, he could be attractive well into his seventies. And if he had a lot of money, he didn't even have to *be* attractive. Not so for women. After forty, it was an uphill battle just to keep from going downhill. The only successful strategy seemed to be cosmetics, a good pair of Spanx, and keeping your age a secret for as long as possible.

Now, thanks to Tino, any feminine mystique I had managed to create had been replaced by a big neon sign flashing *6-0* over my head. The sexy clothes, the efforts to keep up my appearance, all of it, had been designed to make me look as young as possible. Who was I kidding? Suddenly the whole thing felt like an older woman's pathetic misguided fantasy.

I climbed the stairs to the lobby and slipped into the elevator before anyone at the desk could ask how my evening went. I keyed into my room, slammed the door, and kicked off the four-inch heels. *All that pain for nothing*. I climbed into bed and brushed away a tear. We were only on day one, and all I wanted to do was go home.

Chapter 25

The Only Thing That Matters

SO FAR, day two of SJ's last-gasp adventure had been a total dud. The rain started soon after we left Florence, and it continued, unabated, for the first hour. It matched my mood perfectly.

At breakfast, I studiously avoided any conversation with Agostino, devoting myself to SJ's needs until he politely told me to quit treating him like a doddering old fool. Tino, realizing his gaffe from the night before, was keeping a respectful distance. When everyone had gone upstairs to pack, Agostino asked me if my headache was still bothering me. I muttered something incoherent and picked up a magazine.

Having had a night to think about it, I felt angry and humiliated. Mostly at myself. I had let my emotions get the better of me; I had let a romantic fantasy develop that was entirely in my own head. In the cold light of day, when the wrinkles looked especially prominent, I could see how ridiculous it all was. The only silver lining was that it hadn't gone too far. I had not made an irredeemable ass out of myself and some small part of my dignity could still be salvaged.

Tino and Agostino were following the A1 route out of Florence, and in another hour we would be in Bologna. The sun peeped out at one point as if deciding whether to make an extended appearance, but then, losing interest, it hid behind a cloud and went back to sleep. Feeling equally apathetic, I followed suit.

When I woke, the car had stopped. We seemed to be in some sort of alley, and there was a big truck blocking the way in front of us. SJ was on the phone.

"What's up?" I called out from the back seat.

"*Cazzo*head," Tino growled, banging his hand on the steering wheel. "The garage the hotel uses is up ahead, but this guy refuses to get out of the way." Another ten minutes went by. Another "*cazzo*head."

SJ put his hand on Tino's shoulder. "Calm down. Let's not lose our tempers. I'll go talk to him."

Agosinto let him out, and we watched the old man walk over to the driver's side of the truck. At first, a few polite words were exchanged, but as the conversation continued, things got more heated. Finally, a string of what sounded like *very creative* Italian expletives erupted on both sides. SJ spat on the sidewalk and got back in the car. "He's a *cazzo*head. You're going to have to back up."

As soon as Tino put the car in reverse, the truck started to move forward.

"Good job, SJ," Tino said. "It must have been your calm, levelheaded approach that got him to change his mind."

The garage turned out to be a ten by 15-foot space next to an auto body shop. Agostino got out and pulled at the steel rollup door. It came up with a rickety clattering sound as Tino drove forward and positioned the car to back into it. We all got out to watch the performance. With inches to spare on either side, Tino guided her in, the door barely missing the Maserati's nose when it closed.

Tino looked around for someone to assist him, but the alley was deserted. "I'm not leaving her here until I know she's safe."

I looked at the sky. It seemed to be waiting for Mother Nature to make a decision. "We should get SJ to the hotel."

"Go. I'll wait here. Tell someone to come with a lock."

"Signore!" A boy, who looked no more than fifteen, was running down the alley toward us. *"Scusi!* You have the car?"

"She's already in." Tino rolled the door up a few feet. "See?"

The boy's eyes bulged. "GranCabrio. *Bello!*"

"Yeah, bello. Got a lock for the door?"

The boy fished around in his overalls and held up a lock with a key attached. "Here, you use this. Keep the key after you lock, okay?"

"Okay." Tino looped the lock through the bars and snapped it shut. I will return it at the front desk when we leave tomorrow."

"Va bene. Ciao." The boy took off down the alley going the other way.

Tino shook his head. "That kid doesn't look old enough to drive and he's the valet? What kind of hotel is this?"

SJ was trying to keep a straight face. "Emilio is Leonora and Julio's son. He just turned sixteen. When we get to the hotel I will introduce you to everyone."

"Happy to meet them." Tino pointed at the receding figure. "But that kid is not getting anywhere near my car."

Tino pocketed the key, and we walked down the alley toward Via Oberdan. It was at that moment that Mother Nature decided to unleash her fury and pummel us with not only rain but also hail. Big white balls were bouncing off our heads and shoulders and rolling down the asphalt like marbles. When we pushed open the doors to the hotel, we were beaten up and completely drenched. The staff, recognizing SJ, quickly took over and whisked everyone and their luggage up to their rooms to dry off. Check-in could wait.

An hour later, I took the elevator to the top floor to SJ's room. I could hear voices inside and an "un momento!"

When SJ opened the door I noticed how tired he looked.

"This is the deluxe suite," he said, almost apologetically.

I walked into a living room with frescoed ceilings and a view of the Basilica di Santo Stefano and the Piazza Maggiore. Looking out, I saw that the storm had passed, leaving in its wake a sparkling city. A pair of towers could be seen in the distance—red brick obelisks rising out of a cleared-out sky.

I was impressed. "I guess you rate. My room is nice, but yours is a *palace!*"

"The owners are in the next room. Come and meet them."

SJ led me into the adjacent sitting room. A couple in their forties stood when we entered. They were well dressed and carried themselves with elegance and authority.

"Leonora, Julio, this is my niece, Anna Wilson. Her grandfather was my father." SJ made the introduction, proudly and without hesitation.

"Piacere," I said, shaking hands and taking the seat SJ offered.

SJ continued, "As I explained to you earlier, Leonora's parents knew the Francobaldis. Lidia, Santo, and I often stayed at Leonora's home when Agatha was away on an assignment. It was Leonora's family that gave Agatha one of her first commissions."

Leonora turned to me, her eyes bright with energy and enthusiasm. "Agatha redid the entire hotel in 1945, after the Germans ransacked it. We still have some of her furnishings in the Atrium Room on the first floor. Even today, our guests comment on the beauty of the white and gold deco-inspired color scheme."

"It is a gorgeous hotel, and Bologna looks like a fantastic city. I can't wait to get out and see it. I was just going to ask SJ if he wanted join me." I looked over and saw that my uncle's eyes were closed. He had fallen asleep in the chair.

"Tonight"—Leonora pressed my hand—"we will be honored to take all of you to dinner at our favorite restaurant."

"The honor is ours, *grazie,*" I said. After we had gently closed the door to SJ's room, I turned to the couple. "Thank you for helping SJ get in to see Star Francobaldi."

"Quite a character, isn't she?" Leonora said, smiling.

"Quite. But she gave us a valuable piece of information, the connection to Turin. It is possible that the Duchessa Sabauda sent Giulia to live … or work … at the Savoia Royal Palace. Because of your help, we have a good lead."

"And I want to thank you for taking this journey with him," Leonora replied. "Despite his fatigue, he looks very content and focused. I think this is something he has wanted to do for a long time."

I squeezed her hand. "My pleasure. Rest assured, we will be with him no matter how this ends."

Back in my room, I contemplated my next move. The city was beckoning, and I was anxious to discover its secrets. I was too embarrassed to ask Agostino to join me, and Tino did not answer my knock. I grabbed my coat and headed down to the lobby and out into the street.

I walked quickly up Via Guglielmo Oberdan to the Piazza Maggiore, where the Centro Storico was just beginning to fill with pedestrians. The large central square, surrounded by important administrative and religious buildings, was a focal point of the city's community. Eager faces, anxious to get a breath of air after the storm, rushed past me. On the south side, quaint bars and shopping arcades, the lifeblood of the city, glinted in the sun. Shopkeepers were opening their doors, and bar owners were wiping down tables, hoping to entice customers back to resume the age-old pursuits of taking refreshment while people-watching.

It felt good to be on my own, away from the constant reminder of Agostino's annoyingly sexy body. No matter how hard I tried, I couldn't get his unbuttoned shirt and snug jeans out of my mind. I had to get this feeling under control before I embarrassed myself again. A brisk walk was sure to do the trick.

I heard a voice behind me. "Anna!"

I turned, and suddenly Agostino's hands were cupped around my face, and his mouth was on mine. His lips were gentle and tentative at first and then more demanding when he felt my body respond. I felt a hunger in his touch that matched my own, but there was a tenderness, too. Inside his kiss, I sensed a yearning, a hope, like a burning candle in a dark tunnel, that this could lead to something more than just sexual gratification. I held on to that thought as we came up for air.

"If you make love anything like you kiss . . ." I said.

He groaned. *"Per carità,* don't say that . . . you will make me want to . . ." He stopped.

"Want to what?"

"Scopabile," he whispered, his hands in my hair and his breath warm and soft against my neck. "Do you know what it means?"

"I do. I looked it up on Google Translate."

Agostino laughed out loud, and his mouth closed in for round two.

<hr>

We walked hand in hand down Via Francesco Pizzoli toward the center of the Quadrilateral market. Crowds pushed past us, trying to get in some last-minute shopping before the clouds closed in again.

"Anna, I need to ask you something," Agostino began.

I tensed, hoping it was not something about our age difference.

"Remember the day when you and your mother visited *Nonna* Gabriella at her house? You were looking for answers about your family . . . whether they were related to mine."

"I remember. She was clear that Georgio and Renata, my great grandfather's kin, were not related to your family. Your relatives came from another town.

"That's right," Agostino said. "They are from Urbino, in Le

Marche. Has Georgio told you anything different since then? Anything that might connect you to us?"

"No, nothing. He did say that we were here first . . . before you . . . and that we are one of the oldest families in Scheggino."

"Good." He sounded relieved.

We stopped in front of a gelato shop, Agostino eyeing its glass counter. "They have *nocciola*, my favorite. Go find a table."

With one tub of hazelnut gelato and two spoons, we settled into a tiny spot just inside one of the many galleries lining the city. I dug in, tasting the cool sweetness and letting it slide down my throat. I licked the spoon, watching Agostino's face.

Agostino groaned. "I am ready for round three. Maybe we can go to someplace more private? Like my hotel room?

I thought for a moment. "I would like that too, but I don't think it's appropriate. What would Tino and SJ think? This trip is not about us. It's about SJ and his quest. I think the focus needs to be on that . . . no distractions. We should wait until we get home."

Agostino's face fell. "You are right, of course."

"It doesn't mean we can't fantasize a little." I gave him a wry smile. "Like where and when?"

"I like to fantasize. I have done a little already . . . about you." His eyes were on my lips.

"How about your bachelor pad the night we get home?" I offered.

"The *villetto?*"

"No. Your room above the kitchen. I can't wait to see it. I will buy some sexy lingerie for the occasion. You can help me pick it out."

"My pleasure, Signorina Wilson."

I put my spoon down and looked at him. "I still can't believe this is happening. That you and me . . ."

Agostino searched my face. "That we could have romantic

feelings for each other? Why not?"

"Last night, in Florence, when Tino mentioned my age ... I thought ..."

"You thought what? That you were too old for me?"

He asked the question with such candor it was hard to take offense. I shrugged my shoulders, embarrassed.

Agostino grabbed both my hands, his blue-gray eyes boring into mine. "First of all, I have never met a woman like you. You can stir up trouble like no one I've ever known." He laughed when he saw my face. "What I mean is you are a woman who not only dreams about doing things ... you *do* them. Being around you makes me feel alive ... more alive than I feel in a very long time. And as far as my body ... this is what you do to me every time I look at you." He scooted my chair over, grabbed my hand under the table, and put it on his crotch. "That should be all the proof you need."

I had to agree with him.

We held hands across the table, staring out at the vibrant scene around us: long, narrow alleyways jam-packed with food, crafts and people under a gray-and-white El Greco sky. Every so often the sun would emerge to gild the clouds.

"So, how old do you think I am?"

I turned sharply. Agostino was grinning.

I rolled my eyes. "I hate it when people say that. It's like they're fishing for a compliment."

"Not me. Just say what you think."

"Forty-nine?"

"*Grazie,* but you are way off. I am fifty-three."

Six years. "That doesn't sound *too* bad," I said out loud.

Agostino chuckled. "It sounds perfect to me. You need someone younger ... to keep up with you."

My phone buzzed.

"Hey bro, where are you?"

There was a pause. "I don't know."

"Tino, are you lost?"

"Yeah. I started out fine, and then suddenly I got confused. I've been walking around for an hour now and can't find the hotel."

"Go to a corner and find a street address. They're usually on the corner of a building."

"I know that. I lived in Europe, remember?"

Tino's voice sounded shaky, and I knew I needed to be calm with him. I waited.

"I'm at the corner of Via degli Arbari and San Nicolo."

"You are just one street over from the hotel and up a block. We'll come find you. Stay there."

Within ten minutes, we had spotted him.

"I know this is stupid of me, but I forgot the name of the hotel so I couldn't look it up on my phone . . . or ask anyone. Then I started to panic because every building looked the same."

"It's okay," Agostino said, putting his arm around him. "It happened to me many times. Just remember, Corona d'Oro."

"Crown of Gold." I repeated, getting in step on Agostino's side. I hooked my thumb around his belt loop and let my fingers slide down until I felt the curve of his nice firm butt.

The transportation arrangements to the restaurant that evening were complicated. Agostino and I wanted to walk, SJ was going with Leonora and Julio, and Tino would meet us there. Emilio had begged for a ride in the Maserati, promising to give Tino a tour of the city beforehand. We would all meet at Trattoria Ciacco around eight.

SJ, Leonora, and Julio were already seated when Agostino and I arrived.

"Where's Tino and Emilio?"

"Here!" Emilio's voice echoed through the restaurant as they came toward us. "Tino took me to the *autodromo*. I got to drive his car!"

Julio sat up. *"Autodromo di Enzo Ferrari di Imola?"*

"I wish," Tino said. "No, we went to the *mini autodromo . . .* where was it, Emilio?"

"Via Ronzani. Tino let me go a couple of laps. *Fantastico!*"

"Well done, Emilio," SJ said. "So far, none of us has even been allowed behind the wheel."

"He wants to be a professional racecar driver," Leonora said.

Julio's face was grim. "My father crewed for Enzo Ferrari's racecars. As a boy, watching from the sidelines, I saw my share of fiery crashes. It is not something I wanted for my son."

Tino nodded sympathetically. "I understand your concern, but sometimes it is not the parent's decision to make. My mother had a hard time with it too, but, seeing my passion, she didn't stand in my way."

Emilio's eyes were darting back and forth between his parents and Tino.

"It appears Emilio shares that passion," Julio said quietly.

Tino looked at Julio. "This is something you may not want to hear, but it is clear that Emilio has the gift."

"What gift?" The boy asked.

"To drive like you could never die. He definitely has a future if you will let him pursue it."

Leonora glanced at her husband. "That is a conversation we will be having in the near future. Thank you for letting us see it from another perspective. Especially from one who shares the same passion." She smoothed her skirt, took a deep breath, and smoothly switched subjects. "What is the next stop on your adventure?"

"Piazza Reale One. The Royal Palace of the Savioias." SJ answered. "Thanks to your friendship with the Francobaldis, we were able to establish that Marco's wife, Duchessa Sabauda, was first married to a cousin of the King. I have a strong suspicion Giulia was sent to Turin."

"And what are you going to do when you get to the palace?" Leonora asked. "You can't just walk up to a guard and tell him your story. Do you have any evidence that Giulia stayed there?"

"Only a photograph taken of her forty years ago in front of the palace gates."

"Your connection to the Sabauda family may help you," Leonora said. "They were once a powerful family. Nobility from Sardinia, I believe."

"Are there any relatives still living?" SJ asked.

Leonora thought for a moment. "I don't know. I recommend you visit the Basilica di Superga's vaults. The crypt houses the Savoia tombs where the royal family are buried. You might get some answers there."

"Excellent idea," SJ said.

"Just be careful driving," Julio spoke up. "There is a storm coming tomorrow . . . maybe snow."

Leonora shook her head. "You have courage, SJ, to travel so far on such little hope."

SJ smiled at her. "I may not have my youth, but courage and hope I have in abundance."

I reached across the table and put my hand over his. "Sometimes that is all you need."

SJ looked around the table. "Thank you for taking this journey with me . . . whatever the outcome. And thank you, my dear friends, for your hospitality."

"Don't stay away so long next time. We want to see you again soon," Julio added.

"And bring Tino!" Emilio piped up.

Everybody laughed.

Agostino picked up a menu, his eyes lingering on me. "Now, for the *second* thing I have wanted to do all day. Taste the *Mortadella di Bologna*. Antipasti for all?"

Chapter 26

Spooning in Canale

THE RAIN turned to sleet right after we passed Piacenza. I could tell Tino was struggling with the road conditions, but everyone knew better than to ask if he needed a break.

"You have chains in the trunk, *sì?*" Agostino had asked him before we started out.

"Yes, but I'm hoping to get to Turin before we have to stop and put them on. I'm not an expert at it . . . especially in the rain."

We turned onto the A33 at Alessandra. It was less crowded than the autostrada, and we made good time. The big white flakes began in earnest by the time we started our ascent into Moncalieri.

"We are only forty kilometers from Turin," I said, consulting the map. "Can we make it?"

Tino didn't answer. The windshield wipers had begun to stick, and the roads were turning icy. He pulled over to the side of the road and stopped the car.

"This is too dangerous. I have precious cargo in this car." Tino turned and looked at all of us. "Is there any place near here where we can stay overnight until the storm blows over?"

"Canale is right up the road, less than ten kilometers from here," Agostino said. "I know a family that own the Villa Tiberti. A big house they have turned into an Albergo. Two years ago I do a *very expensive* wedding reception for their daughter. Last I hear, they are still married. They will take good care of us."

"On short notice like this?" I asked.

"Not to worry," Agostino assured me.

Tino got out and wiped down the windshield and came back in. "Agostino, lead the way!"

Twenty minutes later, we rounded a turn, and the Villa Tiberti, ablaze with lights, came into view. Its massive stone walls and blue, shuttered windows were like a beacon against an angry, turbulent sky. The sound of a live band cut the stillness of the wintry night, and we could see scores of guests eating and drinking in the hotel restaurant. To four weary travelers making their way up the snow-covered road, it looked like paradise.

I gave Agostino a big thumbs-up.

Tino pulled up to the front entrance, and Agostino got out and ran to the hotel. Through the window, we watched him having a *long* conversation with the desk clerk. After ten minutes, Tino cut the motor. After another fifteen minutes, Agostino came back and got into the car.

"We have a slight problem."

Not what you want to hear when you are in the middle of nowhere and snow is gradually obliterating any sign of a road in front of you.

Tino's voice was calm. "Okay, Agostino, what exactly is the problem?"

"Do you want the good news or the bad news first?"

Tino's voice was less calm. "By all means the good news first."

"They have a room for us tonight."

"*A* room," Tino repeated. "Don't you mean rooms?"

"That is the bad news. They are full up . . . except for the suite on the second floor."

"Normally there would be rooms available, but because of the storm, all the guests want to stay another night. It is a wedding party and the bride and groom are here."

"So," I began tentatively. "How many beds does the suite have?"

"One king bed and a couch, and they will bring a cot."

Everyone was silent. We all knew we couldn't raise a fuss under the circumstances. We had to be adults about this.

"I want the couch," I said quickly.

"I'll take the cot," SJ said right after.

"Oh, no. I'm not sharing a bed with *him*." Tino pointed at Agostino.

"Tino, you take the couch. Anna can sleep with me," Agostino suggested.

"Absolutely not," I said. There was no way I was going to go through *that* agony. I wouldn't sleep a wink being that close to him, and I didn't trust my subconscious.

"Well," SJ said brightly, "I guess it's settled. Tino and Agostino get the bed. Now, let's get inside before I freeze to death."

"What about my car?" Tino grumbled. "Where's the garage?"

"They say there is a garage up the road a bit. Anna, you take SJ and the bags up to the room, and I will help Tino."

I handled the bags myself, there being no one around to help us. From the looks of it, the hotel had not been expecting the extra guests for tonight and were short-staffed. I left SJ in the lobby and walked to the front desk.

"Where's the elevator?" I asked the harried desk clerk.

"No elevator," he said crisply and pointed to the stairs.

There were two sets of stairs. One set had thirty steps, the other ten. Forty in all. I counted them each time I took another set of suitcases up to the suite. Fortunately, the cot was already set up, and I found linens and a blanket in the armoire. I took a good look at the room. It was large, no doubt about it, but it was one giant space with no separate sitting room. If somebody snored, we would all hear it.

I heard footsteps clomping up the stairs, and SJ appeared in the doorway. "No elevator," he said.

"I know."

"I may just stay up here and take a bath. Is there room service?"

"What do you think?"

SJ laughed.

The boys showed up looking very wet and cranky. The "garage" turned out to be a stable where the Villa Tiberti's collection of animals had been herded for the night: four horses, three cows, and a slew of chickens.

"God knows what those animals are going to do to the car," Tino grumbled.

"There are barriers for the large animals, and the tarp you found will keep the chickens from jumping up and shitting on it."

"That makes me feel much better, thank you. By the way"—Tino was eyeing Agostino suspiciously—"What do you sleep in?"

"Normally, I wear nothing, but for the sake of the lady present, I will wear *pigiama*."

"I hope to God that word means pajamas," Tino said, drawing an imaginary line down the middle of the bed. "Just keep to your side."

As I watched the testosterone scenario play out, I doubted if any of us was going to get any sleep tonight.

A high-pitched sound like that of a train whistle, followed by a snort, woke me up. The whistle was coming from the direction of SJ's cot but the snort? I peered over the top of the couch. The sound came again, this time a snort *and* a wheeze. It was definitely coming from the bed. I sat up, sucked in my breath, and let fly an enormous *Shhhh!*

Silence.

I snuggled back down under the blanket and closed my eyes.

Woooo, snort, wheeze. Pause. *Woooo, snort, wheeze.*

"Quiet!" I yelled.

This time, the symphony continued without interruption.

I got up and approached the bed. Tino was on his back, legs and arms spread out in luxuriant slumber. Agostino was in a fetal position inches from the other side of the bed. I checked to see where the god-awful noise was coming from. It wasn't Agostino. I sighed with relief. It would have put a serious damper on any relationship I was considering.

I walked over to Tino's side, put my lips next to his ear, and shooshed him with all the strength I could muster. His eyes popped open.

"You're snoring," I said.

"Am not!" came his immediate reply.

I turned him over on his side and went back to the couch. By the time I got settled, the intermission was over, and the symphony was starting again. I flicked on my phone. Two o'clock a.m. I contemplated the prospect of three more hours of Stravinsky's "Ode to a Snore" and grabbed a blanket and pillow and headed for the bathroom. The tub's hard, cold surface could in no way be considered a satisfying substitute for a mattress, but with the door closed, it was at least quiet. I drifted off to sleep.

Toward morning, when I woke and tried to move my body, my neck felt permanently bent. *Great, a crick.* No more sleep for me. I pulled on my running clothes, laced up my shoes, and opened the bathroom door.

The moon shone through the window, spotlighting the figures on the king-size bed. Tino was on his side, his hands tucked under his head, snoring peacefully, and Agostino was snuggled up right behind him, an arm casually draped over his bedmate's shoulder. I stifled a gleeful laugh and I whipped out my phone to take a picture. *Blackmail material for life.*

I grabbed my coat off the hook by the door and slipped out.

A blast of cold air greeted me. There was a pale light glowing in the east, hinting at the jagged peaks of the Dolomite Mountains. The city of Canale lay below me, covered in a blanket of white. With the moon leading the way, I crunched my way down the hill in search of coffee.

An hour later, we all trudged down to breakfast. The dining room was deserted, and all the tables were still piled high with dirty dishes. I bussed the cleanest one myself and we all sat down. I pulled out my phone. "By the way, I saw a strange sight last night. Two spoons in la-la land. Anyone care to see?"

Tino leaned over to have a look. His eyes narrowed. "Who is *that*?"

"If I'm not mistaken, that's you and Agostino looking very post-coital."

Tino shook his head. "No way. You photoshopped that."

Agostino was suddenly curious. "May I see?" He glanced at the phone. "Ah, I remember now. I had a very nice dream about Anna last night."

SJ started laughing, and Tino's hand edged closer to the phone.

I tightened my grip.

Agostino pulled back his chair. "Got to deal with check out. Meet you in the lobby."

"What do you intend to do with the photos?" Tino asked when he had gone.

"Insurance against any bad male behavior directed toward me for the rest of the trip," I replied.

SJ chuckled.

Tino grumbled something about extortion and stood up. "Time to see what the chickens have done to my car."

"Hold on." Agostino came running toward us from the lobby. "I just spoke with the owner. The hotel is empty. He has offered us four of his best rooms for half price. Do we want to stay?"

SJ shook his head. "No offense, but I feel like I've aged five years in one night. I'm looking forward to a good night's sleep and an elevator."

"That goes for two of us," I said.

Chapter 27

Pastry Trail

"WHAT'S THE plan today?" I asked SJ. We were standing outside La Principessa di Savoia Hotel in downtown Turin.

An hour ago, after checking in, everyone had retreated to their private rooms. It felt like a luxury after last night's fiasco in Canale. SJ seemed transformed. He had the look of someone who was near the end of his quest and the answer to a seventy-year-old question was not far behind.

"First, the Basilica di Superga to visit the tombs. When entering unfamiliar territory, especially royal residences, it is best to be as informed as possible. After that, the Palazzo di Savoia," he said.

"Are we walking or driving?" Tino wanted to know.

"The basilica is up in the hills across the river," SJ said, pointing south. "So we are definitely driving."

"Okay, the car is in the hotel parking garage two blocks from here, off Via Roma. I'll go get it."

"Let's all go," SJ said, without missing a beat. He strode ahead, shoulders thrust back and head held high.

Via Roma is one of the busiest thoroughfares in Turin, packed with shops, restaurants, and street vendors. The sun was holding sway over the rain clouds, and the crowds were taking full advantage of it. Manolos and sneakers, fur coats and puffer jackets, sharing sidewalk space without a single thought to class distinction. Agostino and I hung back, taking it all in, glad to be sharing it together. When he slipped his hand in mine, I felt that familiar shot of fire run through me.

"I need another kiss," he said, squeezing my hand. We reached the parking garage and piled into the Maserati. Following the main drag on Via Garibaldi, we crossed the river and started climbing into the hills above the city. Rose bushes and manicured lawns glowed green-gold in the sun. As the homes got bigger, so did the massive limestone walls surrounding them. After a few minutes, the gold domes of the basilica came into view.

⁕

"Now what?" Tino said. We were in front of the basilica watching a knot of tourists walk up the steps to the church.

"When in doubt, follow the crowds," SJ said. "I have a feeling there will be a fee to get into the royal crypt."

As soon as we entered the church, I saw a glassed-in cubicle and a line forming in front of it. I squinted at the sign next to the ticket booth. "Fifteen euros. That's a pretty hefty price. The Medici Chapel only charges ten, and they have four Michelangelos."

"Where are the Savoia royal tombs?" I asked the woman after she took our money.

"Next room down the stairs."

As we climbed down the marble steps, an impressive sculpture of St. Michael the Archangel greeted us at the entrance to the vault. SJ translated the inscription into English: "Gifted by the Sabauda family in 1925."

"Holy crap," Tino said.

Crossing the threshold, we saw several rooms branching off the foyer with carved out letters above three doorways: *Hall of the Kings and the Royal Queens.* A third, more modern wing, was entitled *Sabauda Family Crypts.*

"Jesus," Tino whispered. "These people have their own wing. I say we check it out. The *duchessa* might be in there."

"Savoia's first," SJ said. "I need to bone up on my kings."

"Well, you came to the right place," Tino quipped.

Agostino and I followed SJ into the Hall of the Kings while Tino veered off to check out the Sabauda wing. I thought for a minute I was in Versailles. Marbled walls and inlaid mosaic floors created the framework for the rows of sarcophagi that rose all the way to the frescoed ceilings. Each niche was topped with a gilded crown and sculptures of angels in emotional distress. As we walked, SJ called out the names of the Savoia royalty: "Vittorio Emanuele II, Umberto I." He stopped in front of a coffin inscribed with the words *Vittorio Emanuele III. Reigned from 1900 to 1946.*

"This was the father of the king that abdicated during the years Giulia disappeared. His son, Umberto II, became king in 1946. If she had been sent to the palace, she would have known Umberto."

I wandered toward the back where the less important Savoias were stacked. "I found the *duchessa's* husband," I said, excitedly. SJ and Agostino came hurrying over.

"Eugenio Amedeo Duke of Abruzzi," I read aloud. I looked up at the next tier. "That's his father. Ferdinando Amedeo I. He was the King of Spain."

Tino came running in from the other room. "The bitch is not in the Sabauda crypt," he called out. Several tourists nearby turned to look at him.

"Quiet," SJ said, a smile twitching at the corners of his mouth, "Do you want to get us kicked out of here?"

I tugged at SJ's sleeve. "Let's check out the hall of Queens."

Sure enough, underneath the coffin of the wife of Ferdinando, King of Spain, lay La Duchessa Simona Sabauda di Savoia, 1911–1987.

Tino smiled. "I don't doubt for a minute she lobbied to be buried with the queens . . . instead of with the Sabaudas.

"Next stop, the royal palace," SJ announced as we got into the car.

We parked as close as we could to Piazza Reale One and walked the rest of the way. SJ had no trouble keeping up.

The gates of the former residence of the royal family were intricately designed with an iron filigree of gold crowns and scepters disguising the impenetrable iron security bars. Several groups of tourists were walking through the open gates toward the palace.

"Let's see how far we can get without paying," I offered.

SJ chuckled. "I have a system that has served me well in my life. If I want information, or to gain access, I seek out the oldest employee I can find. They wouldn't have that job unless they had been there for ages, and they usually know everything."

"Brilliant!" I said.

Tino frowned. "Sounds risky. We aren't going to do anything illegal, are we? This is a guarded government building now. I have a nice, and rather expensive, hotel room waiting for me. I don't want to forgo it for a cell in a foreign jail."

"Where's your spirit of adventure?" I chided him.

"I'm saving it for the Turkish steam room and those half-naked ladies I saw going in."

I looked around. SJ was already halfway down the cobblestone path leading to the gardens. "Relax, no one is going to arrest a ninety-two-year-old man . . . or anyone with him. It's your choice, but I'm not deserting him now." I grabbed Agostino's hand and hurried after SJ.

Tino stood there looking after us for about a minute before he ran to catch up.

SJ found his victim right away. A little old man in overalls was raking leaves in the Principessa's garden on the right side of the courtyard.

SJ started speaking in rapid Italian, and the gardener responded with a cackle and a display of more than a few missing teeth. Soon, the two men were strolling in the direction of the back entrance to the palazzo.

"I don't like this one bit," Tino said.

We got as far as what looked like an employee lunchroom before we were stopped. SJ did some quick talking to a uniformed guard almost as old as the gardener, and the three of us stood at a respectful distance and kept our mouths shut. The guard listened without interruption, a hand on his gun holster, glancing occasionally in our direction. I think he was assessing whether we matched up with the story SJ was telling. When SJ got to the part about Duchessa Sabauda's harsh treatment of the two young lovers, the guard looked at him with a mixture of pity and admiration. He curved his finger at us and started down the hall.

We followed him toward the back recesses of the palace where there was an absence of décor and an aura of neglect. I guessed we were in an area where no one went unless there was an urgent need to locate an artifact or check on a piece of information some historian was interested in.

The guard stopped in front of a door that looked like a dozen others we had passed and inserted a key in the lock. The door creaked open. Dust motes danced in the band of light coming from a single dusty window. On the opposite wall, shelves of boxes with labels were stacked one on top of the other.

"This is where the royal family household records were kept," the guard explained. "His Royal Highness, Victor Emmanuel III, was meticulous in his accounts, especially where servant expenditures were concerned. He kept track of every penny that was spent during his reign. Forty-six years of documents can add up." The guard gestured to a section of shelves. "Here are his records, along with those of his son, Umberto II. The records end in 1947."

"Perche si sono fermati?" I asked in my best Italian.

SJ turned to me. "They stopped because the royal family had to get out of town fast. After the monarchy was abolished in the constitutional referendum of 1946, there was a clause that banned any male heirs of the Savoia dynasty from ever setting foot in Italy. They had to leave immediately or face imprisonment."

SJ addressed the guard. "I am only interested in the years of 1943 to 1947, when Giulia might have been a member of the royal household. Is there a record of the names of servants employed at that time?"

"I believe there is. What was her last name?"

"Her full name was Giulia Albani Urbino. I'm not sure she would have used it, though. She might have changed it to avoid detection."

The guard shuffled through a series of files from 1943. "Here." He pulled out a sheet. "Entries of servants hired that year. He ran his finger down the handwritten names. "Here she is. She uses the name Giulia Albani. Hired as an assistant to the pastry chef in the royal kitchen. August 3, 1943."

SJ swayed, reaching out blindly for support. Agostino and Tino were there in an instant, keeping him steady. "I have found her," he whispered.

"Let's keep looking," the guard gestured to us. "After all, the family was at this address for four more years. Maybe she was still here at the end."

With all of us going through the records, we found she had been employed every year until the exile. The last entry was from May 1947, one week before the royal family left for Portugal.

"Aspetti," Agostino cried out. "Look what I found. The last payment for each servant and an address."

SJ pored over the entry: "'Two weeks' severance pay of twenty lire to Giulia Albani.' There's a plus next to her name." He turned to the guard. "What does that mean?"

"It means there was someone else associated with her, working at the palace."

"Someone else," SJ repeated. "A husband, perhaps?"

"Perhaps."

Agostino read the forwarding address: "10128 Crocetta, Turin. Residenza Carignano."

The guard raised an eyebrow. "*Indirizzo fantastico. La famiglia Carignano e molto ricco* . . . the Carignano family is very rich."

SJ looked relieved. "Well, if she went to a nice house, then someone was taking care of her."

I looked at the documents again. "I see a signature at the bottom of each entry involving an expenditure. It is hard to make out, but it looks like Saone Sabauda. Who was that?"

The guard studied me for a moment and then spoke some words to SJ in Italian.

SJ turned to us. "Our good friend here says he may be extending the limits of his job description by telling us this, but history is his passion and he can't let this opportunity go to waste."

The guard walked over to a drawer and slid it open. After rifling through the files, he pulled out a folder and laid it on the table. "These are loan documents drawn up by Banco di Sardinia, owned and operated by the Sabauda family and issued to the Savoias from 1925 to 1944. The amounts are staggering . . . hundreds of millions of lire over the course of twenty years."

SJ looked astonished. "What does this mean? The Savoia family was broke?"

"The fascist regime both families supported had drained the royal coffers by the early 1940s. After Mussolini was assassinated, with the outcome of the war in doubt, the royal family realized they were in deep financial trouble. It was the Sabauda family's banking interests that paid the Savoia bills. Every expenditure, and that included servant wages, had to be approved by the Sabauda trustees. That is why you see their signature on the bottom of each invoice."

"What happened in 1946 when the decree was issued and the royal family had to escape?" SJ asked.

"The Sabaudas pulled up stakes and returned to Sardinia right before the Republic of Italy was formed. As known supporters of Mussolini's regime, the Savoias were vulnerable to a public that could have become an angry mob. I'm only telling you this because the entire royal household, including the servants, was in danger. The fascist regime was over, and the *partigiani* wanted blood. Even though there is a forwarding address here, it is no guarantee your Giulia was safe."

SJ looked puzzled. "I would think that being sent to a wealthy family would guarantee her safety."

The guard shook his head. "I wouldn't be too sure about that. The Carignanos were close relatives of the royal family."

SJ paled. "I understand." He held out his hand to the guard. "I guess there is only one way to find out. You, my friend, have been a great help. If we can ever return the favor . . ."

The guard smiled. "I would appreciate one thing. Don't tell anyone it was me who relayed this tidbit of information you won't find in the history books. I would like to keep my job."

"Where is Crocetta, and how fast can we get there?" SJ asked Tino as we hurried through the corridors toward the exit.

"Hold on a minute." I stared SJ down like he was a small child. "Never mind that my stomach has been growling like a bear for the last hour, but *you* need to eat. You are running on pure adrenaline."

"You bet I am." He glared. "When you get revved up at my age, you put the pedal to the metal until you run out of gas."

"I just want to make sure you don't die before you see her."

Tino gave me one of those *I-can't-believe-you-just-said-that* looks. "What she means, SJ, is you need to eat or you'll collapse."

"I'll eat afterwards. Let's get to Crocetta."

The address the palace guard had given us turned out to be an Art Nouveau pile of limestone in the San Salvario section of Crocetta. We sat in the car, by the curb, deliberating our next move.

"We can't just go up to the door and knock, can we?" Tino asked. "Our information is sixty-eight years old. We don't even know who lives here now."

"It's the only lead we have," SJ said, staring up at the bulbed Russian-style turrets flanking each side of the house. "Who's coming with me?"

We all piled out of the car and walked up to the iron gate. SJ pushed the button on the intercom.

A no-nonsense voice chirped *"Pronto?"*

"Parenti di la famiglia Carignano," SJ answered confidently.

We waited a good ten minutes before the iron gate buzzed open.

As we walked up the steps to the front door, SJ turned to face us. "I said we were relatives of the Carignano family. With all due respect, I would appreciate if you let me do the talking. We don't want to ruffle the old lady's feathers any more than necessary. He pointed a finger at me. "And no asking questions in what *you* think is good Italian."

I could sense the group dynamic was changing. SJ's dominance was slowly emerging, and we needed to be respectful of that. Agostino remained silent, contributing to the conversation when needed, his role reduced to being a supporting presence to SJ. Tino, taking his uncle's request to heart, kept his mouth shut.

A stout woman with beady eyes and a mole on her forehead the size of a third eye opened the door. "Parenti di Contessa Carignano?"

"*Sì*," SJ answered.

We were ushered into a parlor and told to sit on a settee and two chairs that had to be from the seventeenth century. The interior of the house seemed to be clinging to a grandeur it could no longer maintain. The damask covered walls were faded, and the Aubusson rug in the center of the room had a path running through it. Everywhere was an assortment of clutter and mementos that could only come from decades of living in the same place. I shivered, feeling like I was sharing space with the ghosts of a family long since relegated to the dust bins of Italian history.

"You said we were relatives," I whispered to SJ. "Who are we supposed to be?"

"I was going to ask you the same question." A tiny lady in a wheelchair was contemplating us from the doorway.

SJ started to explain.

"Don't bother," the woman said as she wheeled herself into the room. "I knew you weren't telling the truth the minute I heard the word *parenti*. You see, at ninety, I no longer have any relatives. I am the last of that long noble line." She held out her hand to SJ. "My name is Contessa Maria Consuelo Carignano."

SJ kissed her hand. "Many apologies for the subterfuge, but I thought it was the only way I could get in to speak to you. You see, I am trying to find the great love of my life. I have been waiting seventy-three years to tell her something. I am hoping you can help me."

"And who might this person be?" the *contessa* asked gently.

"Her name is Giulia Albani Urbino."

The *contessa* smiled. "SJ. I was wondering when you were going to get here."

Chapter 28

Finding Giulia

SJ STARED at the *contessa*. "How do you know who I am?"

"Giulia told me all about you. And please, call me Maria. Titles can be so dreary."

I stifled a laugh. I was beginning to see that not all noble families were alike.

Maria looked at the four of us. "I can see I'd better start at the beginning. *Nadia!*" The old lady called out. "*Porta me un po di vino!*"

A dusty decanter of red wine that looked like it hadn't been touched in my lifetime, was brought out by the servant who had opened the door. Nadia laid the tray on a diminutive pie crust table and poured the liquid into five tiny crystal glasses. After she had served us, she retreated to edge of the room and stood by the doorway, arms crossed and eyes wary.

Maria positioned her wheelchair close to where we were sitting. "I will never forget the first day Giulia came to us. A slip of a girl, so frightened, so desperate to find a safe place. I had been hired as a nanny to Her Royal Highness Princess Marie-Jose's children. She was the daughter-in-law to the King and wife of the heir to the throne. I had an extra bed in my room, so Giulia bunked with me. I'll never forget how she cried that first night."

SJ put his hands to his face "God, please don't. I have suffered enough, thinking of her in the hands of strangers."

Maria gave him a stern look. "As well you should have. Poor girl.

Coming from a shock like that . . . finding out her uncle was her father. And then *you*!" She shook her head.

"Don't you think I haven't thought about my behavior?" SJ said bitterly. "This does not excuse what I did, but there was something she didn't know, something I tried to tell her that might have changed everything."

Maria moved her wheelchair closer. "What was it?"

"My father was a man I never knew. Giulia and I were not related."

The old lady threw up her hands. "And I thought the Savoias were bad. All that screwing around. Maybe it was better, after all, that she left. She had a good life at the palace. They took care of her . . . us . . . even at the end."

"When they had to leave the country, you mean."

"Even when they were afraid for their lives, the royal family found us employment and a place to live. It was a scary time. The people of Italy had turned against them because the King was a supporter of Mussolini. Just a month before we were ordered to leave, the King handed over the throne to his son, Umberto, but it was too late. The Italian monarchy was finished.

"What about the Sabaudas?" SJ asked the *contessa*. "Didn't they try to help?"

Those people had no idea the danger the royal family faced as rulers of a country in shambles."

"I thought they came from Sardinian nobility."

"The Sabaudas?" Maria's voice rose, her eyes blazing. "They were *bankers*. Petty bourgeoisie obsessed with the prestige the Savoias brought them and their agenda of power and hate."

"Here, drink this." SJ handed her a glass of sherry. "Getting all riled up is not good at your age."

The *contessa* gave him a surprised look and accepted the glass.

"Forgive me. That part of our history is still painful to me." She took a sip of sherry. "In those last dark days before the Princess Maria left the country, she managed to secure positions for us here. The Carignano family were relatives. Charles Albert had just lost his wife and needed someone to run the house."

"And you are still here," SJ said.

"Well, I should hope so! A year after Giulia and I came to live here, Charles asked me to marry him."

"And Giulia?"

"She opened a pastry shop. Dolce di Savoia. The best *pasticceria* in Crocetta."

"Here?" SJ was up out of his chair and kissing the *contessa's* hands. "Thank you, thank you. I must go to see her immediately." He was out the front door before Maria could stop him.

As I said my goodbyes, I sensed there was something she had not had the courage to tell him.

Pasticceria Dolce di Savoia was located three blocks away on Via Sacchi. The insignia of the royal family was displayed prominently over the top of the chic black and gold exterior. Large glass windows with cases of decadent sweets worked their magic on the well-heeled pedestrians strolling by.

"The reviews are excellent," I said, perusing the website as we got out of the car. "It is considered one of the most popular and highly sought-after confection shops in Turin."

Tino chuckled. "I'm guessing Giulia's credentials as assistant pastry chef to the royal family haven't hurt her chances for success either. After all, she's worked with the best."

I considered this. The Savoias may have suffered from negative public opinion, but some things, like the appreciation of good pastry, were exempt from political fallout.

SJ, walking ahead of us, was in his own world. Even though he seemed almost oblivious to our presence, I knew he was counting on our support if, and when, it was needed.

As we stepped into the shop, we saw several women in starched white caps serving customers from a display case that ran the full length of the room. Behind it, wooden racks held fragrant loaves of freshly baked bread. On the left side of the shop, with its windows open to the street, there was a place for customers to sit and enjoy coffee and treats. SJ walked over to the elderly woman behind the cash register.

"Buongiorno, Signora."

"Piacere. My name is Carla. May I help you?"

"I wish to speak to Giulia Albani."

Carla paled. "You mean *Marina* Albani, don't you?"

SJ looked confused.

"*Un momento,*" she said, disappearing into the back.

A few minutes later, a petite woman in her early seventies came out. She had dark brown hair and a Mona Lisa smile.

SJ stared at her like he had seen a ghost. "I am looking for Giulia."

The woman's smile faltered. "Who are you?"

"An old friend. My name is Spirito Urbino. She knew me as SJ."

The woman took a step back and grabbed the edge of the counter for support. Carla rushed over. "Marina, *che succede?*"

Signora Marina Albani regarded the old man standing in front of her with cold disdain. There was no tearful reunion, no arms reaching for each other in a warm embrace, only a deafening silence. When she spoke, her voice was like ice.

"You are too late. Mama passed away two years ago."

SJ swayed as if the room were spinning, and two sets of strong arms reached for him as he started to fall.

"Get water," Agostino told someone. SJ collapsed into a chair.

I stepped forward. "Signora Marina, this man has waited a long time and come a long way to say something important to Giulia. If you are her daughter, the least you can do is listen." My Italian was a far cry from perfect, but it got her attention.

She motioned for us to come through the opening in the display cases to the back of the store. The three of us walked SJ to a prep area where supplies and cutlery for the dining room were kept. We sat him down next to a marble-topped pastry table that looked like it could have come from the royal kitchens. A glass of water was brought, and Agostino ordered him to drink it.

"He hasn't eaten a thing for hours," I said. "Isn't there something nourishing you can give him?"

The signora whispered what sounded like "*zuppa lenticche*" to Carla. The older lady nodded, grabbed a copper pan and a jar of something brown and headed for the kitchen.

"Lentil soup. An old Italian cure for trauma," SJ muttered, his eyes still closed.

"Wait, did I miss something here?" Tino looked at SJ and Marina. "Are you two related?"

"Obviously," SJ said. "Why else would she be so mad at me?"

Tino was confused. "How can you be so sure? She hasn't said anything . . ."

"Just look at her eyes."

We all looked. I remembered Agostino's photo of the brown-eyed woman in front of the palace. The woman standing before us had gray-blue eyes . . . the eyes of my grandfather.

SJ sighed. "Other than that, she is the spitting image of my Giulia."

As if to confirm SJ's remark, Marina spat on the ground in SJ's direction. "*La tua,* Giulia?" she sneered.

"Uh-oh," Tino said. "This reunion is nothing like I thought it was going to be."

I stepped in. "Okay, let's try to see this objectively. Marina, has it occurred to you that you wouldn't even be here if it weren't for what your mother and SJ . . . uh . . . did?"

Marina stared at me.

"Agostino, translate," I said.

"That is not fair," he pleaded. "I don't want to get in the middle."

SJ waved a tired hand at me. "I appreciate the effort all of you are making, but this is between Marina and me. I will need some time with her alone. Can you three go and eat some of that incredible pastry out there?"

As we got up to leave, Carla entered, carrying a steaming pot, and she laid it on the marble-topped table. She set out spoons, napkins and two bowls and ladled the fragrant liquid into them. SJ looked at his daughter and patted the chair next to him. Without a word, Carla walked over to Marina, took her by the hand, and led her to the table.

❦

Shell-shocked, Tino and I found a table in the dining room of the pastry shop. I looked around at the happy faces of the customers. The pleasant sound of laughter and tinkling cutlery contrasted sharply with what I assumed was happening on the other side of the wall. Agostino had wandered over to the display cases, looking for something to help lighten the mood.

"That lentil soup sure looked good," Tino said. "Too bad we weren't invited."

"I think they have some serious catching up to do without us hanging around. Besides, that Marina looks like a feisty one. I don't want to be anywhere near her if she decides to dump that pot of scalding soup on him . . . and us."

Agostino arrived with a tiny chocolate cake and three forks. "Sachertorte. My personal solution for dealing with family hysterics."

Our banter felt hollow, a halfhearted attempt to mask the

magnitude of what we had just witnessed.

"I feel guilty not being there to support him," I said after a few minutes.

"SJ made it clear he didn't want us," Tino reminded me.

Agostino's voice was gentle. "They need time together alone. Time to heal."

I nodded. "I keep imagining what it must have been like for Giulia, a young mother so far from home, in those difficult days before her employer's exile. And for three-year-old Marina, seeing the only home she had ever known being ripped apart. I hope she was too young to understand the danger and to wonder why her mother had to handle it all alone."

"Do you think Giulia poisoned her daughter against SJ?" Tino asked me. "There must be a lot of resentment, and although not fair, it is understandable under the circumstances."

"Especially with him turning up seventy years too late," I added.

"We may be here awhile," Agostino said, taking a bite of the Sachertorte and sliding the plate over to me. "No sense in starving while we wait."

An hour and two Sachertortes later, we were still waiting for SJ. I felt like an addict in an opium den.

"I'm overdosing. I need to get out of here before I order the strudel." I bolted for the front door and the sidewalk.

The cold air felt good on my face. Suddenly, I felt a familiar hand steal around my waist. "Don't touch my stomach," I warned. "Too much Sachertorte could have unfortunate consequences."

Agostino nuzzled my neck. "I was going to suggest a kiss on rooftop of hotel later."

Before I could respond, we saw SJ and Tino coming out of Dolce di Savoia. They were smiling.

"So, you told her," I said to SJ. "How did she take it?"

"It couldn't have gone that badly," Tino joked. "He's not covered in soup."

SJ managed a smile. "It will take time. We have a way to go before we can claim a proper father-daughter relationship. Seventy years of resenting what I did to her mother does not magically disappear. What she does realize now is that I was just a pawn in a family drama that started long before I was born."

"Does she want to see you tomorrow?" Tino asked.

"Yes. Tomorrow is her day off. She has invited me to her home for lunch. It is a beginning."

SJ turned to me. "I have you to thank for this. Playing the Deathbed Game has changed my life, and we are just getting started."

I held out my arms, and he came into them.

"Wait for me!" Agostino said.

We all turned to Tino. "Well?"

Tino walked toward us, an embarrassed smile on his face. "You Italians are entirely too sentimental." He opened his arms and joined the hug.

Chapter 29

Rooftop Happy Hour

THE PRINCIPESSA Piemonte Hotel was a delight. The lobby and reception rooms were a stunning mix of Asian-meets-Art Deco, with metal-accented leather chairs and sleek banquettes the color of burnt orange lining the room. Instead of walls, panels of stone separated seating areas, and circular translucent lanterns hung from ceilings like planets in a solar system.

SJ insisted I try the wellness center and have a full-body massage with all the trimmings. His treat. How could a girl say no? There was one stop I had to make first.

Twenty minutes later, Agostino and I were staring in the window of a high-end lingerie shop on Via Roma. One mannequin was wearing a cream-colored jumpsuit, edged in lace, that came to just below the buttocks, and another had on a camisole top and panties in red satin. Agostino pointed to a French-cut black bodysuit with a plunging neckline and a very naughty cut-out crotch. "That is the one," he said. "Shows off your *culo*."

"It shows off a little more than that!" I said, taking a look at the price tag. "They must be charging by the inch."

"I pay," Agostino said shortly. He grabbed me by the hand and led me inside.

The salesgirl was as sexy as the lingerie. "For your wife?" She gave me a fleeting look and concentrated on Agostino. I guess she figured he was the one with the cash.

"She's not my wife," he said, his eyes twinkling.

The girl didn't look surprised. "Something sexy, then?" She was sizing me up now with renewed interest.

"Please bring out the sexiest things you have. I will watch her model them. Then I make my decision."

"*Certo,* Signore. At your pleasure." The salesgirl gave me a conspiratorial wink and walked away swinging her not-too-boyish hips.

"Agostino! That girl winked at me! Now all of Turin will know I am having a scandalous affair with a younger man."

"Nothing but the best for my favorite mistress."

"Your *only* mistress," I said.

An hour later, we walked out with two bodysuits, a red satin teddy, and a black lace garter belt.

"Were you serious about the rooftop kiss?" I asked him as we strolled down the crowded street. "The Principessa has eight stories. How do you even know we can get up there?"

"It is the adventure that is most important. *I* will bring the champagne and blankets. *You* will wear the garter belt."

"Just the garter belt?"

"Why not?"

"Agostino, I told you we were going to wait until we got home . . . and I meant it."

"Okay. Then wear the red teddy. I promise just to look."

"Right."

I left Agostino at the bar while I rode the elevator up to the wellness center. I walked over to the girl behind the counter. "Manicure, pedicure, massage, and hair style," I said.

"Name and room number?"

"Charge it to Spirito Urbino. Room 124," I answered confidently.

Immersed in the mineral-infused bath, I felt a sense of contentment envelope me. I couldn't pinpoint the exact reason for my euphoria, and it certainly did not match up with the fifty-nine-year-old face staring back at me from the mirrored walls of the spa. The truth was, I didn't feel my age . . . I hadn't felt it in days . . . and I was no longer wondering what kind of life I wanted to live, I was *living* it.

I wasn't the only one. I thought of my companions: SJ, willing to trade the memory of a lost love for a daughter he had never met and turn it into a new beginning. Tino, dispelling preconceived notions and opening his mind to possibilities he never would have considered before. And Agostino, looking at me like a besotted lover when I came out of the dressing room in that crotchless bodysuit. We were all flying high on a magic carpet ride called life, and none of us wanted to get off anytime soon.

⁕⁓⁓⁕

We gathered in the Salotto della Principessa lounge for cocktails and then wandered over to the hotel's famous Casa di Savoia restaurant.

Inside, teak wainscoted walls, industrial lighting, and silver tufted banquettes contrasted brilliantly with the white linen tablecloths.

SJ waited until the waiter had distributed the menus and announced the specials before he addressed us. "I have already perused the menu, and if I am allowed, I would like to order for all of us. That way we can all share." He looked pointedly at Tino. "Are there any objections?"

Tino smiled. "By all means, go ahead. Since I've been hanging out with you all, I've tasted brains, entrails, lard, and I've even braved a trip to the Turkish steam baths. I doubt if there's anything you can throw at me that I won't try."

"Good boy," Agostino said. "There is hope for you yet."

SJ motioned for the waiter. "First, a bottle of your best Barolo,

1975 if you have it. Then we will begin with . . ."

As I listened to SJ reel off menu choices to the waiter, I smiled. He had become the leader, the one we looked up to in so many ways. In the last few days, the lonely man living with the guilt of the past had become a man in charge of his destiny.

The wine came, and glasses were poured. SJ raised his. "This has been a momentous day. I have lost a friend . . . and a lover . . . but I have gained a daughter. I am grateful I still have time to get to know her better. Thank you for sharing it all with me. *Saluti!*"

Tino took a sip and addressed SJ. "I'm wondering about something. You told us you were employed by the Urbino Truffle Foundation as a chef. You must have worked closely with Claudio and his family. With the issue of Giulia's disappearance, and the part you played in it, I am surprised they hired you."

Agostino spoke up. "It was my side of the family that carried the grudge, not Claudio's. My uncle was a forward-thinking man. It was always business first with him. Family squabbles were considered less a priority, especially if the people involved were valuable to him. SJ was a talented chef and an asset to the company. That was what was important to Claudio."

I broke in. "But what about the scandal of Agatha's relationship with Spirito? Why was Santo so afraid of leaking it to his father-in-law, and would it have made a difference to Claudio? After all, Agatha was a valuable commodity, too."

Agostino hesitated and looked at SJ.

"My brother was obsessed with protecting our mother," SJ said. More so than he needed to be. I suspect she would have been willing to drop the whole charade of my being Santo's son, if he would have let her."

"Do you think Claudio knew who your father was?"

SJ nodded his head. "Yes. I think he knew … but we never discussed it." SJ looked around the table. "I can't help thinking how ironic it all is. All that pretense hiding my parentage, and in the end, we were only fooling ourselves."

"You did it for the right reasons, SJ, to honor your brother's wishes," I said gently. "That should count for something."

SJ smiled at me. "Yes, it counts for something. Like you said, regrets are for those who look backward. I do not have time for that."

Agostino addressed Tino. "You mentioned the Turkish steam baths earlier. How was it?"

Tino made a face. "Men, women, and several persons of an indeterminate gender all lying around on stone slabs completely naked and being massaged by men wearing nothing but loincloths. Kind of like an orgy without the sex, although I'm sure that could have been arranged for an added fee."

"Sounds delightful," Agostino said.

"I couldn't wait to get the hell out of there. There were some very hairy men who were looking at me in an inappropriate manner … if you know what I mean …"

"Typical American paranoia," Agostino responded. "The hammam has been practiced for many centuries. The high humidity removes toxins … they call it 'ritual purification.' It has nothing to do with sex."

"Don't forget, the Romans did it too," I piped up. "The Baths of Caracalla are famous."

Tino looked surprised. "Come to think of it, our mom had other methods of removing toxins when we were growing up … ones I will not mention over dinner. I would much prefer a good massage with aromatic oils. Perhaps another visit is in order."

After dessert, SJ reached into his coat pocket for his wallet.

"Put that away," Agostino demanded, as three credit cards appeared on the table. "This is our treat."

SJ chuckled. "If I had known you were paying, I would have ordered a third bottle of Barolo."

"By all means," Tino said.

"No, no." SJ put his hand up. "I am joking. I have a *rendezvous* with my king-size bed that I don't want to miss. But don't let me stop you. Breakfast at eight o'clock sharp. We need to plan the day."

⌣

The three of us lingered by the elevators.

"Nightcap?" Tino looked at the two of us and laughed. "Never mind. See you in the morning." He headed off in the direction of the lounge.

I slipped my hand into Agostino's. "Are we that obvious?"

He had his hand on the curve of my backside as the doors opened. An elderly couple stared at us from inside the elevator as we stepped in. "Meet you in your room in fifteen?" He asked, running his finger down my open neckline and rubbing the moisture on his lips. The woman's eyebrows lifted.

I reached up and guided his fingers to my lips and kissed them. "Make it ten."

The woman in the elevator gasped and looked away.

On the fifth floor, the door opened, and I sauntered down the hall, swaying my hips like only an Italian woman can do.

"Shocking!" the woman said to her husband as the doors closed.

Eight minutes later, I heard a knock on the door. I padded over in my slippers and opened it. Agostino was standing there with a bottle of champagne and two glasses.

His eyes took in the fluffy white robe. "Not exactly what I expect."

"It's freezing outside!"

"You are wearing it underneath?"

I opened the robe and gave him a peek. "What is that?" I pointed to a mound of fur he had draped over one arm.

"Blanket to keep you warm. I tell the maid my girlfriend is cold. You know what she say?"

"No, what?"

"She say it is *my* job to warm you up. But she give me this anyway." Agostino wrapped me in the faux fur throw, its satin lining cool and soft against my skin. I took the two glasses from him and started down the hall to the elevator. We rode up to the eighth floor and got off. There were three more sets of stairs before we reached the rooftop door. We set the bottle and glasses down, and I wedged the door open with an empty beer can I found nearby.

"I guess we aren't the only ones who've tried this."

We stepped out onto the roof, the wind whipping around us, the sky full of stars. Within seconds, Agostino's lips were on mine, our bodies coming together with an urgency that surprised me. I felt the pull of sexual passion, but there was something more . . . a connection between us that went beyond the physical. The candle was burning brighter now, and I could see a light at the end of the tunnel. Was it my future? Immersed in the joy of his touch, I held on tight, hoping my heart could tell me the answer.

He took my hand and led me around the corner, pushing me gently against the wall. I opened my robe. His eyes traveled slowly down the length of my body, looking straight through the red satin teddy. I threw my head back, surrendering, as he pressed himself into me. My hips joined his, denim and satin rubbing together with a heat that burned us.

I want to make love to you," Agostino whispered.

"Here?" I asked.

"Here," he said pulling me closer.

I looked out into the void, red lights winking on the tops of cupolas, the spires of churches piercing the night sky. I felt like I was on top of the world, far away from any life I had known before. "I'm so happy I could scream," I said.

"Do it," he said. "No one will hear."

I let it out, a throaty howl full of lust, ecstasy, and joy.

A door slammed. "Who's there?" a voice called out.

We stared at each other.

Agostino tied my robe and wrapped the fur around me. "Stay quiet. Maybe he will go away."

The door slammed again. There were more voices this time and laughter. I heard the clink of glass and the sound of a cigarette lighter.

"Okay, what do we do now?"

"We have to go," Agostino said.

"Like this? Look at your rumpled shirt . . . and my robe. They will know."

The door opened and closed a few more times, and the voices got louder. I peered around the corner and saw close to a dozen men and women in hotel uniforms, drinking beer and smoking cigarettes.

"It's a rooftop happy hour," I said. We both started cracking up.

Agostino put his arm around me. "We will walk past, say *buona sera,* like we are going for a stroll, and walk out."

If the happy hour crowd was surprised to see a fur-wrapped woman in bedroom slippers and a man shivering in shirt sleeves, they did not let on. It was only after the door closed behind us that we heard the laughter.

The champagne and glasses we had left by the door were gone. It was the least we could do for the hardworking employees at the Principessa.

Agostino escorted me to my room and lingered outside.

"I would ask you in," I said, "but we both know what would happen."

"And what is wrong with that?"

"I'm a screamer, remember?"

"I like screaming."

I pointed to next door. "SJ's room," I whispered.

Agostino's face fell.

I reached up and planted a chaste kiss on his cheek. "The bachelor pad at Villa Urbino is soundproof, right?"

"*Very* soundproof," Agostino said, giving me a not-so-chaste kiss on the lips before wandering off to his room.

Feeling guilty about the previous day's indulgences, I forced myself out of bed for an early morning run. I followed the route we had walked yesterday: north on Via Roma to Piazza Castello and then east on Via Giuseppe Verdi toward the River Po. A pre-dawn mist dampened the cobblestones as I carefully avoided the one or two errant stone squares that could have sent me sprawling. At that hour, I felt like I had the whole town to myself. Shopkeepers were beginning to sweep the sidewalk in front of their stores, shooing away stray cats and night stragglers who might have dared to take up residence during the night.

By the time I reached the river, the mist had turned to rain, and one or two bars had opened, the gold light from the open doors shining through the gray. I stopped before one of them and looked in. I could see men at the counter, hunched over grappa laced espressos, talking and calling out greetings to each other. The regulars. Fingering the two-euro coin in my windbreaker pocket, I walked in and sat down at the only empty seat at the bar. The two men nearest me turned their heads, gave me a quick glance and a nod, and went back to their conversation. I looked at their knit caps and frayed jackets and guessed they were maintenance men waiting out the storm. Warmed by the body heat in the tiny room, I listened to the guttural sounds of a working man's dialect and eyed the cross-section of humanity lining up for sustenance and conversation in the hours before tourists took over the town.

I nodded to the bartender and ordered, putting my two euros on the counter.

"Cappuccino, per piacere,"

He smiled at me. "You are American?"

Somehow, the bartenders always knew. I remembered my first trips to Italy and how I struggled to order like a native. *"Sì, sono Americana."*

He rung up my order and handed me back the change. After I had finished, I left it on the counter next to my empty cup. Tipping in Italy is optional and only exercised when the service is considered exceptional. If I came back tomorrow, he would remember me.

Fortified, I started walking along the Corso Emanuele back to the hotel. The rain had stopped, and the clouds were separating. I looked east, hoping to catch the first rays of the sun rising over the hills above the Po.

SJ and Tino were on their second espresso when I joined them for breakfast.

"Where's Agostino?" I asked them.

"I was going to ask you the same question," Tino said, biting into a cream-filled cornetto. "The last time I saw you both, you were making goo-goo eyes at each other by the elevator. I naturally assumed . . ."

"You assumed wrong," I said. It was important to set the record straight if for no other reason than to prove I had the self-control to forgo a night of pleasure for the sake of propriety.

"Ah, here he is," I said as Agostino approached. "Come, have a seat."

SJ pulled out a chair and made room.

"Rough night?" I said sweetly.

"As a matter of fact," Agostino said as he sat down, "I get much more sleep than I plan."

"Good," SJ said, "because there has been a change in schedule. I got a call from my daughter this morning. She wants us *all* to join her for lunch."

Agostino looked pensive. "I am confused, what is my relationship to her? Are we cousins?"

Tino interrupted. "Glad you brought that up. I've been trying to figure out how that changes the Urbino family tree."

SJ thought for a minute. "Well, Giulia was Agostino's aunt's daughter, and Marina is *our* daughter, so … mmm … at least one thing is clear: We are all related to each other."

I choked. Agostino gulped. Tino's eyes widened.

"Wait," I said. "Are you saying *Agostino* and I are related?"

"Second cousins, twice removed, something like that." SJ said.

I sat back, stunned. I couldn't help visualizing our hip action last night on the rooftop … not to mention all that shared saliva. Was having sex with second cousins twice removed … I was focusing on the twice removed part … considered incestuous? I glanced over at Agostino. He looked like he was already forming a family tree in his head.

Chapter 30

A Change of Plan

THE NEIGHBORHOOD of San Salvario, on the outskirts of Crocetta, was an architectural enclave created out of the Art Nouveau wave that swept Europe in the 1890s. Giulia had purchased an entire floor of the four-story Liberty-style building after her *pasticceria* had begun turning a profit in 1960. Back then, real estate in San Salvario was still affordable.

We were met at the door by a woman who was helping Marina prepare the meal. As we walked through the whiplash-style ceramic tile foyer, the colorful designs dominating the exterior gave way to a fresh palette of pale whites, creams, and grays. Swedish-designed sofas and chairs covered in coarse linen occupied the big open spaces, and sheer drapes hung from the tall, oval windows. I was reminded, at once, of my room at Villa Urbino.

Our host met us in the dining room where slim French doors overlooked a stunning view of Parco Valentino. "Call me Mari," she insisted as we sat down. She spoke only in Italian as if her English was such embarrassment to her she refused to attempt it. Tino and I absorbed what we could but insisted there was to be no obligation on anyone's part to translate.

I sat back and watched the interplay between SJ and Mari, a tentative but determined effort to build a bridge over the chasm of pain and misunderstanding.

Agostino, although part of Mari's side of the family, did not interrupt as father and daughter caught up on each other's lives. I watched him quietly refill our water glasses and pass the platters of food, making sure everyone had enough to eat. He even pulled the chair out for the woman who had helped prepare the meal after Mari had asked her to join us. Occasionally, he would lean over and translate a word or answer one of Tino's questions, but he was careful not to insert too much of himself into the conversation. I appreciated the unselfish gestures he was making. He had known Mari's grandmother well; she had been like a second mother to him growing up, and yet he understood that this was not about him. I realized I had done him an injustice by only focusing on his physical attributes. Agostino was much more than just a hunky guy who looked good in a pair of jeans.

After the dishes had been cleared, Mari led us into the living room where a silver coffee service had been set out. Next to it, on the coffee table, was a large cardboard box labeled *Lettere di Marina.*

SJ sat down opposite the box and poured coffee. "I take it these are letters Giulia's mother sent her during the time they were separated. I had no idea. I am so happy to know they kept in touch."

"This is the entire correspondence," Mari said, taking the lid off the box. "Twenty-six years, from 1949 to 1975. Almost one hundred letters."

SJ set down the pot and withdrew a letter from his breast pocket. "This is a photo Agostino found at Villa Urbino." He passed it to his daughter.

Mari smiled. "I took that picture. I was fifteen. I see the envelope has no return address. Is this the only letter you have from Giulia?"

"I'm afraid so," Agostino said. "I searched her room and found only this. It is possible the others are hidden somewhere."

Mari looked at the four of us. "How did you find me?"
"We bribed a guard at the palace to look through the royal family's

records," Agostino joked. "La Contessa Carignano's house was listed as the forwarding address."

Mari laughed. "You are all very clever. I am touched."

I ventured a question. "You were born in the royal household, weren't you?"

"I was. Mama was well loved by the children of the Savoias, especially Gabriella, the youngest. They played together all the time. When my mother found out she was pregnant, the *principessa* made all the birthing arrangements. And later, even with exile looming, she helped us find a place to live."

SJ took his daughter's hand. "There is something I need to ask. Was I the reason you and your mother never returned to Scheggino to visit?"

Mari nodded. "She was afraid to face those who would not approve of what she had done. My existence was living proof of that. If only she had known you were not related."

SJ searched his daughter's face. "There is another question that haunts me. If she had known my true identity, do you think she would have run away?"

"I don't think it would have made a difference. You were not the only reason she left. Her mother's behavior—being intimate with Marco—sickened her, but it was more than that. Mama's relationship with her mother had always been difficult, she often told me. It was the similarity in their personalities that made it hard for them to get along. They both had such passionate natures, they both resisted discipline, and they both fell in love regardless of the consequences. When Mama left that day, she was making a decision to forge a new life for herself." Mari sighed. "Yes, what happened between you two was tragic, but she did well here and found her place . . . and she always had me." She patted her father's hand. "Now I would like to ask *you* something. May I call you Papa?"

SJ flushed at the word and then smiled. "There is nothing that would please me more."

"I want you to have these." Mari gestured to the box.

SJ started to protest. "But they belong to your mother... I can't..."

"I have read them... many times. It helped me get a sense of where I came from ... and the family I never knew. I am ready to give them to someone else to read. I would like it to be you."

"I am honored," SJ said. "I'm sure Agostino will want to read them, too. Marina was his great aunt."

Mari looked at her cousin. "Just remember, when you open the door to the past, you may discover things you never knew. As you have seen, it can change your life."

SJ stepped in. "I hope I speak for all of us, when I say that, by seeking out the unknown, we must be willing to accept what we find... good or bad. When I started this quest, I knew there was the possibility Giulia would no longer be alive. I chose to go anyway. It has turned out different than I expected, but no less gratifying. That's what this adventure was all about."

I shot a glance at Agostino. He had the glassy-eyed look of someone who was re-evaluating a future that had changed without warning. "Life has a way of surprising us," he said quietly.

Amen to that, I thought. Searching for the truth can be a very scary business.

"We have a big truffle festival every year in the first week of April," SJ said, seemingly anxious to change the subject. "Scheggino is beautiful in the spring."

"I have always wanted to visit Umbria," Mari said, smiling.

The mood was subdued as we drove back to the hotel. SJ and Agostino, in the back seat, were discussing the return trip.

SJ called out to Tino. "I think we should stick with our plan to spend another night in Turin and leave first thing in the morning. We can overnight in Bologna at the Corona d'Oro and drive home the next day. From Bologna, it is less than four hours to Scheggino. We could be home in two days."

"Sounds good to me," Tino called back.

No one even asked me what I thought.

SJ made dinner reservations at Guido Gubbio, a well-reviewed trattoria specializing in seafood on the Via Roma. When we got to the restaurant, Agostino chose a seat as far away from me as possible. I pretended not to notice.

It was our last night in Turin. We should have been celebrating a job well done and the prospect of a future relationship with a new member of the family. Instead, the conversation was all about going home. I picked at my food, and Agostino hardly said a word. After the meal, SJ said he had letters to read, and Tino pleaded exhaustion. Together, they walked back to the hotel. Agostino and I stood on the busy street looking everywhere but at each other.

I turned to face him. "Agostino, we have to talk."

He stiffened. I reached out to touch his face, and his hand caught my wrist. "Maybe it is better if you don't . . ."

I withdrew my hand. "Don't what? Touch you? Yesterday you couldn't keep your hands off me."

"It feels different now." His words were clipped.

"Because we are distant relatives? We don't even have blood together. Aren't you carrying this a bit too far?"

Agostino was silent, his face emotionless.

I felt my anger growing. "How can your feelings change overnight? *I* don't feel different, I'm on fire just being next to you."

Agostino's eyes suddenly blazed. "You think this is easy for me? I wanted you more than anything in my life . . ."

"*Wanted*," I repeated. "You just said *wanted*."

"Anna, I can't. You hear what Mari say about shame. You saw what happen to SJ and Giulia. You don't know what it is like in these small villages . . . people and their children sometimes live an entire lifetime here. They know everybody's business. The whispering begins, then the stories change, and before long, they turn into lies. In the church, the stigma of marrying relatives, even distant ones, still exists."

"Marriage? Who's talking marriage? We haven't even had sex yet." The minute the words were out of my mouth, I knew I had made a mistake.

Agostino's face hardened, and his eyes grew cold. "There can be no future for us now."

I stood in the street, tears streaming down my face, as I watched him walk away. "Just tell me one thing, Agostino," I shouted after him. "How do I stop the feeling I have every time I look at you?"

The figure striding quickly down the street did not turn around.

<hr>

It was a cruel winter wind that greeted me as I stepped out of the hotel the next morning. I faced it with only one thought in mind: if I pushed myself hard enough, maybe I could outrun my despair.

I was still reeling from yesterday's turn of events. My relationship with Agostino had gone from playful and romantic to sinful in less than twenty-four hours. A third party had now joined us. It had become a ménage à trois with morality overshadowing our every move.

All night the *what-ifs* haunted me. *If* I had not encouraged SJ to seek out the past, he wouldn't have discovered the existence of a daughter. *If* we hadn't been so eager to accompany SJ to play the Deathbed Game, Agostino and I would have been free to explore our feelings for each other. Could it have led to love? By introducing the subject of marriage, Agostino had made it clear he'd wanted commitment. Was he expecting me to drop everything back home and move here permanently? Was I ready to make that kind of commitment? It was obvious we had fallen for each other without thinking about how a long-distance relationship would work.

Maybe it was better this way. Even though it hurt like hell, by walking away from what we could have been, Agostino had made the decision for me.

I reached the bar where I had stopped yesterday morning. It seemed like a lifetime ago. When I walked in, one of the customers called out a greeting. I put down my two euros, and the bartender turned and smiled at me. A second later, I heard the *whoosh* of the cappuccino machine.

"*Piu triste che ieri,*" The bartender said, putting the cup in front of me.

He saw the sadness that had not been there yesterday.

"*Cuore,*" I said, cupping my hands like a heart and then separating them. "*Spezzato.* Broken."

He nodded sympathetically.

"*Quando senti il dolore dell'cuore, sai di essere vivo.*"

My eyes filled with tears. "*Grazie,*" I told him. I finished my cappuccino and walked out.

The man was right. *When you feel the heart ache of love, it means you are alive.*

I thought about my magic carpet ride. If I was going to accept life as it came, unfiltered and without a safety net, I was bound to suffer a few bumps along the way . . . and if I was really going to *live*, I needed to open my heart to all of it.

Chapter 31

Staying the Course

WE MADE it to Bologna by noon. SJ and Agostino were sharing the back seat, and I had been promoted to navigator, a job description that mainly included making sure Tino did not end up in Austria.

Since yesterday, the dynamics of our little group had changed, and I wasn't just talking about the seating arrangements. At breakfast, there were dark circles under Agostino's eyes, and the conversation felt strained, full of awkward silences and furtive glances that hadn't been there before. Waiting for the valet in front of the hotel, I noticed SJ and Agostino stood off to one side, keeping their distance and not including me in the conversation.

A serious discussion seemed to be taking place in the back seat, and I saw SJ hand over some of Marina's letters. I had the feeling that their choice of dialogue, a lightning quick Schegginese dialect, was intended to keep the information to themselves. *Does their secrecy have something to do with what is in the letters? What is going on?*

Emilio was waiting for us when we pulled up to the garages. His face lit up when he saw Tino and the Maserati. "You have time to go to *mini autodromo* later?" he asked.

Tino smiled and patted the boy's shoulder. "Let me get settled and eat something first."

"Mama make gnocchi for pranzo. Everyone invited!" Emilio said quickly. It sounded suspiciously like a bribe.

Leonora and Julio served us in the breakfast room one level

below the main entrance of the hotel. As soon as the elevator doors opened, the smell of homemade Italian cooking wafted toward us from the kitchen. Leonora came in carrying a tray of Bolognese bread.

"Pizza?" I asked, biting into a crispy wedge.

"Different," Leonora explained. "It is made with chopped meat and spices on top."

Tino reached for a slice. "Close enough for me."

Next came the gnocchi Bolognese, potato dumplings made with a ragù and cream sauce.

Tino wiped the last of the sauce from his plate with the pizza bread. "*Delizioso!* Time for a nap."

"No nap!" Emilio's face looked worried. "Racetrack, remember?"

Julio looked at Tino sympathetically. "He's talked of nothing else since you left."

"I've created a monster," Tino said, getting up from the table. "Okay, Emilio, lead the way."

When I began clearing the table, Leonora stopped me. "Please, you are our guest. Go out and enjoy the city."

SJ nodded. "It will do you good." I cringed at the patronizing tone of his voice.

"I think I will. Thanks." I turned quickly before anyone could see the tears well up.

I left the hotel, turned right, and headed for the Centro Storico and Piazza Maggiore. Maybe a little medieval history would put my personal drama into perspective. I was irritated about the way SJ had treated me—as if I was in mourning. Well, come to think of it, I was. Sappy as it sounded, I was in mourning over the loss of what Agostino and I might have been.

I reached the Two Towers, remembering they had been built by two wealthy families in competition to see who was more powerful . . .

or who had more money. In those days, you didn't win until you had both. *Some things never change.*

I touched one of the red brick columns. It was where Agostino had kissed me for the first time. *That kiss!* A quiver of fire shot through me again just thinking about it. That was when the stakes had risen and the game had turned serious. Win or lose, I had thrown my heart into the ring.

I walked to the Quadrilatero market, the teeming humanity and colorful stalls of food a blur, until I saw the tiny cafe where Agostino and I had shared a gelato. I remembered the taste of the *nocciola* as I licked his fingers.

It was no use. Everywhere I looked, I saw a series of landmarks and memories that we would never share again. I walked back to the hotel, to the privacy of my room, where wallowing was allowed and the pity would be self-inflicted.

Around 7:30 p.m. I heard a knock on the door. It was Tino.

"We're going to dinner. You coming?"

"Go on without me," I called from the bed. "I'm not hungry."

"Not hungry in Bologna? Man, you *must* be sick." Tino's voice sounded worried.

I opened the door a crack. "I'm just tired. I need a good night's sleep."

"Me too, but one of us has to represent the Wilson side of the family. Over a nice plate of ravioli Bolognese, I hope. Nice pj's, by the way."

I fingered the lapel of my pink flannel Minnie Mouse pajamas. I always wore them when I was feeling sorry for myself. I looked at my brother. "Do you have a minute?"

"Sure." Tino stepped inside and closed the door. "What's up?"

"I don't know if you and SJ have noticed what's been going on with Agostino and me . . ."

"We noticed the fireworks have dimmed. We thought when the time was right, you'd tell us."

"Ever since Agostino found out we share some parentage, he's backed off."

"But you are second cousins, twice removed, I think SJ said. Why would that matter to anyone?"

"It matters to him," I said simply. "I just can't understand how he can stop caring so easily."

Tino looked at me. "Maybe his feelings haven't changed, only his willingness to act on them. I think what happened in his family's past has made him wary of relationships. Even if you don't agree with the reasoning, you have to respect his choices."

I sighed. "You are right, of course. Make my apologies tonight, will you?"

"I will." Tino reached out and gave my hand a comforting squeeze. "Just think, in less than a week we'll be home . . . *San Diego home*."

As I got back into bed, I didn't know whether I was happy or sad that our Italian adventure was almost over.

The ringing of the hotel phone woke me up. *What the hell? It is after midnight.* I picked it up.

"Anna?"

My heart flipped over. It was Agostino.

"I know is late but there is something I need to show you."

Despite my best efforts, I couldn't help visualizing what it was he wanted to show me. "Agostino, are you sure?"

"No, not *that*."

I wished he hadn't made *that* sound so unappealing.

"What is it, then?"

"I discover something. Can you come to my room? Three doors down. One twenty-four."

I thought of the red satin teddy still packed in my suitcase, and I looked down at my pink flannel pajamas. If anything was going to keep me from straying off course, it was Minnie. Without so much as a swipe of mascara or a fluff of my hair, I marched down the hall. *This better be good*, I said to myself.

When Agostino opened the door, he just stared at me. "You wear Mickey Mouse pajama?" I thought I saw his mouth twitching.

"It's Minnie, actually," I said, striding into the room. "Now, what is so damn important that you had to wake me up from my beauty sleep?"

Agostino's bed was littered with sheets of paper and envelopes.

"Are these Marina's letters?"

"*Sì*, I have been reading for hours now." Agostino walked over and started putting the letters in order according to their dates. "These begin in 1962—five months before I was born—and end in 1975, the year Marina die. There is much about my mother that I did not know about."

"She died in childbirth, you told me."

"*Sì*. Three of Marina's letters describe what happen." He handed me a letter dated December 10, 1962.

I looked at the small, flowing script. "This is handwritten in Italian, Agostino. You overestimate my abilities." I patted the edge of the bed next to me. "Let's start from the beginning."

The story of Gabriella's son Agosto Urbino and Agostino's father was heartbreaking. Agosto had been a shy, withdrawn child growing up, and his parents worried he would never get married. He was the only child, and an heir was an important consideration for the future of the Urbino estate. Then, when he was twenty-nine years old, he met Cecilia. She was ten years older and a schoolteacher from the Le Marche region of Umbria.

"They fell mad for each other," Agostino said. "Aunt Marina say she never see a love so intense. From the moment they marry, papa never spend one night without her. Cecilia became pregnant but she is already forty years old. It is old for a woman to have babies." Agostino pointed to a paragraph and translated:

Cara Giulia,
I am worried about Cecilia. She is five months along and has been confined to bed for the next four months until the birth. She is very weak and there is blood. I see it when I change her sheets. My nephew is crazy with worry but Gabby and I keep him from knowing too much. God forbid if something should happen to her and the baby.

Agostino handed me another letter. "This one is dated June twentieth. It is very sad, Anna." A tear rolled down his cheek.

"Are you sure you want me to hear this?"

"I am sure." He began reading:

Cara Giulia,
How can I tell you of the sadness in my heart! You are the only one I can talk to . . . Agosto will not allow us to discuss it. The night of the birth, Cecilia's pains came on suddenly. Two weeks before her due date. She was rushed to hospital but it took many hours. She begged me not to leave her side so I stayed, watching her weaken and the pain grow worse. After ten hours and much blood, she gave birth to two babies. One was already dead when it came out and the other was taken immediately to intensive care. Cecilia died in my arms soon after.

Agostino put down the letter. "Anna, the second baby was *me*. I never knew I had a brother."

I reached for his hands and held them. "I am so sorry. But at least your papa had you. Just think if he had lost both babies and his wife. It would have killed him."

Agostino handed me another letter. "The next one is dated two months later."

Cara Giulia,
The baby is healthy and growing! We have named him Agosto, after his papa. Agostino for short. My nephew is completely devoted to him; having the little one around has saved his life. He calls him his miracle baby.

Agostino was sobbing now. I pulled him into my arms and held him. "You were their miracle baby, don't you see? For Marina too. You helped fill the void after Giulia left."

"*Grazie,* Anna, for being here. There is no one else who understand as well as you." He pulled away to look at me. "I need you in my life. Can you stand just to be my best friend?"

The words hurt, but there was pleasure in the pain. I would take whatever friendship he chose to give me and be grateful for it.

Chapter 32

Thicker Than Water

I HAD just hauled my suitcase across the threshold and plopped it onto the bed when I heard pounding.

"Anna, you in there?"

GP. How did he know I was back already?

I swung open the door. I swear he was wearing the same filthy overalls from a week ago, and when he smiled, all I saw was black. "GP, what is in your mouth?"

"Chocolate," he said still chewing.

"At least it's not tobacco . . ." I stopped. *Oops*. I had forgotten about the deal we made. No nagging about our vices.

"I quit . . . how you Americans say . . . cold turkey."

My eyes must have bulged.

"I didn't think I could do either," he said proudly. "But after what *dottore* say . . ."

I looked alarmed. "What did the doctor say?"

"I have little spot on lung. Very small. He say he can remove but no more cigarette. So . . . I switch to food. Every time I want cigarette, I eat Hershey bar."

Rotten teeth are better than cancer, I almost said.

"I'm proud of you, GP. When is your surgery?"

"Two weeks. I finish *servizio* by then. I rest month of January. No good to do plumbing then. Too cold. By end of March, kitchen done."

"Perfect timing," I told him. "I'm returning at the end of March.

But are you sure you can do all this by yourself?"

"I have helper."

It was the first time I had heard of a helper. "Who is he?"

"My son."

"I didn't know you had a son. You never mentioned him before."

"You never ask me before," GP said.

He had me there.

"You busy? We go now to see work, *sì?*" GP took another bite of his Hershey bar and started toward the parking lot.

Why was it we always had to do everything on *his* time? Then I remembered I didn't have a car. I grabbed my jacket and ran to catch up.

We hauled ass up the hill to the top level of the castle. I closed my eyes when the *Ape* whizzed by the stone opening with inches to spare. When I opened them, we were in Leonia's front yard.

She had her hands out in front of her, fingers spread. "*Fermare!*"

I got out.

Leonia's face changed from glowering to beaming. "Anna, you are back! This man, here," she pointed to GP, "never know where my property start. If he run over my begonias I will murder him."

"And then I will *never* get my kitchen built, and I will have to come over for dinner every night." I held out my arms for a big hug.

Leonia gave me the once-over. "You going to tell me what happen? You look . . ."

"Like I lived a lifetime in one week?"

She nodded. "*Caffè* at my house in an hour, *sì?* You tell me everything."

"Done," I said. "But you'd better make it prosecco . . . *and* have some Kleenex handy."

My apartment looked like a halfway house for construction

workers. In the middle of the ground-floor area was a makeshift table where a jigsaw and a Sawzall were set up. There were pieces of cut wallboard and wood scattered all over the floor along with plastic cups, the remnants of a three-day-old lunch, and a fair number of Hershey bar wrappers. I even thought I saw a sleeping bag in one corner. I walked over to the staircase leading to the second floor and sniffed. Not even a whiff of sewer.

"*Servizio*, here, you see?" GP gestured to the drywall now separating the living room space from the tiny bathroom. The doorway had already been framed, and there was a hole where the toilet was going to be. On the other side of the living room, the kitchen area had been mapped out, and the tile we had bought at the stone shop was stacked against the wall. I was impressed. GP might have had some addiction issues, but he was definitely no slouch.

A warm feeling came over me as I listened to GP describe how the kitchen would look. It was all coming together, and my dream of being a part of this village was becoming a reality. I put my arms around GP in a spontaneous gesture of affection. "Thank you, my friend," I said.

GP turned bright red.

I gave the room another sweep. "I can't believe you got all this done in a week."

<hr>

"I had help. Meet Fabrizio . . . my son."

I heard the sound of footsteps coming down the stairs, and a young man stepped into the room. The first thing I noticed was the smile. The pearly whites Fabrizio flashed could not possibly have come from any part of GP's genetic makeup. In fact, there was nothing about Fabrizio's six-foot frame and chiseled features that remotely resembled his father.

"Don't get any ideas," GP warned me. "He engaged."

I laughed. "You give my energy way more credit than it deserves." I extended my hand and addressed Fabrizio. "Can I call you Fab for short?"

"Piacere, Signora." Fab kissed my hand. The eyes were even more matinee-idol worthy up close.

"He take after my wife," GP said, as if that explained everything.

I was on my second glass of prosecco and deep into my version of SJ's last-gasp adventure when my cellphone rang.

"*Fratello*," I mouthed to Leonia. "Tino, what's up?"

"Where are you?"

I was having a déjà vu moment.

"Drinking prosecco with Leonia and telling her about the trip. Let me guess, Agostino is asking for me."

"How did you know?"

"Pure speculation. Tell him to go ahead and start rolling the pasta. I'll be there in an hour."

I could hear Tino hesitating on the other end. "One thing. Can you not tell anyone about the night in Canale when . . . you know . . . the photo you took?"

I winked at Leonia. "Not to worry, bro. I promise to leave out the spooning part."

An hour and another prosecco later, I stumbled out of Leonia's front door. GP's *Ape* was still there in her front yard. I glanced at my watch. Seven o'clock p.m. As I walked by, I saw him sacked out in the driver's seat. I knocked on the window.

"GP, what are you still doing here?"

He woke with a start and opened the door for me. "Signora, you leave *domani, sì*?"

"No. Day after tomorrow."

He was looking at me as if he wanted to say something.

"GP, what is it?" Then it dawned on me. If I was leaving for three months, he would need money to finish the work. I felt horrible. He had probably been waiting for me while I was inside downing prosecco and ruining my brother's reputation as a Lothario.

I got in and whipped out my checkbook. "Let's see, how about an advance?"

I wrote out an amount and showed it to him. *"Va bene?"*

His eyes widened, and he grinned. *"Va benissimo, grazie!"* He stuffed the check in his coat pocket and started up the motor. "You need a ride home?"

I asked GP to drop me off at the villa's kitchen entrance. The minute we pulled up, Tino came out. "Finally." He smelled my breath. "I guess you and Leonia had quite a talk."

I smiled sweetly. "We did." I kept walking. Inside, Agostino was putting the final touches on what looked like a very fine *omelette ai tartufi.*

"We wait dinner for you," he said, without looking up.

I felt bad. Two hungry boys waiting while I dished the dirt about our trip. They were both probably dying to know what I said to Leonia. *Well, let them wonder.*

"I'm starved," I said, finding a nice red Chianti and heading for the table.

Tino poured while Agostino passed the truffle omelet.

"I have been discussing Marina's letters with Tino," Agostino began. "He thinks we should make a trip to the *comune* tomorrow and look at birth records of my family. There should be also a death certificate for my mother. Maybe there is something about my brother too."

"I think it's a good idea," I said. "How do you know they will let you look at these records? In the States, it's not that easy."

"I have a good friend who works in the *comune.* I call her today, and she say if we are there first thing when they open, she will help us look."

"Must be a *really* good friend," I muttered.

Agostino smiled. "She was."

Chapter 33

Family Secrets

AT 9:00 A.M., Agostino, Tino and I were standing in the foyer of the *comune*. After a few minutes, we heard the click of stiletto heels coming down the stairs, and a woman appeared.

"Nice to see you again, Agostino." Ariana Frangipani's voice was a throaty whisper.

"As always, Ariana, you are looking well." Agostino's smile was tight.

There was no doubt in my mind. Those two had been *very* good friends.

Agostino quickly introduced Tino and me as his American guests. I noticed he did not mention our recently discovered family connection.

Ariana's eyes swept over me. Even though Agostino had in no way alluded to my being a romantic interest, I felt her sizing me up as competition. I sized her up right back.

She had one of those well-developed figures that had inspired countless artists in the Renaissance. Botticelli's Venus came instantly to mind. Deep, expressive eyes, full lips, and a tight skirt suggesting long, tapered legs and a tiny waist. Her magenta V-neck sweater was cut low enough to reveal generous cleavage.

With a brief nod to me, she extended a sleek, manicured hand to Tino. "Happy to meet you," she said.

"Piacere. Your English is very good," Tino stammered. It looked like he was having trouble keeping his eyes on her face.

"Tank you. I study in Rome." By the way she lifted her chin, I could tell how proud she was.

Agostino cleared his throat. "I appreciate your letting us have a look, Ariana. If I can ever return the favor . . ."

Ariana held his gaze. "I will let you know. Shall we go up?"

As she started up the stairs leading to the offices, both men got in line right behind her.

The room where the official records were kept was at the back of the building. When Ariana opened the door, the layers of dust and the smell of musty paper made it obvious that the room's usefulness had been eclipsed by modern technology. She walked us over to an entire wall of shelves containing bound volumes of handwritten entries. Each volume represented a year of records.

"This is where birth, marriage, and death records for people of *comune* were kept before 1995. After that, files begin to be transferred to hard drive."

I pulled out the first volume and looked at the date. "It only goes back to 1880?"

"A fire destroyed everything before then," Ariana explained. "Let us look for your mother's dates, Agostino. What year did she pass?"

Agostino extracted two envelopes from his jacket pocket and opened one. "I brought these to verify. In 1962, my parents marry. Let us start there and see what we find."

Ariana took out two volumes, one marked 1962, and the other, 1963. Tino and I began poring over the first one. Monthly entries listing dates of births, marriages, and deaths of Scheggino residents were written line by line in a precise, flowing script down the page. When we got to March, we found Cecilia's name.

Ricordo di Matrimonio tra il signore Agosto Urbino e la signora Cecilia Salvatore. 27 Marzo, 1962.

"Good. Their marriage record," Agostino said. "My birthday is April 14,1963. That is the day she die. He opened the second book and turned the pages. *"Ecco!* I find it! It is in Latin."

"Liber Mortuorum. Cecilia Urbino. 14 Aprile, 1963."

"Why is it in Latin?" I asked.

"All deaths were recorded this way by Catholic Church," Agostino said. He read the next line: *"Angelo Urbino. Nato Morto 14 Aprile, 1963. Antequam Nascantur Morientium."* Agostino looked up. "You understand what *"nato morto"* mean, *sì?"*

"It means stillborn," I said softly. "It looks like they named the dead baby Angelo."

"Angelo, my brother," Agostino sighed and began to close the book.

"Wait!" Tino cried, flipping the book back open and putting his finger on the next line.

"Here is another birth entry: *'Agosto Urbino. 14 Aprile, 1963.'* There are some words blocked out here." Tino turned the book and lifted the page so it shone through the light of the window. "An old trick I learned intercepting notes in high school. A lost art nowadays with the advent of cellphones. It looks like it says, *'Un giorno di vita.'"*

"One day of life?" Agostino looked at where Tino's finger was and shook his head in confusion.

"It say Agosto . . . that is my birth name. . . but I did not die, and why is it blocked out? Is this a mistake?"

Ariana quickly looked through the rest of the page and the next one. "There is no record of another Urbino child born that year."

"It could be someone tampered with the entry," I suggested.

"Impossibile," Ariana said, sounding offended. "No one here would do a thing like that."

I thought it best not to question her statement. I turned to Agostino. "Who else would know what this means? Is there someone still alive who remembers?"

"*Nonna* Gabriella, Marina's sister. She would know."

Tino and I thanked Ariana and walked down the stairs to the entrance of the *comune*. I heard Agostino and Ariana upstairs talking in Italian. "What is this all about? Do you think you are adopted?" I heard her say.

"When I know for sure I will tell you," he replied.

"It sounds like something your family would pull ... falsifying records. Watch out, Agostino. Some stones are better left unturned."

Chapter 34

Gabriella's Secret

AGOSTINO wanted to go right away to his grandmother's villa. The three of us piled into the Maserati, but before he started the motor, Tino turned to face us.

"Look, I have not met this lady yet. I am a stranger to her. This is a very touchy family matter, perhaps an emotional one. I feel it is inappropriate for me to be there."

"Maybe I shouldn't go either," I chimed in. "She has only met me once with Mom. When she heard Spirito Urbino was our relative, we were escorted out. Rather unceremoniously, I might add."

"No." Agostino's voice was firm. "Anna, I need you there as a witness to what is said. Please."

He looked so frantic and confused, my heart went out to him. "Ok. I will go with you but don't be surprised if one of her guards throws me out."

"Aren't you going to call her and tell her you're coming?" Tino asked.

"It is better if we catch her . . . how you say . . . ?"

"Off her guard?" Tino suggested.

"*Sì,* off her guards."

"I just hope she keeps her guards off *me,*" I said.

Tino dropped us off in front of Gabriella's iron gates. Agostino told me that since my last visit with Mom, she had installed an electric gate system with an intercom that did away with extra "personnel." *That doesn't mean they aren't somewhere else on the property*, I thought. As if to confirm my suspicions, I peered through the bars at an older gentleman staked out by the front door. He looked vaguely familiar, probably the same heat-packing guy Mom and I had seen five years ago.

"Agostino," I asked, "are we going to get the old lady riled up with all this?"

"Only if there is something she don't want me to know."

"Have you considered that she may not remember anything? She's, what, ninety-eight?"

"Ninety-nine last November. And yes, I consider it but there is only one way to find out. This is my life. I deserve to know." He took my hands in his. "You are with me, *sì?*"

I squeezed his fingers and nodded. I didn't know whether he was holding on for support or friendship . . . or something more . . . all I knew was that his touch felt as good as ever. When he pressed the intercom and the gates opened, I had the creepy feeling *Nonna* Gabriella's entourage was watching.

"Agostino, we didn't expect you," the housekeeper said in a thick Schegginese dialect and waving us in. "Signora Gabby was having *colazione* when I looked in on her a few minutes ago. She uses her wheelchair now, but she still moves quicker than I do."

When we entered the breakfast room, Gabriella's chair was turned away from the table, toward a window overlooking a small kitchen garden. Her eyes were closed, her mouth was open, and she was snoring like a Sawzall.

Agostino walked over and touched her arm. *"Nonna?"*

Gabby's eyes flew open. It took her a minute, and then she reached out her ring-encrusted fingers. "Agostino, bambino! You are finally paying me a visit!" She peered around him to look at me. "You bring a young lady with you?"

"You remember Anna Wilson. She came here with her Mama a few years ago."

Gabby's eyes narrowed. "I remember her, all right. She's that relative of Spirito's."

Agostino glanced at me and raised an eyebrow. He was testing her. If she hadn't recognized me, we were going to have a problem. So far, so good.

Agostino waited. Sometimes it took a while for old people to find their manners. "May we sit down?" he finally asked.

Gabriella grabbed a bell on the table and rang it until the housekeeper reappeared. *"Caffè per tutti!"* she called out.

After the coffee had been poured and half a homemade crostata eaten, Agostino faced his grandmother.

"What happened the night my mother died?"

Ouch. He wasn't kidding about catching her off guard. Gabriella flinched as if registering the shock of such a blatant question, but her face remained as impassive as stone.

"Why do you ask this? You have heard the story many times." Gabriella waived her hand dismissively. I got the feeling she was buying time.

"I have some new information," Agostino said calmly.

Gabriella pointed a gnarled finger at me. "This one, here, did she tell you about the 'new' information? Those people cannot be trusted."

Uh-oh, I thought. *Here it comes.*

"*Those people*," Agostino fired back, "happen to be related to this family."

The old lady held her ground. "No matter what SJ told you, I suspect he is not our kin."

"I'm not talking about SJ."

Gabriella leaned forward in her chair. "What exactly *are* you talking about?"

Agostino withdrew two envelopes from his pocket and tossed them on the table. "Letters addressed to Giulia from her mother."

With a trembling hand, Gabriella picked up one of the envelopes and examined the handwriting. "You saw Giulia? Where is she?"

"SJ and I went to Turin to find her. We were too late—she died two years ago."

"Then who gave you these letters?" Gabby eyed us both.

"Giulia's daughter." Agostino let the words sink in. "Mari was conceived the night her mother left Villa Urbino. She and her mother have lived their whole lives in Turin."

Gabriella took the news bravely. "Giulia had a daughter," she said half to herself. "My sister knew?"

Agostino shrugged his shoulders. "I am guessing. I couldn't find any of the letters Giulia sent her mother. Are they hidden somewhere at Villa Urbino?"

The old lady shook her head. "I never saw them. I had no idea they corresponded. Why did Giulia never come back?"

"You know why," Agostino said. "The shame of her actions . . . and the consequences . . . kept her from returning home. She never knew SJ's true identity."

The old woman put a hand to her mouth. "SJ was Spirito's boy, wasn't he?" She glanced at me accusingly. "If we had known, things might have been different."

Agostino touched his grandmother's arm. "Giulia chose her life; no one is to blame. Do not grieve for her."

"I grieve for my sister, then. All those years, Marina did not have her daughter with her."

"They stayed together through these letters. Over a hundred in all, from 1949 to the year she died. So, you see, in a way, they were never completely separated."

Agostino lifted Gabriella's chin and looked her in the eye. "It is time to stop the secrecy and the lies. Before you try to tell any more, I want you to know I took a little trip to the *comune* this morning to look at the official birth and death records of our family. It is time to tell the truth about what happened the night my mother died."

As if the burden of respectability had suddenly become too heavy to bear, the old lady's stone-like face crumpled. Her chin sank to her chest, and tears formed in the creases around her eyes. The fight was gone. What remained was the vulnerability of a matriarch who realized she had outlived all the people she had wanted to protect.

"The pains began two weeks before your mother's due date. She was bleeding, and Marina and I decided she should go to hospital. Your father was already crazy with worry. He was never a strong man . . . too sensitive . . . and so much in love with his wife. We told him as little as possible even when—" Gabriella paused to wipe away a tear. "Even when Cecilia started to get weaker. After eight hours of labor, the first baby came out dead. She kept pushing, and another one came. The doctors felt a pulse and rushed him to intensive care. Your mother died in Marina's arms an hour later. When they told your papa, he went out of his mind, raving in the waiting room that he wanted to die too. That was when Dr. Sabatini stepped in to help."

"Alessandro Sabatini? Our in-law?" I blurted out.

Gabriella nodded. "He was in the hospital that night. He arranged for a servant to take my son home, sedate him, and make sure he did not try to hurt himself. Marina and I stayed, waiting for news of the little one that was still alive. We prayed for the one thing that would save my son's life . . . but God is sometimes cruel. The baby died the next day."

Agostino looked puzzled. "Where do I fit in?"

"Dr. Sabatini had an idea. It was crazy, but just crazy enough to work. One of his patients had given birth that same night, an unwed mother who was planning to give her baby up for adoption. Dr. Sabatini told her about our family and asked if we might adopt the baby. He assured the mother he would have the best of everything and be well cared for. She agreed. A contract was drawn up and signed, but the woman insisted there be no money exchanged. Pending approval, and with Dr. Sabatini overseeing the details, we had no doubt the baby would be ours. We told your papa only that the second baby was going to live. In those first few days after Cecilia died, the thought of that child coming home was the only thing that kept him alive."

Agostino sat back, dazed, trying to take it all in.

"Why is there no grave for the first child in the cemetery?" I asked Gabriella.

"Dr. Sabatini arranged for the three bodies, and a coffin, to be brought to my home. It was unorthodox, to be sure, but with the doctor's signature, the hospital released them into his care. Marina and I prepared them for burial, laid Cecilia in the coffin, put her two babies with her, and sealed it up. We wanted no one, especially your papa, to ever see both dead children."

Gabriella's hands reached for Agostino, her face full of emotion. "The day of Cecilia's funeral, we walked back from the cemetery to find you sleeping peacefully in a servant's arms. The miracle baby that not only saved your papa's life but Marina's as well. From that day on, she became your second mother."

"Did you ever tell anyone from Claudio's side of the family?" Agostino asked.

"Never. No one knows."

"Why?"

Gabriella sat up in her chair, her eyes focused on her grandson. "Because if my uncle and his family knew the truth, they might have treated you differently. Not like one of their own. I couldn't bear that."

The housekeeper put her hand on Agostino's shoulder. "I think the signora has had enough excitement for one day," she said gently. "She needs to rest now."

Gabriella's eyes closed, and it looked as if she was dozing off.

Agostino leaned over and placed a kiss on top of the grizzled head. *"Grazie, Nonna,* for taking such good care of me."

The old lady opened one eye. "You're welcome," she said.

The gates closed behind us ,and we started walking up the old Roman road to Villa Urbino.

"Anna?"

"Yes, Agostino?"

"I know this is your last night, and I planned to do something special for you and Tino. But with all that happen . . ."

"I looked up at him. "It's okay. I understand. I'm just glad you asked me to share this with you. How do you feel about it?"

"I need time to think. I do not blame my family for keeping this from me . . . as long as my father was alive, they could not tell me. I just wonder, now, who my mother is. Is she someone we know in the village? It is even possible she may have watched me grow up." He walked on a bit in silence. "And I have many confusing thoughts about us."

I knew what he meant.

We had reached the entrance to Villa Urbino. One side of the gate was still open from this morning. In our haste, we had forgotten to close it. I ran my hand along the wrought-iron letters A and U engraved on the front.

"I'm going to miss this place," I said.

Agostino gave me a tender look and reached out his hand. I entwined my fingers through his, and we turned and walked down the long dirt road toward the villa.

The parking lot was empty, and all was quiet when we got to my door. "Tino must be at SJ's, getting fed," I said.

"There are leftovers, bread, cheese, in the pantry if you . . ." Agostino said.

"It's okay. I'm not really hungry, and I still have to pack."

It felt awkward, neither one of us knowing how to say goodbye. He brushed the back of his hand against my cheek for a second and looked at me, his eyes full of questions. I stared back, equally confused. I turned to open the door, and when I looked back, he was gone.

Chapter 35

Bon Voyage

I HAD JUST wiped off the last trace of makeup and slipped into my pink flannel pajamas when I heard a knock on the door.

"Tino?"

"No. It's Agostino."

I caught sight of my reflection in the mirror. *It figures. Just when I look my worst.* I opened the door.

Standing a little to one side was a bright turquoise blue bicycle. The chrome handle bars glistened, and there were two new tires. Across the bike chain cover someone had painted the name *Anna* in pink letters.

Agostino kicked the stand into place and stepped back. "I've been waiting for the right time to give this to you," he said.

My eyes lit up. "I've never seen anything so beautiful. This is for me?"

"You said you wanted something to ride around the village."

"But I leave tomorrow."

"It will be waiting for you when you get back," he said softly.

I looked into his hopeful face and opened my arms.

It felt so good to hold him again, I didn't want to let go.

"Can I come in?" he whispered into my hair.

I stepped back. He closed the door and faced me. "Anna, I am sorry the way I behave . . ."

I led him to the bed, and we sat down. "You've had a lot going on these last few days."

Agostino took my hands. "Remember that night in Bologna when I asked you to be my best friend?"

"The night you read Marina's letters?"

"Yes. I've been thinking many times since then what I want. I know now that I want more . . . I want you as a friend . . . and a lover."

I took my hands away. "It's easy to say that now. Now that you know we are no relation to each other. Did it just magically come back . . . those feelings?"

Agostino sighed. "I was afraid I was making the same mistake as my family . . . you know how I feel about mixing the blood . . ."

"Maybe there is more to it than that . . . you know . . . if you get too close to the fire, you might get burned. I know something about that. I always chose people I knew couldn't challenge that feeling . . . people who were afraid of committing too."

Agostino's eyes narrowed. "So you think I use this as an excuse . . ."

"Sex is easy. Opening your heart to the possibility of love is the hard part. If we try to make a go of this, how do we know something else won't come between us?"

Agostino took a deep breath. "We don't. There are no guarantees."

"Can you live with that?"

He stood, lifted me to my feet, and wrapped his arms around me. "I have to because I can't lose you again. Are you willing to take that chance too?"

"I looked into his eyes. "I'm not sure. I have my doubts."

He traced his finger along my lips. "We take it one day at a time and see how it goes, *va bene*?"

"*Va bene*," I said.

He bent his head, his lips close to mine. "For the first time in my life, my heart is wide open," he whispered.

I heard the ringing of a cellphone.

"Don't answer it," I murmured.

"Not a chance."

It rang again.

I pulled away. "It could be Tino, lost somewhere on the old Roman road." I retrieved Agostino's phone from his back pocket. "Yep. You'd better get it."

"Our relationship is cursed," Agostino muttered, grabbing the phone. "This better be good."

Paradiso Vinto was all lit up when Agostino and I got there. Crossing the foyer, I saw SJ seated on the sofa in the great room. On his right were GP, Fabrizio, and a very attractive older woman. GP stood up and gestured to her as we walked toward them. "My wife, Beatrice," he said.

I shook her hand. "So good to finally meet you." I looked from GP to Beatrice to Fabrizio. GP was right. Fabrizio took after his mother.

I heard voices and laughter from the kitchen. Agostino lifted his head and sniffed the air. "Do I smell pizza?"

"You do!" Tino came striding toward us with two glasses of wine in his hands. "Pizza Margherita, to be exact. Flavia is working some culinary magic." He handed each of us a glass, put his arm around Agostino, and looked at GP's family. "Come and watch the demonstration."

As the group walked away, SJ patted the empty seat next to him. I sat down and held his hands. I was surprised at how cold they were.

"*Zio,* you didn't need to go to all this trouble. You should be recuperating from the trip. You must be exhausted."

SJ laughed. "Exhausted is the right word . . . but happy too. This sendoff is to thank you and Tino for changing my life. Before you came, I was just a lonely old man with a long list of regrets. Now look at me . . . surrounded by friends."

I smiled. "It was a life-changing experience for all of us."

SJ leaned in and whispered. "Tell me, did I interrupt anything between you and Agostino?"

I patted his hand. "Nothing that can't wait until later."

"You hang on to that one." He nodded in the direction of the kitchen. "I wouldn't be surprised if he was in love with you."

"How can you tell?" I asked.

"I've been there. I know that look."

"*Il fulmine?*" I said.

SJ nodded. "I hope you feel it too."

I let out a shaky sigh. "*Zio,* it's not that simple. I know what my heart feels, but there are other things to consider. How will this relationship work? We live three thousand miles apart. We lead different lives."

"Do you love him?" SJ asked me.

"I have strong feelings for him."

"That's not what I asked you. I asked you if you were in love with him."

"I am afraid of that answer," I said. "To say that would make me vulnerable. That is when the pain begins. What if he has a change of heart again? What if he stops loving me . . ." My voice trailed off.

"This doesn't sound like the woman who told me not to hold back," SJ said.

"I'm the classic example of someone who tells everyone else how to live but can't do it herself." I felt the tears beginning.

"How will you know if you don't try . . . if you don't risk?" SJ said gently. "Love is an expression of being alive. There can never be a bad version of that. You were the one who told me risking it all is the point. Anything less is just cheating yourself."

I searched his face. "You weren't afraid. How does it feel?"

"To have left nothing undone?" SJ smiled. "It feels wonderful. I highly recommend it. You will be surprised at what can be worked out when two people care enough to try. Just promise me you won't let fear hold you back. It is the enemy of a full and meaningful life."

"I promise."

SJ reached out and wiped away my tears. "Love is always worth risking. I know that now."

"Thank you, *Zio*. I needed to hear this."

"Good. That is what uncles are for. To give advice. Now I have something to tell *you*. Flavia and I have been talking about a project. We want to open up Paradiso Vinto to guests, a *casa de vacanze* like Agostino's. There are five bedrooms here. All I need is one."

"*Zio,* are you sure?" I asked. "You will lose all your privacy."

"SJ laughed. "It's about time. I've been alone too long." He patted my hand. "Now, go join the others. Flavia's pizza-making is not to be missed."

I got up and walked to the dual-sided fireplace where everyone was gathered. Leonia and Flavia hovered over a large iron pan resting on a rack inside the flames. On it was a puffy round of dough topped with a thin layer of red sauce and mozzarella cheese.

"*Perfetto*," Flavia said with satisfaction as she pulled out the pan and slid the pizza onto a wooden board. "*Manga quando e caldo,*" she told Tino.

Tino gathered a slice in his hands. "Finally. I've been waiting two weeks for this."

GP and Fabrizio reached for slices as Leonia slapped another round onto the iron pan and shoved it into the fire.

"Save a slice for SJ," I called out looking past the fireplace to the figure on the sofa.

SJ's eyes were closed, and there was a peaceful expression on his face. I had seen that look before . . .

My glass of wine slipped from my hands and crashed to the floor as I sprinted toward the living room. I knelt beside SJ, feeling for a pulse. In the background, as if they were a million miles away, Agostino called for the ambulance in Spoleto and Flavia sobbed in Tino's arms.

Gently, I soothed SJ's cool brow and cradled his head on my shoulder. "Well played, *Zio,*" I whispered, my tears falling unchecked. "I know you said 'no regrets.' but allow me this one. I wish we could have had more time together."

As the fire blazed in the hearth, the group gathered around us, their hands reaching for each other, their heads bent in silent grief. Beyond the immense burden of our loss was the certainty that SJ was already on his way to the next great adventure and that when he got there, someone would be waiting for him.

PART IV

Italy 2016

Chapter 36

Reunions

I GRABBED the keys from the Europcar rental agent before he could ask who was driving. "Being the navigator is all well and good, but If I have to stay awake, I might as well drive," I said. "Besides, I made the reservation."

Tino steamed and my sister Terry broke out in a cold sweat.

I looked at both of them. "I have driven in Italy before, in case you were wondering. I drove Mom from Rome to Umbria and back, and no one got hurt."

"A miracle," Tino and Terry said at the same time.

We walked to the Europcar counter of the airport parking garage.

An agent pointed to the far end where the more prestigious cars were parked. "Fiat Abarth, nice car." The agent winked at me.

"Oh cool." Tino's eyes lit up. "Way classier than the Panda."

Before he got any ideas, I slipped into the driver's seat. "Not exactly a GranCabrio, but it will do. How is the old girl anyway?"

"Beautiful as ever."

I turned to my sister. "Did you know that, three months ago, Tino actually *bought* the car we rented on our last trip . . . and had it shipped to the States?"

Terry rolled her eyes. "No, but I don't doubt it. Did he form an emotional attachment, by any chance?"

"You bet," Tino said. "We went all the way to Turin and back with her. We shared some pretty amazing moments, and she never let me down. I had to own her."

"Spoken like a true romantic," I said. "Your relationship reminds me of a certain baby blue *Ape* and a plumber I know."

I roared out of the airport parking garage and downshifted into fifth gear as we hit the Autostrada A1. "Everyone relax! In less than three hours, we will be at the apartment in Scheggino."

Terry spread out in the back seat and closed her eyes. "If we're going to crash, I hope it will be quick and fatal and I don't need to see it coming. "

I snuck a glance at my sister in the rearview mirror as I drove. I still couldn't believe she was here. Ever since Mom died, we had been exploring a new connection and getting away from the *which-sibling-has-it-more-together* game we'd been playing most of our lives. Priorities were changing, and ideas we had clung to in our power years meant something different now. Contentment with oneself and acceptance of others' imperfections now defined success. If my adventure to Turin had taught me anything, it was that mistakes and grievances from the past have no place in the future. When Terry had suggested coming out to meet our relatives, I hoped it signaled a desire to take another step toward a relationship we could both be proud of.

Oops! Almost missed that quick turnoff at the Autogrill. I tried to keep my mind focused on the familiar landmarks: the Sette Bagni straightaway, the big tunnel with the trattoria next to it, and the exit right before the turnoff to Orte where Tino had gotten lost.

After a while, like so many times in the last three months, my mind drifted to the irreplaceable treasure we lost. SJ would not be waiting for us when we arrived in Scheggino. I missed him, but I knew he had left this world feeling fulfilled. He had risked the pain and uncertainty of the unknown and had been rewarded. His daughter was a confirmation of the love he had shared so many years ago with Giulia, the girl with the Mona Lisa smile.

My mind drifted again, this time to a certain pair of blue-gray eyes and an unbuttoned shirt. I couldn't help wondering what it would be like when I saw Agostino again. One thing was clear. With different cultures and three thousand miles separating us, an effort on both sides would have to be made to bridge the gap. On one of our many long-distance conversations, he had suggested coming to San Diego for a month in September. It was a good start. We both knew there was no guarantee that our relationship would grow into something serious, but if we were willing to take a chance on finding happiness, the reward could be life-changing.

That was what the game was all about.

Right after the Orte turnoff, I looked for the toll booth lane with the white sign of coins and a man. Cash and a live person . . . always the safest lane for tourists. I handed over the euros to the nameless face, and the bar in front of me lifted.

"Forty-five minutes and we are in Scheggino," I called out. Tino—who had finally accepted that his cries of "Did you see that car?" or "Maybe you should stay in the slow lane" were having no effect on my driving skills—was slumped back in his seat in a glassy-eyed state of denial.

Terry mumbled something that sounded like "Wake me when we get there."

We rolled into the Piazza Pietro Urbino around noon. The parking lot was a beehive of activity: Wooden booths with canopies lined the edges of the piazza, and men unloaded equipment and supplies from trucks. Down by the river, an enormous iron saucer rested on the grass next to the kayak shack.

"I almost forgot," I said. "The truffle festival is tomorrow! There will be singers and music. I pointed to a temporary, raised stage at the far end of the piazza. "And did you see the waffle iron? That's where the truffle omelet will be made."

"You told us five times already," Tino reminded me. "That's why we're here."

"Hold on," Terry said as we got out of the car. "I'm here for more than a giant omelet. I want to see the town where my grandfather was born. When you told me about your adventure to Turin, it got me thinking about my roots . . ."

Tino rolled his eyes. "Here we go again."

"Yeah, look where it got *me*," I said. "Owning property halfway around the world."

Terry looked at me. "Any regrets?"

I was thinking back to a day, almost six years ago, when Mom and I had first sat on a bench in the piazza and heard an amazing story about my grandfather and a woman named Agatha.

"Not a single one," I answered.

The sound of staccato heels rang out across the piazza. Tino's antenna was already tuned.

"The sex goddess is headed this way," I muttered.

"*The what*?" Terry sounded like she hadn't heard right.

"Sex goddess. The unofficial title all the men in this town have given the woman walking toward us," I said.

"The mayor's name is Pamela," Tino said.

⌒

"*That's* the Mayor of Scheggino? Terry asked.

"Yep," Tino answered.

"Anna, *Come stai*? You are back!" Pamela Urbino smiled and kissed me on both cheeks.

I beamed. It's not every day one gets kissed by the mayor of your village, male *or* female. I brought Terry forward. "This is my sister, Terry . . . uh . . . *Teresa*. She is here to see the apartment now that it is finished."

"Benvenuti. It is good you have come in time for the festival. You will not be disappointed." She turned to Tino and gave him a special smile. "It is good to see you again, too."

Tino blushed, shoved his hands into his pockets, and dug his toe into the ground like a schoolboy.

"I need a strong man to help with the turning of the omelet tomorrow. Can I count on you?" I was sure I saw her bat her lashes once or twice.

Tino puffed out his chest and grinned. *"Certo.* I would be honored."

"We start at noon. Bring gloves, and don't dress up. Clean-up duty after everyone has eaten. *Va bene?"*

"Tino's smile faded a notch. *"Va bene."*

Pamela waved her freshly manicured hand and was off, heels clicking and hips swaying.

I looked at my siblings. "And *that's* why she's the mayor of this town."

My cellphone rang. When I looked at the name, my heart skipped a beat.

"Ciao, Agostino!"

The voice on the other end sounded cranky. "Flavia and I have been waiting for your call all morning. Mari's train got in two hours ago. She is here for the festival."

"Mari? Great! Can you bring her and Flavia to the apartment tonight? We will have a welcoming party."

"At your service, *Madame.* Anything else?"

" A fold-out table and some chairs."

I heard an exasperated sigh.

"Oh, and can you make something good to eat? For a dozen people?"

"A dozen? How many is that?"

My thoughts flashed back to Villa Urbino and a certain

conversation about an *idraulico.* "It means twelve. You had better memorize that word. You may need to use it in the future . . . in *my* country."

There was a long, thoughtful pause and a "I'll take care of it" before he hung up.

"Mari is here?" Tino asked.

"She came in on the train this morning." I turned to Terry. "SJ's daughter has come to visit. You will meet her tonight."

Tino looked worried. "We're having a party, and you don't even know if the place is finished?"

"It will be finished," I assured him. "GP promised."

We crossed the bridge toward the castle and started climbing. Terry was a runner, too, so she had no trouble negotiating the three levels of stairs leading up to the apartment. Tino was taking his time.

"This place needs an elevator," he said between gasps.

The heavy wooden door with the Cardinal Graziani crest over the top was open. Seeing the charming wrought-iron gate, the garden, and the two-story residence overlooking the valley, Terry exclaimed, "This is gorgeous! I was expecting a shack."

"Uh . . . my place is next door." I pointed to the sliver of stone that shared the same wall.

Terry quickly tried to make amends. "How quaint."

The word "quaint" didn't sound as good as "gorgeous," but it was a damn sight better than "shack," I decided. I held my breath and turned the key.

The door swung open, and the first thing I saw were pristine white walls and a little door marked *"Servizio"* at the far end of the great room. To my right, the kitchen, with its rosy tile veneers and rustic, open shelves, looked like it had been there forever. The travertine surrounding the fireplace was polished, and the hearth was stocked with wood. Except for an absence of furniture, it all looked beautiful.

Terry pointed to the door marked *"Servizio."* "May I use it?"

"Certainly." I smiled broadly. If GP had been here, I would have hugged him, filthy overalls and all.

"Anna, sei arrivata!" Leonia stood in the doorway. "Look who I found on the way here." She pointed to a panting Tino.

When Terry came out of the *servizio*, I introduced her to Leonia. "This lady and her papa were the first friends Mom and I made when we came here."

"Piacere," Terry said hesitantly and held out her hand.

Leonia reached over and kissed her on both cheeks. "With those brown eyes and olive skin, you look more Italian than your sister."

Terry beamed.

My phone rang. Agostino again. "How does *osso buco* sound? It has been roasting in the oven all day. I have been saving my best calf for three months, especially for you."

I made a face. "You really didn't have to . . . ."

"And *tagliatelle con tartufo?* Flavia and Mari can make it."

"Truffles?" My eyes lit up. "Perfetto. And don't forget the grappa . . . and glasses."

I pulled Leonia off to one side. "The beds have all arrived, right?"

"Yesterday, GP and Fabrizio bring them. I made them up this morning."

"You are a treasure. I need to find you a good man and bring him over from the US. He will be all over you." I told her.

"I already meet someone. May I bring him tonight?" Leonia's eyes twinkled.

"Of course! I can't wait to meet him."

We scrounged around for as many chairs as we could find, including some from Leonia's house. "Agostino is bringing a fold out table but there are not enough chairs. Maybe the neighbors? Do you know them?"

"*Sì!* They are from Rome. This is their vacation home. I will ask but then I must invite them."

"By all means! The more the merrier!"

Roberto and Teresa turned out to be excellent partiers who were not stingy with their wine and or their dining room chairs.

Like a fairy godfather, GP showed up with a couple of surprise housewarming gifts. He parked his *Ape* in Leonia's front yard and he and Fabrizio carried a beautiful antique dining room table down to the apartment. Beatrice followed behind with a pan of homemade ravioli and several loaves of bread to slice up for crostini.

I pulled GP aside. "How was the surgery?"

"It go well. No more cigarette, no more chew tobacco. I have only one vice . . . well maybe two . . . now."

"Chocolate?" I asked.

He pulled out a small packet, unwrapped a tiny cube and popped it into his mouth. "Chewing gum," he said. "Sugarless."

A few tears escaped and rolled down my face as I hugged all three of them. With the new table, and borrowed chairs, we had room for everyone. I just hoped there would be enough food.

"Agostino is bringing the *osso buco,*" I told everyone. " He said he's been saving his best calf . . ."

Tino held up a hand. "I don't want to hear about it—I just want to eat it."

"I think we need salad," Leonia said, rushing off to her apartment to find some ingredients.

The wooden door to the foyer swung open, and Agostino strode through the courtyard holding a lumpy burlap bag, his right bicep rock hard with the weight of it.

"My man, he come through today." Agostino turned the bag

upside down and let the little black balls roll out onto the table.

"Ahhh ... truffles!" Everyone sniffed the air and clapped their hands.

A moment later, Mari appeared with a package in her hand. Agostino gently brought her forward. "This is my cousin from Turin. She is SJ's daughter."

Mari smiled as she handed me a box. "Sachertorte," she said.

Agostino turned to the door. "Where's Flavia? She came with us."

"I is here!" A no-nonsense voice called out from behind the door. A tiny woman pushed it open and stood there, panting. "This place need an elevator. I just install one at Paradiso Vinto. I heard the American tourists do not like to exercise."

Agostino laughed and put his arm around her. "Flavia has some good news. She will be opening Paradiso Vinto to guests in June. We are joining forces!"

Everyone rushed forward to congratulate her. She thanked each person personally and invited them to her grand opening in late May. *"Pizza al forno,"* she promised.

"Where's the *osso buco?* And the grappa?" I asked Agostino. "We have people to feed tonight."

"Hold your horses," he said to me, his eyes twinkling. "The food is in my truck, three floors down. Someone want to give me a hand?"

"I will," Tino yelled. They took off down the stairs, with Fabrizio right behind them.

"We heard there was a party!" A little gnome-like man was standing in the doorway smiling broadly. Next to him was an auburn-haired beauty with a bottle of red wine in her hands.

"Giorgio and Renata!" I cried, opening my arms for a big hug. "Come in, come in. Just pull up a rock if you can't find a chair. Mari! I have more relatives for you to meet!"

"Ensalata mista." Leonia announced. She had returned with a big bowl of greens and a shy looking man in his fifties. "This is Carlo."

I smiled, extending my hand. "Now I can see why Leonia has been keeping you a secret. She wants you all to herself."

Carlo blushed to the roots of his snow-white hair and returned the handshake.

The three boys were back, their arms full of food and drink.

"Grappa, anyone?" Agostino set down the groceries, extracted three bottles, and started pouring. Luckily, he had remembered to bring glasses.

It was the Italian way—everyone pitching in to make a beautiful moment come together. I felt blessed to have made such good friends, and even though I had just moved in, their warmth and generosity made me feel like I had lived there all my life. Thirty minutes later, everyone sat down to dinner.

Tino tapped a spoon against his glass for silence.

"Thank you all for being here. We are celebrating a milestone in Anna's life. As of today, her dream of owning a place in Italy has come true. She is officially a Schegginese!"

"To dreams!" Terry called out. "May we never stop having them!"

Everyone raised a glass. "Here, here… *Saluti… in bocca al lupo. .*." The cheers rang out in a cacophony of languages around the table. I even heard a familiar voice say, "Down the hatch!"

After the meal, Tino tapped his spoon again.

"I want to tell you about a game our dear uncle SJ taught me to play… It changed his life, and it is changing mine. We call it "The Deathbed Game." A strange title, I know, but an appropriate one." Tino paused and scanned the faces at the table.

"Who wants to think about the end of your life? You keep it at a distance, hoping it will stay there, but what if, instead of putting it off, you pictured yourself lying there, waiting for death to come? What would be going through your mind? The *what-ifs*, the things unsaid, the time wasted *not* doing the things you really wanted to do? So, my friends, I challenge you to ask yourselves this question: 'How will the rest of my life change if I start thinking about the end of it now?' You will be surprised at how much that thought can motivate you. Dreams are great, but they are just dreams if you never make them a reality . . ."

Agostino was mouthing some words to me across the table, but I couldn't make them out.

"Your game sounds a lot like the bucket list," Terry said.

I was watching Agostino's lips. B-a-c-h-e-l-o-r something.

"It's like the bucket list, but different," Tino was explaining. "You aren't just ticking off one event after another on a list. This is a game you can play anytime . . . every second if you wish."

Agostino pulled back his chair at the same time I did, and we walked toward the door and out into the courtyard toward Cardinal Graziani's wooden gate. The sounds coming from the house were fainter now.

"The more you play the game, the more you are living the life you truly want to live . . ."

We climbed down the stairs and walked along the river toward the old piazza. The moon shone on fields of farrow waving like silver feathers under the darkening sky.

Agostino slipped his hand into mine. "Anna?"

"Yes, Agostino?"

"I have made a decision to try and find my real mother. What do you think?"

"I think it sounds like another great adventure."

"One I hope you will share with me." Agostino stopped and put his arms around me. "I know we have a lot to figure out . . ."

I put a finger to his lips. "SJ told me anything can be worked out if two people care enough to try." I lifted my chin and closed my eyes.

"A kiss would feel very good right about now."

He took my face in his hands. "When a man is in love, he kisses differently. May I show you the proper technique?"

I opened my eyes. "Are you saying you are in love with me?"

"Ever since the day you walked in and told me you broke the furnace. Then, I knew for sure when I saw those ridiculous Mickey Mouse pajamas."

"And I knew when you brought me the bicycle all fixed up. All those hours you worked on it you were thinking about me. I knew your feelings were real."

Agostino looked at me tenderly. "It's been waiting for you for three months."

The kiss felt indulgent, wrapped in layers of emotion and hinting at a passion held back for too long.

I nestled into him, the touch of his body sending shock waves through me like a bolt of lightning. *Il fulmine.* The end of the tunnel was just ahead, and the light on the other side was magnificent.

"Agostino?"

"Yes, Anna."

"I can't wait to ride it."

His arms tightened around me.

"The bike, I mean."

Agostino threw back his head and laughed, the sound lusty, free, and full of joy. It ricocheted off the mountain-tops and echoed through the valleys, leaving behind a silence so profound it felt like the entire countryside was listening.

He stepped back and looked at me, his eyes intent. "Why don't we take it for a test ride ... down that road you're always talking about."

"The one less traveled?"

Agostino nodded. "That's the one. Are you ready?"

"I'm ready."

Hand in hand, with the moon lighting our way, we walked up the old Roman road to Villa Urbino.

Acknowledgments

A SPECIAL thanks to my family, Tony Wilcoxson and Tess Wilcoxson Nelson, for their insight and willingness to take the journey down memory lane with me … no matter how many skeletons we uncovered in the process.

To Sergio Proietti, my go-to source for all things Italian, including some interesting, if undocumented, stories of Scheggino's past.

To Agostino Lucidi (Centro per la Documentazione e la Ricercara Antropologica in Valernerina e nella Dorsale Appennimica Umbria) for his contribution and verification of Scheggino archival information.

To my editor, Molly Lewis, for her willingness to challenge me to dig deeper and not settle for anything less than a novel I can be proud of.

To the team of Acorn Publishing, in particular Leslie Ferguson, for continuing to guide me through the ever-increasing technical demands of publishing with patience and good humor.

To Tess Wilcoxson Nelson for her help with marketing and the social media connection so essential to today's writers. I would be lost without you.

About the Author

ANNA WILCOXSON grew up in San Diego, California, in the 1960s and began her career in 1975, dancing with the original San Diego Ballet, the Santa Barbara Ballet Theatre, and the International Ballet Company of USIU. In 1991, she received her BFA in dance at the USIU's School of Performing Arts. In addition to teaching in private ballet schools, Miss Wilcoxson served on the faculty of Mesa College, Mira  Costa Community College, and Chula Vista Middle and High Schools. In 1995, Anna opened her own ballet school, where she taught and directed classical ballet productions for children.

In 2009, when she assumed the role of caregiver for her ninety-five-year-old mother, Anna's creative passion shifted, and she began writing short stories based on her life and experiences in the performing arts. A trip to Italy with her mother in 2010 sparked the idea for her first novel, *Secrets and Promises: The Story of an Italian American Family,* which centers on the stories she had heard as a child about her immigrant ancestors. *The Deathbed Game* is its sequel.

Anna divides her time between San Diego and Scheggino, Italy.